MIGRATIONS

Migrations: New Short Fiction from Africa

Published in 2017 by
New Internationalist Publications Ltd
The Old Music Hall
106-108 Cowley Road
Oxford
OX4 1JE, UK
newint.org

First published in South Africa by Short Story Day Africa in 2017
Registered NPO 123-206
http://shortstorydayafrica.org

Edited by Helen Moffett, Efemia Chela, and Bongani Kona
Cover collage and design by Nick Mulgrew
Design by Nick Mulgrew
Typesetting by New Internationalist

Printed by T J International Limited, Cornwall, UK
who hold environmental accreditation ISO 14001.

British Library Cataloguing-in-Publication Data.
A catalogue record for this book is available from the British Library.
Library of Congress Cataloging-in-Publication Data.
A catalog record for this book is available from the Library of Congress.

Print ISBN: 978-1-78026-405-9
Ebook ISBN: 978-1-78026-406-6

MIGRATIONS
NEW SHORT FICTION
FROM AFRICA

NewInternationalist

CONTENTS

INTRODUCTION

*T*he past year may have been exceptionally bleak in terms of geopolitical events, but it provided rich soil for stories. At a historical moment when global travel is ubiquitous, people – desperate, hopeful, pragmatic, brutally displaced – are wandering like never before.

People on the move are threatening; at least, this is the anti-migrant narrative heard around the world, particularly in countries once known for their humane attitude to refugees. But this collection of twenty-one unusual and imaginative stories provides alternative perspectives, demonstrating how varied and inventive responses to or accounts of migration can be, the potential they open up for new ways of seeing and understanding. In an era of disquieting xenophobia, these stories provide relief, reminders that human history is the history of human movement, whether in search of a new world, or wrenched from home and hearth by darker tides of war and slavery.

The SSDA anthology has since its inception in 2013 included a mentoring component. This year, for the first time, this expanded beyond the writers to the editors of the collection. Publishing a collection of the finest short stories from the continent involves identifying and nurturing not only writing talent, but editorial skills. Helen Moffett worked alongside Bongani Kona and Efemia Chela to polish the selected stories to a high shine. Editing, however, is far more than a matter of rearranging words; it involves partnering with authors to enable them to hone their skills. The contributors to this volume responded with enthusiasm, and the editors thank them all for the learning opportunities they afforded us.

The SSDA team are particularly grateful to the judges for making the hard decisions – each story had merits, surprises and quirks that surely marked it as a contender for the SSDA Prize. The judges agreed, describing the stories as "outstanding". Ultimately, they chose Sibongile Fisher's "A Door Ajar", a reinvention of the traditional tale of the prodigal sibling leaving the bright lights to return to the remote location of childhood, as the winner. Fisher's hypnotic prose turns an account of a horrifically dysfunctional family into a subtle, rich, and complex work of art. TJ Benson, the first runner-up with "Tea", likewise upends convention by turning the grim subject of human trafficking into an endearing and unusual love story. And Megan Ross's "Farang", the second runner-up, transcends the traditional travelogue as it uses the structure of learning a foreign language to describe romance and loss in Thailand in intimate detail.

As this already indicates, one of the joys of this collection is the range of interpretations given to the prescribed theme. Some were pressing: for those seared by the photo of toddler Alan Kurdî's drowned body on a Turkish shore, there is comfort to be found in Mirette Bahgat Eskaros's exceptionally moving account of an encounter between a boy on a boat and the story's rather unusual narrator, whereas in "Teii mom, win rekk lah", Francis Aubee tackles head-on the double hope prevalent in parts of the African continent: that a better life is possible abroad, and that sport (in this case, football) can offer a golden ticket to that better life.

The authors' imaginations conjured journeys without and within, sometimes in alternative versions of the cities and countries we know, sometimes in terrain readers will recognise. Familiar themes, such as the utopia that is in fact dystopian,are burnished anew in stories like Blaize Kaye's moving and witty version of a world in which humans and computers finally merge, and Anne Moraa's chilling account of a young woman's journey as a "vessel" to ferry a wealthy older man to another world.

Many contributors used the framework offered by ordinary journeys to tell powerful and poignant stories of the spillage of the human heart, the pain of leaving home, the possibility of fresh starts. Mignotte Mekuria's lyrical and lush "Of Fire" presents a journey around the varied landscapes of Ethiopia, and a return to home and healing. It is convincingly told from the perspective of a child, as is Aba Asibon's "Things We Found North of the Sunset", in which a girl's bold trip towards a dream world is witnessed from the viewpoint of the child left behind. In "The Castle", Arja Salafranca turns a day trip around the historical sites of Cape Town into a melancholy meditation on the separation of lovers and the yearning for connection, while Izda Luhunmyo's "The Impossibility of Home" transforms a quest for an absent father into a dazzling account of connection and friendship between two women wanderers. In contrast, Lauri Kubuitsile's "Movement in the Key of Love" charts the turbulent passage through marital betrayal towards self-reliance and healing In Nyarsipi Odeph's "My Sister's Husband" and Gamu Chamisa's "Bleed", bereavement and unresolved grief respectively draw their heroines home from foreign countries, to build or destroy family ties, to confront demons and overturn expectations, while the evergreen theme of the stranger abroad is cheekily subverted in Fred Khumalo's "This Bus Is Not Full!", in which an African scholar on a bus trip in Boston turns an anthropological eye on his fellow passengers.

But not all journeys involve travel: the narrator in Stacey Hardy's "Involution" ventures on an interior exploration that is both wickedly funny and queasily erotic; and the lone lighthouse-keeper in Karen Jennings's "Keeping" has become so self-reliant, he dreads evidence of the world beyond washing ashore. Likewise, not all journeys end well: in Umar Turaki's hallucinatory assembly and exploration of words from a rich range of sources, "Naming", the simple tale of a breakdown on a lonely road at night becomes a Gothic tour de force; and in Edwin Okolo's "The Fates", siblings displaced to the home of an aunt experience trauma that is all the more disturbing for the normalcy of the domestic setting. Mary Ononokpono's exquisitely written "Ayanti" intertwines two classic narratives – intrepid children who venture into the jungle to discover a ghost town and the hideous journey of the slave trade. Okafor Tochukwu's "Leaving" likewise explores wounds of displacement and difference in a coming-of-age story that is both heartbreaking and hilarious.

These stories, by both seasoned and emergent authors, offer an invigorating sample of the talent, imagination and energy of contemporary writing from Africa. They demonstrate a flair for observation, engagement and solutions that bodes well for the future. The SSDA team looks forward to following the authors' careers and thanks them, and all those who entered, for their trust and enthusiasm.

Helen Moffett
MENTORING EDITOR

Exodus

Mirette Bahgat Eskaros

*D*rained. Bored. Sick and tired. It was about time to change my regular route and the everyday view of endless blocks of cement, sickly scrawny trees, and the mounds of trash simmering on almost every street corner. It was absurd to live in a coastal city like Alexandria, yet not enjoy the sea view. Most days, I had no energy to move beyond my little neighbourhood in the northwest of the city, dull and stale as it happened to be. Yet, that day, I woke up late afternoon with one thought in mind: *I'm going to the sea.*

After shaking my drowsiness, I took off into the air. The stiff muscles gradually loosened, and the sunlight freshened my body after so many days of snugging up in my nest. Flying across several side streets and alleyways, I finally reached the corniche. *Ah, the sea.* The breeze carrying the smell of salt and seaweed blew on my body, shaking the soreness from my fatigued wings. My pupils narrowed upon meeting the naked sunlight and the vastness of the space threw me off balance for the briefest of moments. Upon reaching the grand old square, I flew down and rested on the shoulders of Saad Zaghloul's statue – a popular refuge for old crows like myself who need a break from flying – to linger and soak in the charm of the scene. *This is as close as I can get to the sea, I guess.*

My gaze wandered between the pedestrians, the cars rushing along the road like bullets, and people loitering at street cafés, smoking shisha or staring at nothing in particular. At one corner of the square, a friska seller stood calling out his fresh, crispy, honey and nut- filled wafers. *Mm, let me get a taste of that.* I flew over towards him, and as he reached into the blue glass stall to grab a piece of glazed caramelised wafer to give to an old man standing across from him, I swooped down and snatched the wafer from his hands, leaving both men in a burning fury. I flew back to my watchtower on the shoulder of the statue and savoured my little piece of dessert.

How come I never thought of crossing the sea? A thought popped up, enticed by the deep blue waters that looked from above as soft as the breeze brushing against my feathers. The urge to get closer to that indigo surface filled me. It was an unfamiliar desire for a risk-averse like myself who wouldn't go out of his way to make new discoveries; a desire intensified by a haunting thought that most of my life had been wasted living in a stinky nest on top of a stinky tree – or what remained of it – in a stinky neighbourhood. I had no story to tell.

What are you waiting for, then? Another thought popped up. Clearer. More intimidating this time. *If you want to cross the sea, then cross it now. You have wings to fly. All you need is to flip them. Flip. Flap.* I had no answer to that. Everything in and out of myself welcomed the adventure. The horizon looked enticing. The weather was serene. I felt ready to leave the safety of the shore and fly deep over the sea. Looking around and beyond me, everything was the same as it had always been – people smoking shisha at the café, the friska seller lounging by the corner, and Saad Zaghloul's statue standing tall and firm, its arms stretched sideways like a soldier, and a frowning face looking down at the world. I knew I would go and come back to this never-changing scene.

I flapped my wings while standing still to make sure they were strong enough to take on the long ride, and before my head became too overwhelmed by my cautious self telling me how stupid this idea was, I leaped into the air, straight ahead, seeking a new destination. It was the first time in so long that I had flown towards the edge of nothingness. Only the sky and the sea surrounded me.

*T*he evening sun middled the sky like a piece of glowing coal taken out of fire and left to cool down. It held back its flames, yet made sure to cast its blazing shadows on the surroundings before it set. I flew closer and closer to the sun, yet it didn't hurt me to come that close. It was a cold sun, old, just like myself; and as I was starting my voyage, it was getting ready to leave for another destination.

The vast space was embraced in perfect stillness, void of any movement except for the nomadic birds passing by, greeting me with a side glance or a wag of tail. Beneath me were scattered oil ships and fishing boats that appeared from above like puffs of cloud floating in a lower sky; a perfect reflection of my upper surroundings.

It dawned on me that I was completely alone – no humans, no nothing. I felt alarmingly free, and that scared me, and the only way to shake the fear was to keep on flying towards nowhere; and I did it for long hours until there was no light to be seen, except for the navigational beam of the distant lighthouse, and some glowing unidentified shapes beneath me.

After long aimless flying, I gave in to fatigue. My stomach rumbled with hunger. I needed somewhere to land and something to eat. A couple of scattered boats beneath me glowed amid the darkness. *One of these boats will do,* I thought.

I swooped down towards the closest one: a wooden blue boat with a cabin in the middle of the deck. From above, I could see countless bodies crammed on the medium-sized deck, and even more lounging on the cabin roof. I wondered where all these people were headed to. The cool night air sent chills through my worn-out body as I flew down to land on the roof of the boat's cabin. It was deep in the night, and as soon as I landed, the cleanness of the upper space was replaced by the stink of human flesh mixed with sweat and ammonia.

A couple of fluorescent bulbs flickered on the roof, casting their faint light on the deck. Some people grouped together in small circles, chatting lightly and occasionally sharing a laugh or two. Someone was humming in the background. My stomach growled with hunger. I surveyed the roof and spotted half a sandwich left unattended next to a young lad who sat in a corner all by himself. I hopped cautiously closer, trying not to catch attention, but before I could get close enough to grab a bite, the lad's tiny hand was quicker than my beak in reaching out to the bread.

"This is mine!" he said, glaring at me with eyes wide in his brown-skinned face. I glanced back at him; he looked harmless to me.

"Can you give me a bite at least?" I asked as meekly as I could. "I've been flying the whole day with nothing to eat, and I'm afraid I might die of hunger very soon if I don't eat right now."

The boy switched his serious gaze between me and the sandwich before he decided to tear out a big chunk and throw it to my side. I hopped towards it and gobbled it down. The boy watched me in amusement, and as if satisfied with me, he opened his rucksack, got out a flask, and poured water for me to drink on the wooden deck. I felt rejuvenated.

The kid watched me for another couple of minutes before losing interest and going back to what he was doing earlier: folding a sheet of paper.

"What are you making?" I asked.

"A paper boat," he answered without looking at me.

"A paper boat! Why?"

"To take me back home."

"And where is your home, boy?"

"It is far away from here. But the paper boat should know the way back."

"Is that where this boat is heading?"

"No. My brother told me this boat is heading towards Italy."

I looked at him in silence, and then shifted my gaze towards the dozens of people covering the deck. They all looked so different. Some had pitch-black skin the colour of my feathers; some were brown like the lad by my side; and others had fair skin and blonde hair, like milk and honey. *Who the heck are these people?* I wondered.

I shifted my gaze back to the boy. "And what does your home look like, boy?"

He finished another paper boat before placing it next to the others he had made. "A long river flows across our village. Ibrahim, Nur, and I would feed the ducks every day after school. There were lots of ducks. And Mohamed, my brother, the one over there…" he pointed towards a young man sleeping on the far side of the deck, "…he would come and pick me up from school every day and take me back home. We had a big house where we lived with my family. My grandmother would gather us every night to tell us stories about the ghoul who used to roam the village at night, kidnapping the children who stayed out late. Of course I didn't believe her, she was fooling us." He paused for a few seconds before taking another sheet of paper to start another boat. "But she couldn't make it here with us. Mohamed told me she was killed when those men came and attacked our village. I wanted to take my dog with me, but Mama grabbed me by the arm and we ran away. I slept and woke up in a strange place – lots of tents and babies crying and sand everywhere. It was a desert."

He paused to open his rucksack and get out the water flask again for us to drink. My throat was dry.

"What about you?" His eyes locked onto my face. "Are you going to Italy with us?"

"Me! No way," I laughed. "No, I'm just here for a short adventure, and then I'll be going back to Alexandria."

"Are you from Alexandria?"

"I was born in Alexandria. But I had a grandmother just like yours who used to tell me stories of our homeland before we moved to the city."

"Can you tell me one of these stories?" he beamed.

I rolled my eyes, trying to conjure up my memories. "Well, I remember her telling me that my ancestors used to live in the Sahara hundreds of years ago. They built their congregations of nests in the crooked branches of the rising acacia trees, drank from the flowing waters of the oasis springs, and soared high in the limitless sky. There were all sorts of flying, crawling, swimming, and walking species. In the early morning, and with the first rays of the rising sun, snakes would come out of their caves looking for food, birds would leave their nests and fly towards the clear horizon, and swarms of insects would mingle with the golden sand particles. At night, the silence would be perfect except for the occasional sounds of howling wolves, night crickets, and hooting owls night-guarding the desert under the moonlight."

"And what happened? Why did you leave?"

"Well, covetous humans is what happened, my young friend. The dwellers of the desert wanted to expand their powers to further lands, and so wars erupted between different races. Thousands of humans died, houses and temples were destroyed, and lands were set on fire. My grandmother told me of a great famine that occurred during that time, followed by mass starvation and disease. There was no food for humans or animals to eat, and death crawled heavily on the surface of the earth. Many species of animals, birds, and fish were said to have disappeared forever after the great famine. Life was never the same again, and we had to flee and find a refuge somewhere else. My family were among the migrating birds. They fled to the east towards Alexandria. It took them ten days to arrive in the new land and settle down. There I was born."

"Do you like your new home?"

I twisted my beak. "Well, it's nothing compared to the image I have in my imagination of my homeland, but then again, it's the only home I know. But some days come when I feel a deep longing to go back to where my ancestors once lived. I sometimes feel sick of living in the chaos of the city."

*W*e had spoken long into the night, and the position of the moon in the sky alerted me that it was past midnight. The sky was starless, and the still waters reflected the dim light of the crescent moon hanging low over us.

"It's getting late. I'd better fly back home," I said.

"Which home?" asked the boy, smiling.

I smiled back. "I'm not as adventurous as you are, my little friend. I'm just an old bird with a limited number of days left in my life account. I'm going back to my shaggy nest."

The boy fixed his eyes on mine. "Will you visit me one day in my new home?"

I was silent for a moment. "I wish my old wings could carry me that far. One day maybe." I plucked out one of my feathers and offered it to him.

As I was getting ready to set off, I heard the revving sound of a motor vessel coming our way. The people on our boat became disturbed. "Is that the coast guard?" one of the passengers yelled. A hubbub broke out and people started standing up and cramming to one side of the boat to get a better glimpse of the approaching vessel, making the boat sway and tilt. "Everybody go back to your places right now. I order you!" a sturdy man urged. "This is our boat, you idiots," he snapped.

The new vessel stopped close to our boat. It was less than half the size of ours, and carried around twenty men who looked like fishermen in dirty wrapped pants, cotton vests, and bucket caps.

"Yalla, grab your stuff and move your butts to the boat. Hurry up!" Half a dozen men started yelling at the passengers and pushing them out to the new vessel.

"What! Are we going to move again?" The shouts of the men and the crying of women and children rang through the silence of the night. "Come on. Have mercy on us. This vessel can't even hold half of us. We will drown before reaching the shore," one old man pleaded.

"Well, I'll make sure to kill you with my own hands, you bastard, if you don't move right now," one of the men in the fisherman outfits burst out. "Don't you understand, you fool? The coast guards will be here any minute, and then you'll be back to where you came from."

People started dividing between those who resisted moving and those who succumbed to the orders. They started pulling and pushing each other: mothers clinging tightly to their children, husbands clutching the hands of their wives, grandparents calling in the pitch darkness for grandchildren.

After the vessel was filled with almost half of the people, while the other half remained in the wooden boat, one of the fishermen started the engine and the vessel started to move away.

"What about us?" shouted the people in the first boat. "You can't leave us!"

A deafening noise erupted as a machine gun fired towards the boat. "You want to stay here? Fine. Stay forever."

The second vessel headed off into the darkness of the sea, leaving the wooden boat drenched in the blood of dozens of bodies, pierced by the bullets, lying on the deck. The night was filled with wailing and hysterical screaming. Those who miraculously escaped the bullets rushed to cut pieces of cloth, breathe life into the mouths of still bodies, or bury their crying faces in the warmth of the newly deceased. The boat started to sink as water started to pour in where the bullets had penetrated its sides.

I stood frozen on the highest point of the cabin's roof. The cold night air cut into my bones, and the smell of blood bit into my nostrils. I was too scared to move. Too numb. Half of the boat was already submerged and the remaining people – around twenty of them – started blowing up their life-jackets and deconstructing wooden planks out of the hull to help them float on the surface of the water, while a couple of them flashed rescue lights. I thought of going to call for help, but where and how? My head was spinning. I was hardly able to carry myself. I hopped onto one of the floating objects and blacked out.

After who knows how many hours, I opened my eyes a crack. I was still groggy and not quite alert to what had happened before I had lost consciousness. The rays of the dawning sun stroked my eyes and body, and out there, far on the horizon, I glimpsed a scene that to this day remains a mystery. There, across the skyline that separated the waters from the sky, hundreds of paper boats were floating, or flying, I could not really tell. Each one of them carried a soul, and oh my, I saw the young lad in one of them. He was smiling and waving at me, and I heard him saying, *I'm going back home*.

It started raining lightly; soft drops plopped onto the surface of the water. I drowsed again, only to wake this time to the noise of a siren; a ship carrying people in formal attire and others holding cameras, caught in a frenzy of shooting the still bodies floating on the surface of the sea.

Involution

Stacy Hardy

*W*hen she first discovers the thing, she reacts with fright. It isn't just its outlandish appearance but also its proximity. Why, considering all the suitable nooks and crannies, the possible hidey holes in the vicinity, has it chosen her? In truth she might not have noticed it if it wasn't for the itch. At first, barely noticeable, more like a humming, a low-level vibration somewhere in her nether regions, then louder, more insistent.

Eventually she has no choice but to give herself over, to make her way to the bathroom, shut the door and strip down. She sits on the toilet – lid down – kicks off shoes and peels leggings, thrusts hips forward and bends head. Even from this position, bum balanced, legs akimbo, she has trouble discerning anything. It isn't so much that the thing is well hidden, as it is that its very form resists easy definition. Much about it is familiar: its colour – pinkish, brownish – its jowls and dugs, its convex shape. All these things are easy to describe, but how they are assembled evades logic.

Her first reaction is to snap her legs shut, get dressed, and pretend she has seen nothing. She tries to calm herself. To breathe. She isn't usually scared by strange animals or creepy-crawlies. She grew up outside the city, a semi-rural area known for its biodiversity. Her childhood was spent collecting worms and beetles, chasing after frogs and meerkats. It's only recently that she moved to the south, a coastal metropolis. She tells herself that the thing is probably like her, some poor rural animal that has strayed from its natural environment. It is nothing to be afraid of. After all, there must be all sorts of species, and subspecies she has never encountered before. Small mammals alone come in a number of varieties. There are rodents, tree shrews, and the eulipotyphla made up of moles, hedgehogs, and solenodons; and each of those categories has its own variants and deviants, its smallest incarnation.

When the pamphlets on mammals and reptiles that she obtains from the local Parks Board office reveal nothing, she extends her search. It is possible that the animal is not from these parts, not indigenous, as the books call it. That it is an alien or an immigrant. Cases like this are documented all the time. On the internet, she reads stories of vervet monkeys and miniature hippos smuggled across borders. A rare sea snake, usually only found in the waters of Mauritius, pops up in an aquarium in a restaurant in lower Manhattan. A cat travels aboard a research vessel all the way to the Antarctic.

She tries Google, but it yields nothing. The problem is in her search terminology. She has difficulty finding language to describe the thing. It is hairy, but the hair is neither long nor soft; it isn't furry exactly, but it seems to have a sort of fuzzy quality, a kind of fluffy pertness that could be considered cute under the right circumstances.

Mostly, though, it is ugly. Its hair stands up in a shadowy tuft framing a sad little naked face that might have resembled a puppy had it not seemed so bunched up, so awfully scrunched. She feels almost sorry for it, a warm prickling in her stomach. No wonder the thing is hiding – a tiny lonely Frankenstein creature with no protection from the outside world.

She clicks a link and finds herself looking at pictures of rabbits: Bugs Bunny next to the white rabbit from Alice, and a man-sized cyborg rabbit ghost from some movie she doesn't recognise. The final picture isn't of a rabbit but rather a man covered with bees from top to toe. The picture is titled "Beeman". She stares at the photo and then the caption. Something about it, the combination, makes her stomach knot. What is the relationship between the bees and the rabbits? And the man and the bees? Is the caption meant to suggest a new species, a coupling of man and insect into a vibrating human swarm? She thinks about evolution. Ape skulls and how human embryos have an extra jaw that fades into the skull, early on in development. She bites down hard, clamps her teeth shut against the memory that rises.

She considers that the thing might be a type of mole. It seems to be blind or rather, if it has eyes, she has yet to see them – at least anything that resembles the eyes she's seen on other animals: the hooded eyes of lizards, the soft brown balls of cows, the red obsidian beads of the rat, the cat eye, fish eye, eagle eye, each so distinct.

But sometimes the eye is not an eye. Seeing without perceiving, for example; sight as an act of creation. In addition, there are all sorts of species that are eyeless. A quick search reveals cave wolf spiders and sea urchins and all types of shrimps and salamanders. Most of them are underwater dwellers, but she is sure more will appear if she searches deeper, if she delves into the underground caves and abandoned mine shafts that litter the local landscape.

Later, looking at a blind naked mole rat makes her think that maybe the thing is a hybrid. She has read reports and seen pictures. Genetic modification is leading to all kinds of permutations. At the shops, she buys cherries the size of pawpaws and oranges with edible peels and a new fruit that combines a pomegranate and an apple. The fruit is expensive and ultimately disappointing. It lacks the apple's crunch or the pop of pomegranate rubies. She remembers a vegetarian friend who warned her that they were already breeding chickens without wings and limbless cows. Picture it: just the central mass, a cow torso or trunk, clumped and inert. Could it be that her creature is such an experiment?

She thinks of how pearls form in oysters or how a tumour grows in a body, a clump of cells without differentiation. And then her creature. She imagines it beginning life as a ball of tightly packed radioactive flesh, raising itself up from the bottom of some medical waste truck, swimming through the debris of polluted biological matter, swamps permeated with the discarded waste of every living process. Emerging, its body limp, face exposed, hauling itself on to the tarmac, the hum of the sliding liquid. The sucking sounds it makes as it drags itself towards her...

*H*er bladder feels hot and tight. She closes her laptop. Head throbbing, she walks to the bathroom. Pees without looking, holding her legs clamped together. She listens to the sound of her piss on the water. Sits like that awhile, then slowly spreads her thighs, peers downwards and gasps. The creature seems to have grown; its features are more distinct, more pronounced now.

A shudder goes through her. She quickly balls up some toilet paper, touches a wad lightly to it. The paper comes away wet, but she has no way of knowing if it's her pee or the creature exuding liquid. She recoils, hurriedly pulls her pants up. Flushes, holding down the handle until the paper disappears.

She considers her relationship with the thing. What is she to it? Is she a friend? A habitat? A habit? A home? Or a safehold, a place of refuge, somewhere warm and secluded away from the city, like a hole or nest? But if she is a nest, then is the animal nesting? Creating a safe place so it can breed? The thought drops down to her stomach, hangs there a moment, then births a dozen small creatures, tiny replicants of their mother with pink, crinkling faces and a tuft of soft downy hair that scrabble in her belly. She touches a hand to her stomach, wonders what will become of them once they are fully grown. Where will they go? She doesn't have space to house them. The enclave between her legs is the only really private nook of her body, unless of course one counts the armpits – but surely even those are exposed countless times in everyday activity, in lifting and carrying and calling for attention.

She lies awake in bed, her senses on high alert. The room is filled with shadows, monsters hiding under the bed, ghosts that run lights across the ceiling. The shadows in the room are still when she fixates on them. But when she looks away, they move subtly in the corner of her eye. They're breathing, she thinks, and closes her eyes, then opens them an instant later.

She is sure that as soon as she sleeps, the creature will awaken, begin some kind of secret nocturnal creaturely activity. She tries to lie very still, to hold her body inert. Her limbs are heavy and tacky with sweat. She listens. Finally, when nothing happens, she reaches down. Her hand gropes under the sheet, slides inside her panties. It seems somehow less scary, and she folds her hand over it. Initially it is warm, almost body temperature, but as she presses down, she feels it swell, grow hot and distended. Immediately she pulls back, uncertain if she is somehow smothering it. She waits a while before she slides her hand back down, this time cupping it gently so its little hairs tickle her palm. She falls asleep like that, her hand between her legs, mouth open, saliva gathered in the corners.

In the morning, the bed has a sweetly fetid smell and the sheets feel damp. She balls them up and throws them in the laundry. In the shower, she scrubs herself down. She uses the disinfectant soap that she usually reserves for the kitchen. She scrubs her armpits and her breasts. Washes her feet and behind her knees. She rubs the bar of soap between the lips of her crotch, sliding it down to the groove of her arsehole. She rubs back and forth until her arms ache from reaching and her crotch burns. She repeats the motion until her thighs are red and splotchy from rubbing. Positions her body so the hot water scalds her stomach and streams down between her legs.

She should take action. Report the animal. But to whom? Should she go to a doctor? That's where you would go to get a tapeworm removed – but her creature is not a tapeworm. She has no indication it's parasitic. It does not suck sustenance from her body, at least as far as she can tell. She hasn't lost weight recently or experienced any undesirable symptoms. No hair loss or broken nails to indicate a vitamin deficiency. If anything, she is looking rounder since the thing arrived. Her breasts seem heavier and firmer and her cheeks have a new sheen. If the thing isn't feeding off her, what does it eat? The question unsettles her, the idea of the thing eating. But of course it must eat! What else would be the use of the mouth? What she thinks is a mouth. The thing doesn't seem to use it for sound. It is very quiet, unnaturally so. Since the initial itch she has heard nothing. She listens intently. The silence unnerves her.

She conducts several experiments. She wets her fingers with different things: fruit juice, honey, the bloody effluence of a steak she buys at the butcher. She unbuttons her pants and rolls down her panties, slides a finger between her legs, angling along the thing's surface until she reaches the small hole of its mouth. In each case, the response is the same: nothing; not itching or twitching, no change she can gauge in the thing's temperature.

She pours a saucer of milk, balances it on a small bench, and sinks her buttocks in the cool liquid. Sits like that a while, motionless, the pink and dark flesh of her creature submerged. Finally, she stands, the milk dripping down her thighs. She examines the saucer but there is only a small change in the liquid's level, probably caused by the displaced milk that now pools on the tiles below her.

*I*t's cold inside the Natural History Museum, quiet. She spends hours wandering the hallways. Lingers in front of stuffed lions and hyenas, an ethnographic display featuring Khoisan hunters, passes snakes adrift in jars of formaldehyde, petrified insects entombed in stone. The display cases are giant aquariums emptied of water. She stares at the predatory jaw of a coelacanth, the ancient bottom-dwelling fish that was believed to be extinct until a scientist found it at the mouth of the Chalumna River. The locals laughed at the discovery – how can something that has always been, lived long amongst us, be discovered? She runs her fingers along the glass case surface. Stares into the fish's eyes, its ravenous mouth, traces the snapping urgency of its teeth. Feels a welling in her stomach as a museum guard approaches. "Can I help you? Is there something specific you're looking for?"

She shakes her head. Just looking.

The guard's presence makes her nervous. She imagines her creature would be quite a find for a place like this – an institute or research centre. For the first time she thinks of the thing's worth. She goes to the information desk and asks about the price tag attached to rare animal displays. The stuffed riverine rabbit or Ethiopian wolf, say, or the hairy-eared dwarf lemur from Madagascar. The woman doesn't understand the question. She is just a help desk jockey, trained to dispense brochures and pinpoint areas on the map. She points the girl to the curio shop.

She has no interest in curios, but walks in the direction indicated so as not to arouse suspicion. She buys a bottle of water and a plastic bat on sale as part of some special focus on cave-dwelling mammals. Once outside she wonders if she chose the bat because she sees an affinity between it and her thing. She thinks about her body and its caverns and sinkholes.

She resolves to keep her thing secret. To tell no one, certainly not anyone involved in the study of science. After all, it doesn't seem to be doing any harm. It demands very little. It doesn't need to be fed and it makes no sound. As far as the rest of the world is concerned, it doesn't even exist.

As if to prove this to herself, she phones a man she met at a party she attended when she first arrived in the city. The man, if she remembers correctly, was introduced as working in wildlife conservation, some sort of research into endangered species. She dials his number and says, "I don't know, I was just thinking of you." He seems flattered. "How about a drink sometime?"

She has had little social contact since discovering the thing, and is afraid that it might somehow show, be visible to others. She wears an old pair of black jeans that keeps everything neatly tucked in without riding too close to her skin, too near the panty line. The restaurant they meet in is crowded. They find a table, squashed in the corner, and face each other. As it turns out, she was wrong about the man's field of expertise. Yes, he is in conservation, but he is mostly concerned with legislation. His background is legal. She tries to focus while he tells her about a case study he is working on, examining how recent trade agreements with Chinese shipping companies have affected the perlemoen population in local waters. He tells her about the plight of local fishing communities, the tiny motorised fishing boats that carry pirates, armed gangs that run the illegal perlemoen trade.

The word "pirate" catches her attention. She feels a shudder. It is as if the setting or the man or what he is saying has upset the thing. She doesn't know how she knows this. It is not so much a feeling as a sudden twitching, a sort of pull-itch that makes her slide her arms across her belly and hug them tight. She wriggles in her chair, overly aware of the sucking sound her bottom makes on the seat's vinyl cushion. Eventually the pressure is too much. She excuses herself and rushes to the bathroom.

Her bum hugs the toilet bowl, pants around her ankles. Her

panties are slightly damp – not wet exactly, not like she peed on them – but clammy, coated in a viscous substance. Her mouth is dry. Could there be something wrong with the creature? Is this how it bleeds or maybe some weird form of weeping?

She is overcome with a flush of emotion. It starts in her stomach and radiates out until her whole body is filled with small warm fuzzy things. She reaches down and gently cups the thing. She begins to stroke, very slowly at first, then faster.

The thing grows taut under her touch. She feels its warm mouth open, the liquid excretion saliva, not blood. It coats her hand, stringy tendrils that seem to pull her deeper. She slides a finger in, just one, then another. She roots around, scratching at the top, the soft yielding sides that bulge when pried. She pushes harder, discovers a funny sound made by squishing the walls in. She starts to laugh. Her body tingles. Her skin shudders and her jaw trembles. The thing pulls tight, spasms into a hard knot and then goes slack. Everything becomes indistinct. The air is hot and thick. She sits on the toilet breathing. The thing is quiet. Her belly is flat and relaxed. She stands slowly, legs shaky beneath her, wipes herself off and cleans her panties with toilet paper. At the small enamel basin, she avoids the mirror, washes her hands twice, dries them under the hot stream of air from an electronic hygiene drier.

*A*t the table, the man is drumming his fingers. They sit in silence. She is sure her face is flushed, and she looks down to avoid his gaze. Finally, she looks up and asks: "Do you have any pets?" She doesn't know why this question.

He shakes his head. He doesn't like the idea of animals being domesticated. He says something about corrupting the animal spirit.

She says: "And cockroaches?" Cocks her head and watches his face. Obviously he doesn't get it. She tries to explain that there is no urban and rural divide any more, no pure, incorruptible nature. She asks him to try to imagine dogs before they were domesticated. Or rats in the wild and pigeons in jungles. Of them all, the pigeons seem the most unimaginable to her. They seem so stupid and placid.

She hopes her thing never becomes like that. Docile and dependent. She likes its wildness, its skittishness. How it cowers below her, seemingly afraid of the light, the hard air. She slides her hand between her legs under the table. Her thighs are hot. When the waiter comes she orders steak. The man orders the grilled line fish. "I don't eat red meat," he says, as if needing to explain.

She watches him slice carefully into his fish and take the bones out. The meat is pale and flaky, gives easily. The spine comes out clean. He impales a forkful, brings it to his lips. Between bites he talks about problems with the Chinese shipping industry. Certain practices: sharks brought up in nets, their fins ripped off, thrown back, still living, to sink like stones. She watches him eat and thinks sharks do not have bones, only cartilage. The thought makes her seasick or at least feel something like seasickness, that same lurching. The smell of the man's food is suddenly overpowering. She can see his jaw moving. A deafening noise around her: the sharp sound of metal and porcelain, high-pitched voices.

Outside it is raining lightly. She declines the man's offer of a lift. She wants to walk, to be outside, to feel the air and water on her face. She walks quickly. In the distance, she can see the silhouettes of the cranes in the harbour against the sky, the lights of the ships far out at sea. The wind rips through her and blows her hair in her face. She is soaked when she gets home.

She decides not to phone the man again, pushes him out her head. That night, he keeps coming back to her. She thinks of the fish dish in front of him, of him eating then talking, of his lips opening and closing. The spine left on the side of his plate, its spikes and serrated edges. She goes through to her bedroom and undresses slowly. She sits in the centre of the bed and spreads her legs. Her heart beats quickly as large red splotches spread across her thighs. She breathes, reaches down and feels a quiver. The stirring grows so strong it's as if her insides are tiny animals, gnawing and scratching the walls of her body. She runs her fingers across the creature's skin. The mouth feels like a little wet cave under her touch. She wants very badly to stick her finger into it. She peels open the lips, very wet suddenly, lubricated so her index finger slides in easily. The whole thing cleaves as she penetrates it, goes in with three fingers, pushes deeper, rocking and thrusting.

In that moment she realises that her understanding of the animal has been very limited. What she took to be its body, the bulk of the thing, is really only an exterior. Buried just below that is another whole extension, an animal holed out or turned inside over. It is not clear if it's mammalian or reptilian or amphibian. It could even be fish or a plant. It has no bones, or perhaps she just can't feel them. Its muscles, or what might be muscles, are coiled in spasms that knot and loosen as her hand strokes them. Its skin is hot and wet, a mucus membrane covered in a thin layer of slime. It doesn't make a sound, but as she thrusts deeper she becomes aware of a vibration, low and metallic, like the hum of insects, a soft buzz at a pitch that human ears shouldn't be able to hear.

She listens closely, tries to imagine the shape of what's inside her. She navigates like a bat sending out signals. Does it go on indefinitely? Does it have many parts, chambers, like a heart? Is it contiguous, or are parts of it cut off from the other parts, sealed away, unreachable and silent? Are its parts solid, defined, or do they simply take on the shape they inhabit, like liquid? In that moment she thinks she smells it, a smell like fish, like seaweed on the beach in the morning, but after a time she cannot remember that smell, or seaweed, or morning. Her ability to compare anything with anything else is slipping. There is nothing to compare. They are no longer separate creatures.

Leaving

Okafor Tochukwu

*D*on't ask me how I know these things.

*O*n a hot, dry afternoon in June 1993, they left the city in a dust-eaten Peugeot truck. Six children and many oversized bags and tear-filled eyes. The mother perched in the vehicle's wide back, shivering, pleading inwardly for safety. Gunshots rang in the air, hitting people, cracking walls, splintering glass.

The man who had won the presidency in what had been deemed to be the country's free-est and fairest elections was denied the power to rule. Enraged, his supporters took to the streets to express their anger. Roads were blocked. Shops were looted. Cars lay abandoned. Stern-looking soldiers, called in to quell the unrest, filled every corner like termites building a new colony, shooting protesters, squashing women and their babies under their boots. Death saturated the streets, and those who could, ran for dear life.

This was weeks before Obioma Aniocha came into the world.

*T*he family returned to the city two years later, when things had returned to normal. Well, normal enough for people to carry on with their lives. The man who would have been president had been imprisoned for treason, and the city looked safe again. But it was a difficult homecoming for the family. The house they once lived in had been packed with new tenants, and most of the property they had left behind had either been stolen or thrown outside and left to rot. It took the generosity of the landlord for the family to spend the night in a dank, cockroach-infested storeroom. They lived there for about a month, not without many nights of cold and bouts of fever, not without the landlord grumbling for them to find a new apartment. Their life was now consumed by fear and uncertainty, but just like every other person who had returned, they had to survive.

*T*heir survival is a story for another day. For today, I tell this story of my Obioma.

$\mathcal{F}$or little Obioma, life started in a spacious three-bedroom flat on Mission Street. A long narrow expanse of street frequented by police and area boys and vagrants who found homes alongside open gutters and sunbaked dumps. As the months fattened into years, Obioma grew used to not going outside to play. He loved sitting by the ant-eaten cupboard where old books were piled one atop another. He would pull out book after book, shredding them, the shi-shi-shi of each page's rip making him laugh until his eyes, big as globes, gleamed with caged moistness.

His mother set up a small stall in front of their compound. She sold Nasco biscuits and soft drinks and plastic toys, but not cigarettes and beer which, ordinarily, would have fared better. His father opened a shop at Trade Fair, where he sold motorcycle parts, all thanks to the Men's Progressive Union which, after much consideration of the weight he had to bear, pooled money to help him start a small business. As for his siblings: they left home to start school in other parts of the country. Soon the memory of 1993 washed away like a bad dream, and life for the Aniochas returned to what it had been.

Obioma began school at age four. It wasn't surprising to his mother that he never cried when she turned to leave after placing him in the care of his teachers. Signs of a genius, she thought, and would tell her husband her wondrous predictions of what Obioma would become. True enough, Obioma did well in class. He was a shy, quiet boy who gained the love of his teachers and peers. He was hardly ever seen playing football, like the rest of his schoolmates, or the neighbours' children, who spent their afternoons basking in the sun, running after each other, the way cats chase hapless rats. Obioma kept to himself and his books.

In Class Three, he became fond of a boy who sat next to him. The boy's name was Adebola. Adebola had a table-top forehead and thick eyebrows that loomed over moody eyes. His skin, a burnt black, reflected in the sun. He was soft-spoken and had an air of mystery about him, such that when he was made fun of, you could never tell his reaction. His face betrayed no emotion.

And just like Obioma, he was quiet. Unlike Obioma, however, he struggled to pass his subjects.

During lunch breaks, Obioma would move close to him until their bodies were almost touching, and each could feel the other's warmth seeping through their faded red and white chequered uniforms. Obioma would say something like, "What did you get in the maths assignment?" or, "Can you read this sentence?" and then point to a line in one of the many colourful pages of his storybook. Obioma loved colourised stories: stories about lost children who could talk with neem trees and pigeons; a family of three that lived in outer space and had superpowers and were earth's superheroes; stories about white people in America. He read them over and over, reciting paragraphs in his head until the characters in the stories were real enough to be dreamt of. Through the retelling of such stories to Adebola, he became his closest friend.

One bright afternoon, Obioma sat staring at the blackboard. The writing seemed to roll off the edges into wobbly chalked forms. He shut his eyes, opened them. He hoped Adebola would start a conversation, and when he didn't, he picked up his pencil, rolled it between his fingers, and tap-tapped on the wooden desk. When this didn't work, Obioma dropped the pencil, picked up a notebook, and slapped the desk here and there, while his other hand drummed on the chair he sat on. Adebola still wouldn't look up. Obioma stopped and drew close to his friend, close enough to hear his muffled breaths, as if he were drowning in a sea of his own thoughts, close enough to see scarlet welts across his arms and along the back of his neck.

"Ade, are you okay?" Obioma asked in a voice like his mother's – a soothing voice, soft and gentle. He touched Adebola. Adebola withdrew, turned his face away to the window where senior pupils chattered as they passed by. "Ade, look at me. It's me, your friend. Your good friend. It's me, Obi."

For a moment or two longer, Obioma thought the world was too full and noisy for people like him and Adebola. He imagined that only he and his comforting words existed for Adebola. He felt like taking him away, to another world where only the cool wind blew, and birds sang songs, and the sun wasn't always red hot. He imagined Adebola taking his hands in his, reassuring him that everything was all right, hugging him the way his mother did every morning, tightly.

And when Adebola turned to look at Obioma, sad eyes meeting lost eyes, Obioma's thoughts crumbled like a sand-house by the seashore as he watched streams of tears race down Adebola's cheeks. He felt Adebola's suffering, bone-deep. He knew someone, or something, was depriving Adebola of his joys of childhood by lashing at his skin, leaving reminders all over his lean body.

He inched closer and closer, locked his slender fingers in Adebola's, his free hand sliding up Adebola's thigh – kneading, probing, longing. A strange feeling; strange, but warm. Adebola relaxed breath by breath, allowing Obioma to caress him; after all, the world was not watching.

*D*on't ask me how I know these things.

A month before examinations were due to start, Adebola disappeared. It happened after his mother came to visit their teacher. Days drifted. Obioma waited and waited, hoped and prayed, but Adebola never came back. Sometimes, Obioma would fix a long stare at where Adebola used to sit, as if staring would summon Adebola, as if staring would make the glaring reality of his absence easier to bear.

Then one orange-lit afternoon, a white reverend sister visited the school. The whole school dashed out to see what she looked like. Some said she was Indian, because a mole the size of a pebble sat right on her forehead. In the ensuing commotion, Obioma walked up to his teacher and asked her what had happened to Adebola, why he had stopped coming to school. The teacher looked away, hesitant. Then she told him Adebola had gone up to heaven to join his new friends. Shocked, he forced himself to get angry at Adebola for going to heaven. He found it difficult to listen in class, and, for the first time in many years, he failed his examinations. Years slowed, while he awaited Adebola's return from heaven.

The year he turned twelve, Obioma understood what going to heaven meant. It meant abandoning friends and never returning. It meant transmigration. It meant leaving. *Dead sleep.* It meant his distant cousin Chikwado dying in a riot in Jos, where Muslims and Christians attacked each other, burning mosques and churches, charred remains of corpses littering the streets, a vast gloomy sky the colour of blisters.

That same year, he felt the same way he had felt about Adebola for a boy named Nnamdi. Nnamdi was a boy about his age who lived in the next compound. His mother sold okirika clothes at Yaba market, and Obioma's mother spent most evenings with her, pricing clothes and discussing outcomes of the Christian Mothers' meetings. Whenever Nnamdi came by to drop off the clothes his mother had bought, Obioma would watch him from behind a door. He watched the small muscles of Nnamdi's arms and legs contract and relax, skin glowing like mbuba as he heaved the bag of okirika clothes. And when he turned to leave, Obioma observed the worn fabric around Nnamdi's buttocks crease, folding in and out as Nnamdi walked away in bold strides.

Obioma's imaginings of Nnamdi fell in his favour one quiet Saturday. Nnamdi had come to charge his mother's electric lamp. He sat on the sofa in the sitting room, legs parted, back straight, and watched television. A kung fu movie was playing. He loved such movies. He shook his fists every now and then, and voiced Japanese-like sounds and bared his teeth. His face contorted with rage like one of the fighters in the movie – a deep fold formed by the skin between his eyes, nose crinkled like a withered leaf, jaws clenched.

"Now, I'll take you down. *Tee-chuu. Huan,*" mimicked Nnamdi. This made Obioma explode into fits of laughter as he walked into the room, bearing a sweaty glass of water.

"You really like this movie, don't you?" Obioma asked.

"I don't like it. I love it," Nnamdi said, punching the air.

"Are you hungry?"

Silence.

Obioma went into the house and returned with a plate of steamy jollof rice, two pieces of fried goat meat hidden underneath the reddened, curried grains. He placed the food on the round glass table, his fingers smarting from the hotness, and settled on the far end of the sofa. He coughed and coughed, but never claimed Nnamdi's attention. He gave up and sat with his thoughts, looking at the television, then looking away, his gaze shifting from one wall photo to the other, waiting for the movie to end.

By the time the movie ended, the glass of water had lost its chill, and Nnamdi was sweating like a thief being pursued. He drowned the contents of the glass in big, throaty gulps. Obioma edged closer. His nose caught a strong whiff of Nnamdi's underarm, and twitched. He moved again, and when the hairy skin of their thighs grazed, he whispered into Nnamdi's ear, "I like you." Obioma felt Nnamdi's body stiffen, like sun-dried meat, as he turned to look away. He followed Nnamdi's gaze to where the walls met, where dark lines of cobwebs draped the wall and two geckoes lingered, eavesdropping.

Obioma inched towards him. He felt a tightening in his throat, a million butterflies fluttering in his belly, strange sensations he could not understand, now sweet like mmiri ukwa, now clawing like hunger. He let his hand travel from Nnamdi's hair, down his back, to the hairy line just above his shorts. And when he used both hands to cup the back of Nnamdi's head, willing their lips to join, it was no longer just the two of them in the room.

"What is happening here? Obi, what do you think you are doing? Eh?" Obioma's mother raged, her voice rattling the still room. You could see the bright fire of anger as her whole body spasmed.

Obioma stuttered. Only air, and more air, escaped his mouth. Nnamdi shot up from his seat and clasped his hands, rubbing heat into them, pleading. He knelt and said, "Sorry Ma, sorry Ma," until the saliva in his tongue ran dry and his heartbeat sounded louder than his voice.

"These children will not kill me. You will not kill me." She disappeared into the house.

Nnamdi stood and sprinted for the door. Obioma had unbuckled his belt and his shorts fell below his waist as he ran. He did not stop to say goodbye. Obioma's eyes had started to redden and swell with tears, and his head ached from so many thoughts, thoughts of what his mother might do to him. She returned with a cane in her hand and chased him round the room.

"Get out of my house. Get out," she said, froths of spittle dribbling from the corners of her mouth. She succeeded in kicking him out of the house and locking the door behind him. "Stay outside till your father returns. Nwa nzuzu. Stay there," she shouted, facing the door, as though it were the door that had offended her. When she walked to the window and saw him crying, resting his back against the newly plastered fence, she said to him, "The sun will heal you. It will heal your senses. Useless child."

Hours later, she sprinkled holy water round the house, stashed all the male fashion magazines in a small corner behind the house, lit them, and listened to them cackle under the bright red and yellowing flame. In Obioma's room, she emptied his school bag, pulled his cupboard apart, and shredded the poster of a well-built, half-naked man slouching against a new model Yamaha motorcycle. With Obioma's room upturned like a slaughterhouse, she sank on her knees, face forward, body shivering, and prayed to God in three languages.

I know that woman, Obioma's mother. I see her every day. Hell is in bed with her.

And yet the sun didn't heal Obioma Aniocha. It didn't heal his senses. After that day, he apologised to his mother. She told him that such a thing should only be done with girls. He had wanted to ask her what she meant with the thing she said about the sun. Did the sun take away one's feelings? Or would the sun burn away his affection for boys?

It doesn't matter now, not after years of clandestine love affairs. He grew up to become a medical doctor, and now he lives alone in his own flat. He is in love with a new man. This new man is in America, waiting.

*O*bioma stood outside the US Embassy on Walter Carrington Crescent. The wind lapped across him a fresh scent of magnolias. He needed an American visa. He walked into the embassy. The security men didn't stop him, didn't ask him anything. What person in his right mind will hassle a well-known medical doctor as if he is any ordinary civilian? He walked into the office where he would be interviewed. He sat and stared at the interviewer who simply stared back at him. An impregnable silence gripped the air-conditioned room. Only the clock hanging high on the wall ticked away. He looked at the practiced smiles on the faces of former Heads of States, whose pictures in gold-rimmed frames hung like shiny accolades on the walls of the room, and he remembered a conversation he once had with his father.

FATHER: My son, I come from two wars.

SON: Papa, how?

FATHER: I come from two great wars. Great wars, my son. Not
        even two. Many great wars. I come from the entangled
        space between life and death. Remember this: not all
        wars have blood and gore. Each day comes with its own
        war. Ah, but 1993! Protecting you while you were in
        your mother's belly was a war on its own. My struggle
        in raising you and your six siblings, another war. Living
        is war itself. This is why, my son, you must learn to fight
        your wars. Don't run away like a chicken. Don't cry like
        a little girl. Face your wars like a real man. You will be
        strong that way, my son. And when hope seems as thin as

your fingernails, you must sing this song, for it is a song
of power, and of glory, and of praise:

> *Onye akpakwala agu aka n'odu*
> *M'o di ndu*
> *M'o nwuru anwu*
> *Onye akpakwala agu aka n'odu.*

SON: Yes, Papa. Thank you, Papa.

FATHER: You will be a light to your generation.

SON: Amen, Papa.

FATHER: You won't live to see another war, the kind with guns.

SON: Amen, Papa.

FATHER: Even if war comes, you will stay and fight like a real man.

SON: Amen, Papa.

FATHER: You will fight. You will not run away. Your chi will also
fight for you.

SON: Amen, Papa. Amen.

And so be it.

*I*t was the interviewer who interrupted the flow of Obioma's
thoughts. He asked if everything was okay, if he would like a
drink of water. Obioma stood up, his eyes unblinking. He walked
out of the office, the interviewer shouting after him. He walked
past the long line of people waiting outside under the light rain.
He walked past the security men and the birds that sang songs. He
reached his black suv, looked back before he slid in, revved the
engine, and drove slowly away into the noisy streets of the city.

Movement in the Key of Love
(or something that sounds like that)

Lauri Kubuitsile

LOVE: THE ORIGINAL

I sit in the dark leaning against the rough wall of the rondavel, watching the dancing shadows caused by the paraffin lamp. I'm bored by the expat talk – *them and us, us and them* – and getting drunker every minute: the solution and, unfortunately, the problem. I can't leave now because I rode my bike here. I'm drunk and home is further in the dark and further still with every Castle down my gullet. I know they invited me because I'm white and they felt bad for me being out of their circle in this strange new place. I'm not a group person, though, never was.

She likes having no circle. She likes being on the outside.

Yes, I know this, but I came, didn't I? I tried.

I'll wait (as if I have a choice now). The Do-Gooder with the illegal bakkie says she'll drop me at home. So until then, I add a word or two where I can so they won't think I'm stupid or judgemental or suffering from some other disease whose symptom is quietness. Mostly I space out and drink and admire the shadows morphing on the opposite wall.

The door opens and, without speaking, the woman who enters screams insecurity in a rude and blatant way; I hate her instantly. Is it her posture? Her clothes? Her face? I can't say – maybe everything – all I know is she stinks of it. She should try harder, the rest of us do. Why does she think she's special? It makes me sick. She could have washed some off before going out in public. Unfair to subject us to all of that shit; her psychological baggage is just too heavy. Too fucking heavy. I look away; my eyes aren't made for seeing that.

Doesn't matter anyway. Irrelevant. Something more exciting to look at behind her.

He's tall and thin and dark, wearing a tie-dyed orange shirt. Strong wide shoulders, long piano-player fingers. He is sick with quietness too. The good kind.

Done. Nothing more to discuss. I must fuck him. Not tonight. Sometime though. It is fundamental, destined, visceral, decided. It is the beginning.

He follows Miss Insecurity around like a trained dog.

Don't look at that; don't see it and it's not there. Make up a better story. She doesn't like ugly things.

That last bit, the compliant bit, that part where he is a shadow of someone else's image. Yeah, her – *me* – she ignores that.

LOVE: PART II

*W*eeks. Months. Days. Later in any case. Time has moved along. Accidentally, he is there again. We stand on the veranda of the post office. People passing, letters, stamps.

"Excuse me, I need to post this."

I shift myself awkwardly, not completely in my own body.

I don't like accidents. I don't like not having a script. I can't seem to stand comfortably. My shirt is crooked. Are my legs uneven?

What should she do with her extraneous arms?

There are his hands again. His shoulders, his smile. *His hands.* Is my heart beating faster? I tell myself it is.

"Meet?" he asks

"Yes," she says.

"My house?" he asks

"Yes," she says.

Oddly, it's my birthday – *did I tell him?* There are lots of murky underwater bits. Hard to see anything through all of that. Nothing is clear, at least with the eyes. Smells and touches are laser-edged to precision. Time is malleable. Sequences forgotten or made up, she's not quite sure. I tell her that, but she doesn't listen. I warn her to pay better attention, but she's singing and dreaming happy, pornographic dreams of her rainbow and puppy-dog future.

Stupid girl. Get some sense before it's too late, I warn her.

Do you want some mango? she replies.

He brings small presents. A Cindy Lauper tape. Flowers picked from his garden. It's sweet. Sweet like love books and romantic movies, so I'm sure it will all be fine; happy endings are a given. It's how the story goes and goes and goes.

I've cooked. No time for food. We kiss and grab at each other. I think maybe I shouldn't, maybe I don't want to, but he is insistent. I'm hesitant for unknown reasons. Is she telling me to stop? Telling me to take a closer look? Maybe.

I can't articulate it even to myself. He is rough and I like it, I think, but I'm scared too. He pushes his hands into my jeans, under my pants. Piano-playing fingers are not as adept as expected; she pretends they are though. I moan and say I like it. It's okay, everything is okay, I tell her.

She wants to stop. Does she? She can't decide.

"Stop," I say.

He does. Then he begs. I say I want it. I do. I do. I do. I know it for sure this time. She won't change my mind again.

He enters me with his silky, beautiful cock, and it's lovely and she agrees. She always wipes away the ugly things. Life is so much nicer that way she's found.

I love him. I do. I do. I do.

LOVE: PART III

I'm married. We are married. To this man? To this man. The steps that got us here are obscured. What happened during all of those days from then until now? Stuff. Undefined stuff. Mostly good stuff.

Don't pick at it, it will only bleed, I tell her.

Maybe this is when blood is needed, she thinks. Lots and lots of blood.

Stop all that thinking, she orders.

It is love because that is what marriage means. It's not just me who thinks it; the world is behind me on that one. One hundred per cent. Buy one, get one free. Couple. Joined. Inseparable. Indivisible. Soulmates. The entire world says it is, so are you going to stand there, one minuscule, insignificant person and shout to the seven billion others that they're lying? Don't be silly, she says.

Okay, I won't.

One where there were two. Hide and seek – *where did I go?* Where did she go? Where am I now? Piece by piece I'm dripping away. I'm sure of it. I feel smaller.

Am I disappearing?

You're fine.

I'm fine.

You're fine.

In the photo of that day I stand, arms hanging; he's next to me the same way. What do our faces say? Finally it is here, this day. We are in love, they say, until death do us part.

What path got you here? she asks.

I look around, confused and disoriented, is *this* the place then? Is this the real solid manifestation of that love word? Have I arrived? Does it feel like this? Is this how it is meant to feel?

She doesn't answer me. Her face is stern. Don't ask me such things!

Who should I ask?

No one, she says and turns and leaves.

I look at him. Husband. I force the feelings that are not there. Fake it until you make it bullshit; it's all I've got, and you've got to have something.

"Should we go back to work?" he asks.

"Yes."

"And then?"

"We're married, what else do you want?"

He looks confused, which is not what I need so I leave. He stands. Alone on the stoep. Hands hanging. Piano-playing fingers still and awkward. He has been cast in a mould, just as I have. His is stuck, it keeps him in one place, which is sad. At least mine lets me move about, but it is still binding. I'm sure my legs have fallen asleep.

It's done now.

Don't cry over spilt milk. If wishes were horses, beggars would ride. The grass is always greener on the other side of the fence. It's a big heavy bucket, this marriage one. Full of history and expectations and pressure and requirements and rules and lots of clichés that I find, surprisingly, do not help.

Pick it up, she says.

It's so heavy.

Don't be a pussy. Pick the fucking thing up; it's yours now.

But how will I move carrying all of that around with me.

Wrong time to ask now. Pick it up, it's yours, she says. Get along now. Your path does not end here.

AMBIVALENCE: PART I

*H*e has condoms in his pocket when he comes home.

"They're for us. When we went away. I forgot them."

I'm too tired not to accept his barely disguised lie. Two babies, work and then work, work, work. I can barely see through my cloud of fatigue. Yes, okay. Wipe the guilt off your face at least. At least have the courtesy to do that.

Each year I am less and less and lose more and more. Melting in the sun, seeping into that deep Kgalagadi sand. Where do I go? Me, the me-part, *where's that?* Did I leave it in my old home? I'm like an electron: not there and not here, nowhere, can't be found – but existing.

My home far away is gone forever. I tried to go back but I stood with odd strangers talking languages I couldn't decipher because my eyes had changed, my ears could no longer hear that frequency. She told me it would be that way, I should have listened.

Here I am hovering on the edge, one foot, on tip-toe, wobbly, unstable. What sort of home is that? I ask.

The kind you chose, so shut up, she says.

The edge is so near, the drop so far. I can't take a step; the fear will swallow me up, I'm sure of it. I must just stay where I am no matter how bad where I am is.

Gone and here. Loved and betrayed. Hurt and cared for. Kind and mean. Everywhere and nowhere. The fury about it all builds and builds. I want to scream, but she insists I swallow it.

Quiet, quiet. Be very quiet on the ward. The patients don't like sudden moves and loud noises.

I step carefully and keep my words to myself, my doubts, my fears. Things are crumbling, though, even my good behaviour won't stop it. The first pebbles are falling. Tumbling, tumbling; weakening the entire structure. Tiny little sounds in the far distance moving nearer, ever nearer.

Watch out, she says. The monster is waiting. Either pull your shit together or welcome him in. Give him tea, get acquainted. You don't want him barging in unexpectedly, do you? You know you don't like surprises. *Take care!* Pull it together before it's too late for everyone. People are depending on you.

But what can one woman do against a crumbling mountain and a monster?

ANGER: PART I

I see him drive past. He's not alone. I follow. They stop. He has her sitting on the bonnet of the car, her legs spread wide. He is kissing her with my lips. He is wrapping her with my arms.

Red. Blind. Fury. I waited too long; the monster has arrived like a surprise party.

This *isn't* a party, she says.

I think we all know that, I spit back.

I take the metal bar from under my seat. I walk towards them, banging my feet into the ground that is now me. I feel the vibrations through my body, each reinforcing the next, making them stronger and stronger, making me stronger and stronger.

Crash. Window gone. Crash. Another gone. They see me now. They *really* see me now. I will kill them. It is not a thing I fear. I will kill them both and wash myself in their blood.

She will wash herself in their blood, warm and sticky.

The fury is rolling and rumbling, it is its own thing, away from me and inside too. Huge and unfettered. Fed for years with late nights and limp cocks and unidentifiable smells and love-words with no meaning. It is loose and ready.

Monsters really have very bad manners. And they eat you up completely if they're hungry enough.

Yes, but what do people expect from monsters?

AMBIVALENCE: PART II

*H*e begs and she relents. Not much left, but she gives it over anyway. She will have faith. Faith. Hallelujah. Amen. The grey-bearded old man watching out for us, floating on his cloud. Fuck. I can believe that – *why not?* Other people do. I can swallow shit as well as the next person.

You're not other people, she says.

This time I'm other people. For this once I'm other people.

He will be good. He loves her. She loves him. Love plasters over the bumps and the stinky bits. Too much time has passed. Too late to start over. Too-too late. Too late for Mama and every other fucking person. It's just too late to start looking at shit clearly.

I'm not sure I'm who I thought I was. I was not a person like this before.

Sure you were, she says. You've never liked the ugly bits; don't you remember?

It all looks ugly now. I decide to say home is here. Nice is not. Summer is winter and yes, Jesus loves me. Right? Right?

She walks away, shaking her head.

Where are you going?

She keeps quiet. She stops and looks at me. Are her eyes kind? I don't trust anything anymore.

(Tell me later what you saw? Okay? You're on my side, right?)

Was my journey to here? What was I supposed to be learning?

Forgiveness? Selflessness? But at what cost? What have I had to pay for these lessons?

You had to pay everything, she says. She blows on her nails and rubs them to a shine on her T-shirt. A smear of purple remains behind.

Was it worth it?

They say it's worth it.

Who are they?

She shrugs. Maybe you are they.

LOVE: THE FINAL ACT

*W*e travel through the icy towns. Sleep under down duvets. Make love morning and night. Kiss and hold hands. Everyone can see: *they are in love.* The right sort. The Julia Roberts and Hugh Grant sort. How sweet. Like honey on top of a sugar ball. Sweet, sweet, sweet. And it feels just like that. I know I've done the right thing. Sweet is always the right thing.

I love you so much. Please don't ever leave me, he says. He is ardent (with a capital A) and honest (with a capital H) and desperate (well … you get it). I know he's broken inside, always has been. I must make allowances for that. He doesn't know love, real love, reliable love, loyal love. The love I offer. He doesn't know The Right Kind of Love. I'll sort him out.

You'll sort him out.

Yes, I'll sort him out.

(Is she smirking? I can't see. Tell me later when she's not around. It's important.)

He suspects all love is using love, deceptive love, destroying love. This makes him lash out first. Defensive play, it's an option, a game plan. I understand that. I want to help him heal. I want him to love like me. But instead, I'm starting to love like him.

Ignore that last bit, she says.

Why?

Ugly. You remember, akere?

Yeah, okay. Forgotten.

I told you she never likes ugly things. Throw that thought away. Bury it deep. You've got a lot of work to focus on. Huge job. Get busy or you'll never finish. A woman's work is never done.

Oh, it was incredible though! When we are good, we are like magic, like healing, like liquid hot love. The sex is perfect or nearly or enough. Like a gorgeous drug.

Drugs are great, she says.

(Is she smirking? Tell me later, okay?)

ANGER: PART II

A phone call. I explode inside and out. Broken me-pieces scatter around the house, in the garden, over the fence. I scream and it doesn't help. I cry and cry and it doesn't help. I am the first to feel such pain, the first in the entire world, in the whole history of humanity. Don't placate me with your fucking stories. They don't even touch the place where I am.

Fire. I burn everything. Myself and him. A conflagration that pulls the entire world inside. Nothing can be fixed. All must be destroyed. It must be given its proper spectacular burial. He has caused this and his punishment will be death.

My punishment will be death too.

So we walk away from each other – dead – can you see that? Can you see the death in our eyes? In our souls? In the place where love lived?

I want to pound my chest and say: *Look!* Look what his love did to me! I have been fatally wounded. Look you fucking people! You who applauded marriage: *Look!* I am pieces and dust. Nothing more of what I was at the beginning – because of all of you. Take some fucking responsibility. Your Marriage Box is full of poison yet you push it like some sort of happy healthy heroin. You must also be blamed. Because of you I am here. Because of you I am dead.

Because of them? she asks, one eyebrow arched.

Yes! Fuck you! Don't ask me such things.

She keeps quiet. Too late for words, it seems. Too late for lots of shit.

Just fucking too late.

THE WAITING ROOM

*I*n our waiting room we have many lovely magazines. We accept that waiting is not what you want to be doing with your time, so we want to make it as pleasant as possible. Help yourself to coffee and tea in the corner. There are biscuits too, *the good kind.* Feel free to have a biscuit. Some hot coffee and a tasty biscuit will make the time fly. You won't even notice that you've been waiting for hours, days, months, years. It's nice like that, you'll see.

We have a wide selection of magazines, puzzle magazines. Try a Sudoku. That will fill some time. Or take a *Cosmo* quiz: *Are you the best sexual partner you can be?* Scores out of one hundred. Aren't these quizzes fun?

The wait will be over before you know it and everything will be fine. Everything will be just fine. Would you like a spoon?

HARMONIES IN THE KEY OF SURVIVAL

*T*he land is barren, so finally I can see without a single distraction; such a relief to see it all clearly. Everything is exactly as it appears now. The truth of it feels like medicine. I walk unhindered. The freedom is overwhelming. I can swing my arms and legs. I want to spin and do cartwheels. I feel like yellow and summer and birds in the blue sky.

As we walk, she points out the important bits, here and there, the bits I thought I'd lost. A love for beautiful things. The courage to take chances. The peacefulness of silence. I'm happy to see they survived it all, they were just misplaced for a while. I put them in my basket, which grows heavier and heavier as we walk.

The sun is warm on my face and the sand soft on my feet. We are together, walking in companionable silence. The sky is as big and blue as it has ever been in this home of my heart. I am thankful and happy in this place, finally I am me and I am home.

As we walk, slowly, small grasses appear. Green and fresh after the first dusty rains. Then some spiky thorn bushes. And trees: tall marula and scrubby mophane, yellow acacias with their smooth golden trunks. Their shade is welcome, and we stop in their coolness, in their calmness, and it feels like they were waiting for us to arrive; they receive us like lost friends.

Do you like it here now? she asks.

Yes, yes, now that I can see things clearly, I like it very much.

She rubs my heart with her hands of silk healing all of the broken edges, mending the wounds, dabbing up the tears.

I look at her and smile. Then I pick up my basket, and we continue with our work.

Diaspora Electronica

Blaize Kaye

*T*here's someone else on the underground train today. He's sitting near the door and reading something. Whatever it is, it's serious. Aqua clothbound and hardcover. A thousand pages at least. He waved at me when he got onto the train. I waved back. I wonder what's wrong with him.

It's still early and it's damned near freezing. When I was a boy, you could hardly find an open handrail on the early train into the city. I'd catch it with my dad on those days he'd let me take a sickie from school. He'd give me some pocket money and the sandwiches that Mom had made for him, and he'd drop me off at the cinema. Most days I'd be able to buy a medium-sized bag of sucking mints and two, sometimes three, tickets. The cinema manager, a big man with brown teeth, would ignore my sneaking into other films when I'd run out of money. I know he saw me, but I guess he liked me. Maybe he just felt sorry for me because I was always there on my own. I don't know.

I haven't been to the cinema in years. It's not that I grew out of it. It's just that they don't make films any more, not the kind I can watch. I've got a whole stack of old movies on file though, and most nights I'll stay up late watching the ones I really like, but it's nothing like going to the cinema. Nothing like the lights dimming and that grey rectangle coming to life. You could forget things there. You could forget what it was like outside, how frustrated the teachers got, how frustrated *you* got, how the other kids would laugh behind their hands. But Dad understood. He never cared that I missed school.

Just before we get to the city, the train travels a short way above ground. The winter sun is low and bright. Here at the city limits are what's left of the informal settlements. I see an old shaggy dog scratching around. It ignores the train as we pass. When people began to leave, these squat dwellings of corrugated iron and chipboard were bequeathed to the wind and ocean air. There isn't much left, and those small houses I can still make out stand like hollow teeth amidst the rubble. I suppose that those, like me, who couldn't leave just moved into the city once there was enough space.

The man with the book gets off at one of the earlier stops. I'd thought that maybe he was going to the Institute too. I guess not. He stands on the platform and waves at me before the doors close and we move off. I wave back at him. He's wearing a scarf. Maybe I should have also worn mine.

I step out onto the platform a few more stops before we reach the central hub of the underground. It's warming up. That, or there's still some attempt at climate control in this part of the city. Near the 172nd Street exit I see a woman in blue overalls sweeping the floor. At first I think she's calling me, but then I realise that she's muttering to herself. The same phrase, over and over. That'll do it. Whatever's making her speak out loud to herself will be what's keeping her out. Some, like her, wear their disqualification out in the open. Mine isn't as obvious. I wonder if it's easier that way. Easier if you have no expectations.

The Institute dwarfs the surrounding buildings, making them look dumpy and squalid in comparison. Here there is some movement, although not human. The square outside the Institute is abuzz with drones and bots. They pay me no mind. They expect me to be here. Or, rather, the Institute, the building itself, expects me. If I were an intruder, of if I were carrying some kind of weapon, I could expect a very different reception.

The entrance to the Institute is carbon black and perfectly flush with the wall. I step in front of it and for a moment I see myself reflected in the dark surface before the door opens along some imperceptible seam. There is no sound as it slides apart.

The first time I visited the Institute with Sarah, the lobby was an actual lobby, with an information desk and people with suits and clipboards herding visitors into the appropriate queues and waiting rooms. I'd come out of curiosity, to see what Sarah – and everyone else – was so excited about.

What was then the lobby now consists of a series of lockers and showers. Illuminated strips set into the floor lead me to the locker designated for my use. I undress and step into a narrow glass cubicle. Warm water that smells of bleach and antiseptic sprays from the roof, walls, and floor. A woman's voice tells me to wash my face and hair with a gel from a dispenser that appears from the wall. The water stops abruptly and the driers engage. Within a minute I'm as clean and dry as I've ever been. No dust can be allowed to enter the Institute.

I put on the gown I've been provided with. It's pure white and open at the back. I skip the paper underwear. After doing this a few times, one grows not to care.

I met Sarah through music. My mother thought, somehow, that sight-reading classical piano pieces would be easier than reading novels because "it's not letters". Obviously it's not letters. That doesn't make it any easier. Not that I couldn't play, mind you. I could, and I was something of a natural, if you don't count my trouble reading sheet music. I just did what I did in school when someone called on me to read out loud, I memorised it all. Still, it was painful, the recitals, the tuxedos, the tails, the bowing, the polite clapping.

It was Sarah who'd kept me at it. I met her at one of my recitals. "Listen to this," she said, and removed the white bud from her left ear and handed it to me. It was Coltrane. She stood, listening in mono, smiling as though she expected me to say something, or to pass out from sheer delight.

There are moments that change everything. Moments that teach you something about yourself. Sarah and I listening to Coltrane's "Giant Steps" together, standing so close we were almost touching, was one of those moments. Before then, I hadn't realised that I was lonely.

*D*espite its present look and feel, the Institute was never a hospital. There were psychologists and neurophysiologists, yes, but there were also AI researchers, people with double doctorates in Machine Learning and Biology, MBAs who held degrees in abstract mathematics. The Institute for the Future of Humanity was the result of unlimited computing power meeting exponential population growth. It was a joint initiative between some of the biggest names in technology. They approached the problem of human overpopulation the same way they approached everything, as another scaling problem to be solved with better algorithms and faster hardware.

Sarah worked at the Institute for a while before she left; most graduates did. She got a job as an immigration officer – that's what they called themselves, I don't know if that was her official title.

She helped people with getting the right forms filled out, and told them who they could get clearance from. She also helped them understand when and how they would be leaving. We moved to the city, she worked at the Institute, I got a regular gig playing in a small coffee shop in the arts district. Things were good for a while. Then Dad got sick.

I remember the day my dad told me that he was going to leave. Mom had invited Sarah and me to their one-bedroom apartment in the city – they'd downsized since I'd moved out. Mom had made a potato casserole for lunch. She'd bought fresh tomatoes too, which none of us had had for years. Now people were draining out of this world at a rate of many thousands a day, and so things that used to be luxuries, such as tomatoes, had become commonplace.

After dessert, Mom asked Sarah to help her with making coffee, and Dad led me to what was once a balcony but had been closed up and converted into a small sitting room. It smelled as though the thick, green pile carpet had never been vacuumed.

"I need to show you something," he'd said, pulling down the collar of his shirt to reveal a dark mole about the size of a small coin, but not nearly as round. Its edges were ragged and white with dry skin.

Stage 4 melanoma. The prognosis was bad. Dad told me that his doctors had urged him to look into the Institute. They'd said, rather cheerfully, that "it was putting oncologists out of work." He hadn't wanted to worry me until he and Mom had made a decision, but they'd reached out to Sarah a few weeks earlier for information. She was, in his estimation, the right person to turn to, since "she actually worked at the place, you know?"

I was shocked and furious on his behalf. I was also, somewhere below, in a quiet, selfish place, more than a little hurt that Sarah had kept something so vital to herself, that she'd been able to fall asleep next to me for weeks knowing that my father was ill. She worked at the Institute though, and I suppose she saw cases like this all the time.

The doctors were right. He didn't have to die. The technology that was meant to get the world's population under control had the upshot of making death voluntary. At least, that's how it had seemed to me at the time.

"Mom is coming too," he'd said. It made sense. They'd already been together forever.

On our way home, Sarah suggested we think about leaving too, at the same time as my parents. Hers had already left; they'd crossed the threshold nearly a year earlier. Our friends were leaving weekly. I understood the attraction, really. You're never sick, you never get old or die. And with every upgrade, every new server added to the cloud, your consciousness was supposed to expand, to deepen.

"It's simpler than buying a washing machine on credit," she said. I told her I'd think about it, and she asked about it every day for a week before I gave in.

A small drone, the size of my palm, flies up to me. In a voice too loud for its body, it says: "Please follow me, we'll begin with socialisation tasks." I nod, it turns and moves off towards one of the open platforms that act as lifts here.

As I follow, I feel the floor beneath me vibrating. As high as this building is, it's only the tip of the proverbial iceberg. There are thousands of rooms below, each housing hundreds of thousands of computers. Long, anonymous racks of machines. Below that, the power plant drawing from geothermal vents. Entirely self-sufficient. The surface of the planet could be scoured clean by a super-volcano or asteroid, or anything really, and Suhkavati – that place inside the cloud – would keep ticking over.

Sarah and I were evaluated on the same day. We'd planned on telling our friends together and throwing a combined leaving party. I'd waited for her outside the Institute. "The 7th of June," she said, waving a copy of her contract an inch from my nose. I wanted to be happy for her. Really. I said nothing and handed her the blue slip that the doctor had given me. I'd failed some of the neural examinations.

"I don't understand," she said. "It's *just* dyslexia."

It's strange how someone can know you half your life and still say something like that. It was always just dyslexia, wasn't it? Maybe if I'd just tried a little harder, I'd be neurocompatible? Maybe if I could just read the fine print? Sarah was like that sometimes, making the hard things sound like they should be easy, even when they really weren't. Even when they'd never be easy.

"They're making progress with the tech all the time," is what she said a week later, when I realised that she hadn't cancelled her June appointment. "I'll be there for a month at most before they work out how to pull you over."

But what if it took longer, what if they never managed to figure it out?

"Nonsense. And It's not like we won't be able to talk," she said. "We can mail, and voice chat. We can date, I've heard people still date across the threshold, if one of them can only leave later. That's what the people who work in interfaces tell us."

I'd tried to convince her not to leave.

"I've already signed my things over to the Institute. Do you know what a hassle it is to get that reversed?"

With that, the subject was closed. A simple matter of transfer of property.

The 1st of June. Her leaving party. It was at our place, and not well-attended. Most of our friends had already left. There were a few people from the coffee shop, and some of Sarah's colleagues from the Institute. I got very drunk early on, and spent most of the night in our bedroom closet, covering myself with blankets and jackets to drown out the music.

A week later, I dropped her off at the Institute. It felt like we were at an airport, but she had no luggage. I held her tight, and then she was gone. She didn't cry.

I've never seen anyone leave. They don't let you. Althoug Sarah explained it to me once. They lie you down in a vat, with electrodes covering most of your body. Then, somewhere in the network, there's an empty model, a mirror image of you across the threshold – in the cloud. The syncing takes hours. At first, you think, and the mirror image thinks in turn. Then, you and the model begin to think together, and it becomes a part of you.

Eventually, you can't tell if it's you or the model that's thinking, and that's when they start shutting down the biological parts of the new hybrid consciousness. First your limbs, then your torso, then, by degrees, the brain. And all this time, through the syncing, your consciousness has expanded into the machine, and long before there is no trace of electrochemical activity in your body, you've already slipped all the way into the network. Sarah said she didn't know what happens to the bodies, not *really* – not that it matters.

I suppose time works differently in there. They send messages at first, trying to explain what it's like in Sukhavati, how you're reborn inside a lotus bud and how everything is made of light. They're all bowled over at how they *think* now, how quickly they can read, argue, understand. Amazed at the kinds of music and art they can make.

Dad sent me a symphony he'd composed. There were half a million parts. When I played it, though, I couldn't understand it, it was cacophony. He explained that the piece worked along nine dimensions at once, he knew it might seem complex to me, but that everyone on that side agreed that it was a masterpiece. This from a man who'd never shown the slightest interest in music, who hadn't had a musical bone in his body. When he still had bones. And a body.

Soon they forget to send messages, or they give up in frustration because they're that much further along than I am. I understand. I'm only human. They're so much more, now. And less.

*O*nce the testing regimen is done, I'm led by the drone into a room with two low chairs.

"The doctor will be in in a moment," it says before departing.

"The view is gorgeous, isn't it?"

The doctor, late forties, balding.

"It is," I reply.

"We're half a kilometre up, if you can believe it?"

He gestures to the chair closest to the window. I take a seat. The chair is more comfortable than it looks.

"You're the first person I've seen at the Institute today," I say.

He smiles, "I'm not surprised, the roster has really thinned out over the last couple of years. Almost all of the permanent members have left."

"And I only am escaped alone to tell thee, eh?"

"What's that?"

"Nothing, just something I heard once. I liked it."

"Oh, right, well," he shifts himself in his seat, straightens up to deliver the verdict. I know what he's going to say.

"I'm afraid we weren't able to certify you this time around."

"Still not?"

"You score fine on most metrics, but on information processing…"

"I'm ND, yes, I know."

"Yes, and we can't risk it."

I look down at the floor for a moment and see the doctor's shoes. They're old brown oxfords, I think, scuffed almost white at the toes.

"Okay," I say. "Can't I sign something, a waiver?"

He explains that even if he thought it was a good idea, there are legal issues and that he is very sorry. Et cetera. He shakes my hand and I'm alone in the room again. It's only when I see the afternoon sun hanging low above the horizon that I realise I've been here the whole day.

I wonder what's wrong with the doctor. I wish I'd asked. Why is he still here when everyone else has left? Is it contractual obligation, or is it something more? Almost everyone I've asked has been neurodiverse. Sometimes those on the spectrum can't sync. Some kinds of aphasias. My dyslexia. Whatever the Institute considers wrong. Of course, he needn't have something "wrong" with him to stay. I've heard that there are some people philosophically opposed to it, shaken by the thought that what is on the other side of the threshold isn't really going to be them. There are some criminals, too, who have been refused entry. But most of us still here in the cold, riding trains, watching the sun set, are simply a little different.

I ride a platform down to the lobby and head to my locker. I change back into my own clothes and step outside. I begin walking to the underground entrance, but it's so cold that I decide I'll stay in the city tonight. I don't want to be alone. I find an information kiosk and ask for the location of the nearest shelter. When it was clear that the majority of humanity had been absorbed into the network, the Institute set up a series of shelters and food depots for those left behind. They spared no expense. They didn't have to. There were very few of us to care for anymore.

It's two blocks to the shelter and I pick up the pace to warm myself. I know the place. I think I've stayed there before. An old hotel, automated to run without human intervention. The sound of my shoes against the sidewalk echoes against the high walls about me.

How many of us are there left here, I wonder. How many of us will still leave?

I'll continue to make this trip to the Institute, every few months, as I have ever since Sarah left me. I'll make this trip again and again until they eventually say "Congratulations, and welcome." And then? I haven't thought beyond that.

The shelter is up ahead, a yellow light streams from the glass doors that face out to the street, and I think I can hear voices. And music.

Naming

Umar Turaki

I'Kokulok (Taroh)
Rooster. Between two feet in the car where four people are hunched with pounding hearts because the sky has turned to ink and their tyre has turned to flap. The bird is one of those bald ones with feathers that begin only from their necks. They are mainly found in that lowland of neem trees and decorated warriors.

☙

Wanduni (Temne)
Man. The driver. Standing and staring and standing. Thinking. How to change a tyre in the middle of this godless hour without spare or spanner?

☙

Culicidae (Latin)
Mosquito. Night hunter. Probing the depths of the flesh found wanting.

☙

Twa! (Human)
She slaps her neck and misses. Scratches with nails as tough as nails and just as sharp. Those same hands demonstrate a peculiar, desperate tenderness, travelling south to rest on her hump. She whispers a secret song in a tongue that no one around her knows. The same tongue he used to whisper to her as she slid down his throat to quench his thirst on a hot night: the one she chooses to believe is the father of her unborn child. Airy words. *Mi alma. Amado. Angelico.* In the haze of the love ballooning inside her, she began to learn it, that lilting, succulent tongue that fills your mouth like honey. Now she knows it, and it is of no use to her. She inflicts it like a lash upon herself, calling herself names.
Puta (Spanish)
Whore. She slept with the white man in return for a promise; to be taken to his own land. She never took a pledge for the promise, and she never saw him again. Two days later, a man who was black

like her pried her open even though she begged him not to and also spilled himself into her. Now, as she sits in this car and stares down at this hump in this darkness, she has no idea what colour her child will be. She does know for certain, though, that men, black or white, are dicks. In the future she is planning for this child, he is male, his skin is as bright and soft as overripe pawpaw, hair black and wavy like his father's. He becomes her totem of achievement, a ticket to heaven. She thinks she draws envy and admiration in pails from the hearts of the watchful; she does not know that she is a soiled skirt in their eyes. She tells herself she is happy; she does not know she isn't. Her happiness is an armour that imprisons her. In another future, the true future, the one that would materialise if she could only reach the end of this black road, she thinks to herself that her son is a dick. But tonight there shall be no futures. And her son, for now, is only a piece of toughening tissue inside her womb.

☙

Ole inu aboyun (Yoruba)
Male unborn child. Suspended inside the woman who calls herself a whore. In that true future, the boy is as black as this snaking road. When he becomes a man, it is his heart that will know what true blackness is. He will know many things. That he is unhappy. That his mother hates him. That women are a sickness to be cured. He will grow to become a man suspended, as he had been in his mother's womb, between two natures, between someone who writes and someone who erases, between living and dying, endlessly, until he surrenders to his unchangeable spots. By the time he spills himself into his first victim, he is already blaming his mother for spilling *him* into this existence, for not undoing him from the moment she knew he was a clot in her belly, for allowing him to be the son of a rapist, for allowing him to become a rapist. He does not blame his father, an ellipsis that precedes the sentence that he is, the sentence that ends in an ellipsis trailing into space as he becomes frozen in this present night of no futures. He will

remain a foetus forever.

∽

Gurum (Ngas)

Man. Half his head is on fire. He grips it with one hand. There is more than one reason for this, but they don't come all at once; they take turns tormenting him. The other hand slides a thumb down his Facebook photo section. He has been looking at images of his three children, and their mother, uploaded to curate the sham of his happiness. Now there is no way to take them down without encountering the questions that will point to the other woman and her child waiting at the end of this black road.

The world is a place of wonders, he thinks to himself. So he wonders at many things. How the phone signal picks up in this least likely of places. How his white collar commands reverence in the faces of his sheep. How it haunts him. How it isn't enough to keep his faith from ebbing. How he tried to transcend the base desires tickling his frayed edges in Jesus' name, and how even that name could not pluck him out of his human mire. How his fall was so predictable; it could only have been a woman. How it is impossible to run away from your true nature. How it all reminds him of touching himself on the cusp of puberty in a toilet stall in the three-minute gap between Math and CRS periods, training his mind to hold the image of the breasting Samira as he climbs and climbs, finally spilling into a heaven of pure white softness that lasts only a moment before giving way to the graffiti on the toilet door and cleaning up in a haste fuelled by regret. How the guilt is what he remembers more than the pleasure, how the idleness of sitting in this car finally brings him understanding: in the showdown between wanting and regret, he has chosen to be crushed by the weight of guilt rather than be licked by the flame of desire. Every time. Whether it is in his own well-lubricated palms, or the truer, incomparable softness of a woman. Mighty, wondrous things.

Yet his true curse remains that he found love after the fact. His wife and his three sons are the fact, and facts cannot be erased or ignored. The woman at the end of this black road and her child are his light. They tip the scale. Two people against four. They tip the scale. The choice he is making is a continuum, and he is in the middle of making it. Once he reaches the end of the road, the choice will be complete. He will take off his collar and surrender his flock and take a boat south with the woman and the child who tip the scale against the whole world. But he can't finish making the choice, because there are no futures tonight on this black road.

∽

Akuko (Yoruba, Twi)

Rooster. Shitting like a shit factory on the shoes of the man to whom the chicken does not belong. It belongs to another man who begged and begged until the first man said yes. An undue thank-you to another man, a big man in a big house who has sent yet another man to wait for it at the end of this black road. The air around a rooster in transit is a problem, a stench crawling up noses and nipping at joy until there is no joy left in the small car. In the joyless wake of the stench, somebody is thinking thoughts of sweet vengeance against the ugly chicken, imagining roasting its plucked body marinated in groundnut oil and groundnut spice on a spit. But the thinker of the thought shall never again eat chicken or think about chicken. For the thinker of the thought and the rooster and the man who agreed to ferry the rooster to the end of the black road have become equals in the scheme of things. On a night when there are no futures, a rooster and five human beings are about to have the same end.

∽

Nwoke (Igbo)

The man whose shoes are covered in shit. He now regrets the decision. He has been a bad man his whole life, or for as long as he can remember. If he thinks hard enough, he may come up with one or two past good deeds. He thinks and he remembers: he once found a boy wandering in the streets, lost, and he found the boy's home and made sure he was safely under the beam of his mother's restored smile, before turning away. That is the only good deed that sparkles in his sea of dark memories. Any other good deed would have been accidental, unintended, a cosmic ordering – like stealing someone's car only to have delivered them from a fatal accident the very next day.

He has been many bad things; he has even been a hypocrite: he once broke the jaw of a thief with a single blow that left the man's mouth gaping like a useless door. His last bad deed was of biblical proportions, Cain and Abel, earth and blood. Blood is crying out, blood is chasing him, and he is running. Running to the place where he will not hear the voice of blood calling his name. He will cross the desert, and then the sea, and he will plant himself in that land of snow and women who have flat buttocks and long straight hair. His friend married one such woman. His friend who sends pictures of his new life, but has never sent money. He will join his friend where the sound of the crying blood cannot reach him. It is on the heels of his last bad deed that the chance to be good again presents itself. An ugly rooster and a begging man. This rooster, ugly as it is, could be the beginning of his redemption, he tells himself. He decides that he will take the rooster and deliver it to its intended recipient as promised, and he will be kind to the rooster, even though it is only an animal. This will be the beginning of his kindness to all creatures, and he prays that this kindness, this goodness, is what he will be remembered for.

But your true nature is a hard thing to run away from. In the only future that he sees for himself, he does not see the armed desert bandit who revives his hate and his badness, or the platinum watch he steals from the wrist of a dead-drunk fellow migrant, or the lonely white woman he marries with the pretty face and small breasts he wishes were bigger, only to divorce her once his papers are ready. On a night when there are no futures, none of these things matter. All that matters is that he is a good man on a black road that shall never end.

ભ

Homo sapiens (Latin)

Boy. His exam is in seven hours. But seven hours isn't enough time to traverse the length of this black road. In the future he is planning and willing to happen, he sits in the examination hall and writes ferociously, like a tiger caught in a fight for survival against the other students and the supervisors and the examiners and his teachers all put together. He fights and he wins. What this future also contains, although he cannot see it, is that he will sit between two girls in the examination hall, one in front and one behind, while a crush collects in a pool behind his lungs for the plainer of the two, whom he will marry on a windswept Saturday afternoon in the month of December, eleven years later.

There are two forces at work on him now as he sits in the car on this black road. One is behind him, propelling him forward; a force composed of a dead father who had only one child, a mother who continues to dress in black and sweep street gutters just after sunrise and weep through the wall in the middle of the night for everything that God gave her yet still took away, and the onus on him, not to become the full stop in his family line, not to allow his name to die. This force looks at him every day through the photograph of his father he carries in his Velcro-strapped wallet.

The second force is in front, beckoning. Sometimes it taunts him, tells him he is nothing. But it is smiling all the time. It looks like a white coat and a stethoscope, and sparkling white tiles under brilliant white light where poor, sick people are healed; it looks like a long driveway guarded by snow-laden maple trees and a magnificent sprawling house that sits so close to the ground you would think it sprang out of it. Filled with soft, golden music that seeps through the walls, and woods in the backyard, and a dark blue passport, and seven children – seven, to be sure – to run around and grow up and see to it that his name doesn't die.

Two forces, and they are constantly at work. This is why he fights like a tiger in an examination hall. This is why he is unstoppable. This is why he must get through the night, to the end of this black road. But tonight is a night that can't be moved. It is an immoveable night. It is a night that has no futures.

∾

Direba (Hausa)
Driver. He has travelled many roads to get here. Along the way, he has seen many things. He has seen a pregnant woman ripped open like a birthday present. He has seen diamonds as big as a child's skull. He has seen a man urinate on the body of a woman he has just devoured. He has seen his own head in the mirror, uneven like a cracked egg, hair forever trying and forever failing to conceal the machete scar that runs in a furrow along his temple. So he forever wears a black woollen hat with a tufted tip. He has seen a night in which so many people died that when he closed his eyes and listened, he could hear their spirits rising through the roofs. The sound was like the small hiss a hand makes when it breaks the calm surface of water and slips under it. He heard it a thousand times that night. He left the next day with nothing but his clothes and walked until the roads turned brown and red and green, and when he was certain he had crossed the border, he found the nearest home and asked them for anything to drink.

A week later, he was still alive. So he decided that he would travel far and forget this land and all the blood. This is how far he has come. Here he has found a woman who loves him in spite of the shape of his head, and five children who fill his heart with a pure, earthen joy. He has learned a new tongue and has donned a new name and has become a new man. Now they call him direba. He has seen both ends of this snaking black road more times than he can count, and he knows it the way he knows the scar on his head. Three or four times a week, he wrestles with this black road for the food he will bring home and place like a sacrament in each of their mouths, each one he loves more than they shall ever know.

He is so confident he has taken to lending out his spare tyre, even with an impending trip, because he knows God will take care of him on this black road the way He took care of him on many other roads. He is a happy man, but the memories of death linger in his head like a song that refuses to fade. This is even what keeps him happy. His suffering distilled his ambition; he has no room for rarefied dreams. His dream is peace, a bed, a wife, five children, and some food. If he can achieve this dream for more days than not, it is enough. Though he is fearless tonight on this black road, he has one secret fear. Smack as he is in the centre of his happiness, he fears that his life is a palindrome patiently unfolding, that the same pain that burned him as a youth will return to finish him off as an old man. This possible symmetry troubles him, and sometimes he finds himself thinking of quitting while he is ahead, wishing that his soul would rise from his sleep and slip through the roof like a hand slipping into water, and drift to that impossible mountain place beyond the town, inside the door that cuts through a rock not far from the place he was born.

∽

Dare (Hausa)
Night. Shrinking around them like a vice. The night is a home for many things. Dreams. Demons. Skulking hooded figures with guns and knives. Hooded figures that fly and drink blood in wooded enclaves (these are no vampires). Short, leering creatures that crawl out of folk tales and challenge you to a wrestling match. The night is a home for the fear that grips five stranded travellers, a home for something the size of two elephants that now hurtles towards them. A home for this moment that becomes a breath drawn into the chest and held there.

∽

There is no name in any language for five people, a foetus, and a rooster in a small car with a flat tyre on a black road in the middle of the night, who are about to die.

Things We Found North of the Sunset

Aba Asibon

Saaku ran away. Well, she did not literally *run* away. I watched her strut down the dusty path, carrying a frayed raffia bag, making no attempts to hide between the shrubs, lacking any fear of being caught. I looked on until all that was left of her was a speck, and until that too eventually disappeared at the point where the sky meets the earth.

She left on a Saturday because she knew our mothers would be busy with housework, and our fathers caught up in their weekend gambling under the acacias. On a Saturday, the other children would be at the weekend bazaar, pilfering sweets and trinkets with high hopes of going unnoticed. The day my best friend ran away, the sun hung low like a saffron medallion, guiding her path while I looked on with hands shielding my eyes.

Now, looking back, we should have run away together, hand-in-hand, our brown bodies camouflaged by the shrubs, because that's what best friends do. We had heard our mothers say Eden was a long way from home: several bus and boat rides away. When they spoke of this place, they spoke of it reverently, pointing towards the horizon, north of the sunset.

Many had left before Saaku, mostly men, because the women said they could not bear to leave their children behind in search of greener pastures. Wearing their Sunday bests and carrying nothing but raffia bags filled with maize and dried fish, things that would not spoil, their families saw them off amidst prayers and tears. After several months, the travellers would send photos of themselves decked in heavy jackets that fell all the way to their knees, standing shin-deep in what looked like a blanket of white ice. Sometimes, these pictures were accompanied by short letters and crisp green bills that had to be exchanged in the city for money their families could actually use. In these letters, they said Eden was a place of abundance and that sometimes you had too much choice. Even bread, they said, came in several varieties.

Saaku and I pictured this Eden, a place with crisp green bills hanging from trees and ice falling from the sky like soft wafers. Everything we knew about this place we had heard from the families of those who had left, and Saaku's father – who, might I mention, had never been to Eden himself. Saaku and I would sit around his radio while he listened to the news, which was usually read by a deep-voiced woman who swallowed half her words. We heard of the incredible things the people in Eden had achieved, how they had sent men to the moon and how their buildings were so high, they almost touched the sky.

"Do people in Eden die?" Saaku had asked her father once. She had a tendency to ask questions children should not ask.

Her father chuckled, which surprised us because he was not the sort of man who chuckled. "Yes, they do, but not like us. They don't die because their doctors are on strike or because there is drought. They die because they choose to."

Saaku and I looked at each other, puzzled. Her father was not a man of many words. Not to us. Not even to Saaku's mother. Papa Saaku was a stout man with a stern face, who relayed his expectations succinctly and expected to be understood.

Saaku and I were fascinated by this place where people chose whether or not they wanted to die. For weeks we lay on her bed in her parent's bungalow, comparing life in Eden with life here, where nothing really happened. Here, our money was worn and dirty, and things like milk and soap were as seasonal as fruits and vegetables.

It was at Saaku's house that we did all the planning because she did not have siblings running around causing chaos. At my house, my parents' seven children filled every space and every corner with shrieks, name-calling and fistfights. My mother, in between constantly doing the laundry and cooking for nine, would yell threats at us, and when she had had enough, she would grab the first child in sight, drape them over her thighs and spank them foolish.

At Saaku's house, we could huddle on her lilac-covered bed in peace, sketching directions and making calculations in our double-ruled notebooks.

"It will cost us a whole year's worth of lunch money to be able to afford this trip!" I exclaimed once we had tallied the figures for bus fare, food and lodging.

"No, dummy!" Saaku responded. "Only a third of a year."

She was better at mathematics.

"I'll find us the money," she proclaimed.

And find the money she did, day after day, that is, until her father caught her with her hands in his wallet and left her buttocks with welts the size of baby okras.

One afternoon, while we dug twelve little holes in her backyard for a game of bao, she placed a hand on my shoulder and announced that only one of us would be able to go to Eden.

I argued against this. It would be safer if there were two of us. Saaku argued that we had only been able to raise money for one, and then offered to be the one to go. I wanted to be brave too, to offer to venture alone into the unknown, leaving behind the familiar, but I let her win; she was better at arguing anyway.

So Saaku ran away. I walked her all the way to the ridge of termite hills where our town seeps into the next. There was no need for hugs or kisses or emotional goodbyes because Saaku would soon send back money for me to join her. Instead, we hooked arms and twirled around till we became dizzy and collapsed on top of each other, laughing until there were pins in our sides.

"Write, will you?"

"Of course I will, on lavender-scented paper."

"With a picture?"

"With a picture every month, I promise."

We lay there in a small heap, listening to the rise and fall of each other's chests, until the amber edges of the sun began to fade and the sunset revealed itself.

"Promise you won't tell anyone I'm gone, or they'll come looking for me."

She pressed a finger to my lips, turned around and disappeared with the sun.

So later when I saw Mama Saaku crying, her hands folded on top of her head, calling for someone to bring home her only child who had not shown up for supper, I could only look on. I stood by and watched her roll herself around in the red dirt, her shrieks drawing attention and gathering a crowd. A hush fell over the town, people whispering in soft timbres, wondering what could have happened to a woman to make her pull at her own hair with such ferociousness. And once they had been briefed, they placed their hands over their mouths because such things never happened in this town.

A search party, twenty men strong, was sent out to find Saaku. They perused the area, calling out her name every day until nightfall for a whole week. They searched houses, turned the market square upside down, and cut through the thickets with their machetes. Their hunting dogs were with them, their noses trained to sniff out Saaku's scent along the obscure trails that led out of town, and each night they came home with heads hanging low.

Our mothers became fearful; they could not sleep at night at the thought of some fiend prowling around town, stealing their children. They placed curfews on us to make sure we were indoors and under their watchful eyes before the sun took its light away. Thanks to Saaku, our mothers now looked out for each other's children, and if they saw a child straying too far unattended, they grabbed them by the ear and returned them to their parents. Finally, the women of the town had a legitimate reason to stick their noses in other people's business. At school, children spoke of how their fathers slept with machetes and rifles next to them, as if whoever took Saaku might dare come into our homes in the middle of the night.

When Saaku had failed to show up by the end of the week, her parents came to my house. Flanked by my father and mother, they sat me down and searched my eyes for any hint of Saaku's whereabouts.

"Did you see her talking to any strangers that day?" her father asked.

I shook my head, avoiding eye contact.

"In which direction did you last see her go?" Mama Saaku followed, small cracks in her voice.

Mama Saaku was a nice woman, always spoiling Saaku and me with homemade baobab sweets, feeding us until our bellies stuck out. I loved her almost as much as I loved my own mother, and the sight of her sitting in my parents' living room, shoulders slumped, made the truth dance in my throat for a quick moment before fizzling down my gut.

Our parents talked among themselves for the rest of the night. My mother, in all confidence, assured Saaku's parents that if I knew something, I would speak up. And then, in her all-knowingness, she speculated that perhaps their daughter had wandered off and lost her way. They should consult a medicine man, she suggested. There was a good one a few towns away, who was cross-eyed and saw things the rest of us could not.

Mama Saaku touched my arm tenderly on her way out of our house, waiting until her husband was out of earshot to whisper, "Please don't stop coming by to visit."

The night of my interrogation, I pulled out the picture I kept hidden inside my pillowcase, the one of us grinning, our heads leaning towards each other, taken at the previous year's harvest festival. Saaku was the prettier one, her teeth shiny white and perfectly arranged, her skin the sweet colour of coffee. Staring hard at the photograph, I noticed details I had never taken in before: a tiny mole at the left corner of her mouth, the slight dimpling in her right cheek when she smiled.

My father eventually noticed, without thinking too much of it, that I had taken a liking to his weekly post office trips. Every Saturday morning, I rode on the back of his Roadster through the crowded city centre until we reached the rows of little red boxes on the back wall of the post office. Eagerly, I watched him while he fiddled with the lock on his post box, craning my neck to catch the names on the envelopes while he scanned them. There were always religious pamphlets for my mother and stacks of bills for my father, but no lavender-scented paper for me, not yet.

The first few months after Saaku ran away, I had these recurring dreams of us in her bedroom, painting each other's fingers with hibiscus dye, cursing loudly whenever one of us painted outside the nail boundary. The dreams were so vivid I could smell the camphor scent she always carried, hear every note of her wheezy asthmatic breaths. The dreams lingered behind my eyelids, like acts waiting for the stage lights to be dimmed, taunting me until my eyes flew open. And then, the rest of the night, I lay on my back, listening to the chorus of my siblings' snores combined with the monotonous chirping of crickets outside.

Some nights, I worried I would never sleep again because of the deep throbbing in my chest. I feared I would go mad. I had heard stories of people who did not sleep for days until they began to talk to themselves, and when sleep finally came to them, it was for eternity. It was in those sleepless moments that I missed Saaku the most.

I also missed her on the walk to school, when the other children paired up along the footpath, kicking red earth at each other until their black shoes turned the colour of rust. I missed her during religious education classes, when our classmates passed notes back and forth, and made faces when the teacher's back was turned. They looked at me with pity, the way you look at someone who is missing a limb. Sometimes, while I sat by myself in the playground, they came up to me and said they missed her too: her hyena-like laughter, how good she was at impersonating teachers, her sharp mouth. When you miss your best friend, you do not just miss parts of her: you miss the entirety of her existence.

*T*hese days, children are allowed to play outside past sunset, to frolic under the moonlight in the market square. Mothers no longer use Saaku as an excuse to keep their wandering children indoors to help with the housework, and our fathers once again sleep with both eyes closed. Somewhere in all of this, I have found sleep again. It comes without much beckoning, and when I fall into it, it is as if I have fallen into a deep abyss.

I visit Mama Saaku every day after school. While the other kids stay to play soccer, I sling my bag over my shoulder and trot down Tudu Lane. Some days, I find her on the front porch, engrossed in a pan of beans, sorting and flicking bad seeds to the chickens. Other days, I find her mending clothes in the backyard, humming a little tune while she works a tiny needle. Each visit begins with a cup of sweet kernel water, which I gulp down, stray droplets trickling down the sides of my mouth. The kernel water is soothing, ten times better than regular water. My parents would not approve of Mama Saaku serving me kernel water every day, something they reserve only for special guests. But my parents barely notice that I am gone, not with six other children running around the house.

At first, the visits to Saaku's house were difficult. I would smell her through the cracks in the walls, and each moment, from the bleating of the goats in the backyard, to eating Mama Saaku's mashed yams, was déjà vu. Mama Saaku used to stare at my movements so intently that she wept: thunderous sobs that rose from her gut and made her body tremble. During these episodes, which usually lasted about an hour or so, I did not exist. It was just her and the bare floor on which she lay sprawled, arms draped over her face. While Mama Saaku writhed on the floor, I looked around and made quiet observations: the window panes were enveloped in a thick film of dust, the dining table was clearly unused and covered with piles of old newspapers, and the walls which used to be bare, were now covered haphazardly in a child's amateur pencil sketches. When Mama Saaku finally picked herself off the floor, she would dry the snot off her cheeks with the back of her hand and apologise. But if anyone had any apologising to do, it was I.

These days, our favourite thing to do together is to mend clothes. We sit in the backyard, tucking in loose hems, patching up underarm holes and replacing missing buttons. Mama Saaku has taught me to embroider, how to move my fingers to create delicate patterns across dull fabric. She says I am a fast learner, that while it took Saaku roughly six months to learn to embroider, it has only taken me two.

Some days, when I arrive at the house, she takes one look at me and mumbles under her breath that my mother should take better care of my hair. Hair is a woman's glory, she tells me as she summons me to sit on the floor between her legs, undoing the four lazy plaits that have become my mother's signature. I can feel her frustration as she pulls and tugs at my wild curls, her fingers sliding up and down my scalp, smoothing and weaving. When she is done, she hands me a mirror so I can see her work of art, my stubborn hair intricately braided into rows of submission.

"See how pretty you look," she tells me and I feel warmth fill my cheeks.

When we are done with mending clothes, we venture into Saaku's unaffected room, her bed still covered in lilac sheets, a small collection of toys heaped in one corner. The missionaries hand out the toys every year during the Christmas bazaar, right after they teach us songs about snow and holly, things of which we have no knowledge. The girls receive dolls and the boys get rubber footballs, and if a girl asks for a football instead, she gets scolded. Some of Saaku's dolls are streaked with black stains from all the times she tried to dye their golden hair black with ground charcoal to get them to look more like herself.

In Saaku's room, Mama Saaku and I keep busy, organising the closet, dusting the furniture and removing cobwebs. Sometimes, she tells me grown-up things that I struggle to understand. Once I listened to her deliberating what would be worse: if someone found a sandal that belonged to Saaku on the outskirts of town, or if nothing was ever found. She said that perhaps a sandal would give her closure. I wondered what "closure" meant. I wanted to tell her that Saaku needed both sandals in Eden, that people there would laugh if she showed up with one foot bare, but I remembered Saaku's forefinger on my lips the day she left.

Mama Saaku makes sure to shoo me out of the house just before sunset, before her husband returns from work. She says he would not approve of her harbouring me in their house when I should be out playing with other children. My guess is, I am an unwelcome reminder of his daughter.

Before I step out of the door, Mama Saaku presses three coins into my palms and clasps my fingers over them. I have given up trying to refuse the money, because this puts her in a strange mood. The money is tucked away in the patent shoes I wear only on special occasions. Occasionally, I give myself a treat by spending a tiny bit on custard apples and dough-puffs in the market, but the bulk of the money remains untouched, waiting for the day when Saaku and I can buy tickets to see the acrobats perform at Easter.

*T*he return from Eden begins sometime in the rainy season, two years after Saaku runs away. It begins with three, then four, then five, until eventually it seems as if our people are coming back in throngs. We have heard our parents talk about the situation in Eden, and we smell the hidden panic in their voices. They say the natives are upset that foreigners are taking their jobs, their women and their dignity. One of our own was ambushed and killed on his way to work one morning, and without a body, his mother has still not had a chance to grieve properly. The natives lurk in the shadows waiting for anyone who looks a little different, smells a little different, speaks a little different.

The other children and I now play at the periphery of our town, at the very spot where Saaku and I parted ways, craning our necks to see who would return next. They all emerge from the horizon with the same defeated demeanour, carrying nothing but the same half-empty raffia bags they left with. They come wearing those heavy coats we have seen them wear in the pictures, even though they will never need them in this climate. As soon as their shadows appear, one of the children runs back into town yelling, drawing a crowd to meet the returnees.

Each return is tinged with the same bitter sweetness: a murky mixture of relief and disappointment. There are no colourful celebrations to welcome them back; the returnees do not come bearing exciting stories to feed our hungry ears. Most of them spend their days in melancholy, sitting on their front porches, facing the direction from which they have returned. You cannot ask them if they ever saw so-and-so back in Eden, if so-and-so is still alive, because making them remember just seems so cruel. So instead, everyone sits and waits and cranes their neck towards Eden.

The other children stretch their necks out of curiosity, to have something to point at and gossip about, but me, I stretch my neck each time hoping to catch a glimpse of my best friend. I wonder if she too now has breasts the size of small tangerines jutting out of her chest, and if she too has started to feel funny things for boys. I have so many questions for her. Why did she never write? What was Eden like? Did their money really grow on trees? Did she ever find out what people there died from? Most importantly though, I would ask her why she burdened me with keeping this heavy secret.

Sometimes, while Mama Saaku and I sit in the backyard mending clothes, we stop to look at the hens peck lovingly at their chicks. Our eyes follow the brown baby goats running to nuzzle their mothers and I wonder what is going through Mama Saaku's mind. Often, I feel the need to put her out of her misery, and each time I come to a quiet resolve: that this is not my story to tell. One day, when Saaku finally comes back among a throng of returnees, she will see that if there is one thing I am better at, it is keeping a secret.

Ayanti

Mary Ononokpono

*I*n the shadow of the stones of Ikot Nta we built a fortress. It was a large construction forged of shells, wood, flotsam, and sandy clay. We wove a roof from the banana leaves scattered near Little Ekirikok Cove, before furnishing the ramshackle tower with an assortment of treasures. We brought washed-up, sea-worn objects, scavenged from the latest wreckage now adrift off Parrot Bay. The boys carefully cleaned the salty, bloated treasure, collected on one of the weekly canoe expeditions they now undertook with other boys of akparawa grade.

Ntiero and Efiom Junior were inseparable. Though born to different mothers, both wore Papa's face. It was a thing that caused angst amongst strangers, for they were taken to be the living manifestation of the most fearsome of taboos: twins, permitted against all better reason, to live. That they were not at all twins was considered beside the point; and indeed, it was often said of them that they bore the spirit of our founding fathers, twin sons of Okoho, who had not only secretly lived, but had gone on to found the prosperous ward of Ikot Atakpa: our beloved riverside home. It was a place brimming with mysteries, of which it was said that the atmosphere was so rich in old utterances that the faintest of your imaginings instantly took form and walked abroad.

Ikot Atakpa was more commonly known to the hordes of white traders who now frequented the waters of the great Akwa river, as New Town. Though our fathers had settled the country two generations before, establishing our harbour as the principal trading post of the whole nation of Akwa Akpa, we were considered little more than newcomers by the haughty strangers. Yet even they were wary of trespassing upon the property of the family now better known throughout the coastal cities as Duke.

My brothers, the small-small Duke boys, moved as of one accord. Known for wandering off from the rest of their flotilla, they had, on this most recent occasion, discovered a wreckage in the part of the great river that faced Tom Shott's Point, behind which lay the pungent, fish-scented streets of Salt Town. They would later barter their hoard with Inyene and I for little more than a bowl of freshly prepared ekpankukwo, which I would inform them, with a wry smile, had been especially prepared for them by the chief deity of Vulcan City.

*I*t was an easy trade. I threatened Ntiero with telling his mother of his secret excursions to the bay, for I knew that if she ever caught wind that they had broken the mud-larking taboo, there would be infinitely more trouble for him than there would be for myself. That is how I came to sneak two extra portions of Mma's delectable winkle-strewn pottage, delivering it in a large, tortoise-shell bowl to the greedy pair under cover of darkness, before finalising our trade the following morning.

The boys were clever, yet also stupid, and were yet to realise that Vulcan City was nothing more than a product of my imagination. Awed by my tales of wandering spirits escaped from their haunted forest boundaries; of creatures part-vulture, part-giant, with human skulls for heads, they would cower as I whispered of the passing of the dreaded Ekpo Nyoho. Their scavenged store they built by visiting the wreckage over the course of several market weeks; but suspecting them of thieving and hoarding, I relayed the news to Inyene, which meant that it was only a short while before we stumbled upon their hiding place.

Inyene could sniff out anything. She was strange like that, but always proved useful. We were not eyeneka, but were bonded through Papa nonetheless. Our mothers, by some happy stroke of Abasi Atai, got along famously. They had known each other since infancy, when they dwelt in neighbouring compounds in their beloved Raffia City. For years they spilled their shared stories of learning the arts of crafting through observation of carvers and weavers; careworn faces animated as they retold childhood memories by their respective evening hearths. As our mothers spoke, Inyene's eyes would glisten and she would later recount their stories, as though she, too, had wandered the russet roads of Ikot Ekpene; as though she, too, had dwelt for a time in the famed City of the Makers.

"Inyene the dreamer" we named her, for she often dreamt awake. Yet we took her dreaming seriously, for it had led us time and again to otherwise unknowable discoveries. Now it led us to the haul from the wrecked winged-canoe one quiet noon.

*I*t was Akwa Ederi, the first day of the week, when Inyene entered my room as the cocks crowed.

"I saw the dry bones of a tree with a cavernous mouth," she said, eyes wide in semi-shock. "It stood by a clearing in which were left stones from the People of the Sky."

"I know the place. It is half a day's march away, near the Kwa river-road which leads to Oban, down by Little Ekirikok Cove."

"But that is next to the Forest of Ekpo. Mma told us never to enter the place, that it is in the bad part of the bush."

I rubbed the sleep from my eyes but said nothing, for I felt the same dread that flickered for an instant across Inyene's grass-tinted pupils. I said nothing as we walked to the stream and bathed. Said nothing as we returned, dressed in bell-skirts and beads before breaking our fast upon hot, savoury akara and peppery snails. I said nothing as we walked to the shrines for morning prayers. It was only after we had received our tasks for the day, which involved ensuring the slave girls properly tended the cassava, that as I chewed on my chewing stick, I hatched a plan for escape. It was mid-morning and the heat was just about tolerable when I found Inyene with her youngest brother beneath the fronds of Iban Isong. Pulling her from the doorway of the lodge, I made my intentions known.

"We must leave before anyone misses us."

I handed the baby a ball of greasy akara which he chewed as we slipped away. Once we cleared the back of the building, we exited our sprawling compound, making our way south towards the waterway that led to Efut Country. We ran the distance of the road that led to the river, but as we approached the sound of flowing waters, we slowed.

"If we walk, we won't reach Little Ekirikok before noon.

We must pay a ferryman," I said. Inyene's face wore the look of someone who knew she was about to transgress, but was resigned to her fate, for she had already transgressed a step too far.

The ferryman turned out to be a ferry boy, one of the slippery-haired creoles now populating this part of Creek Country. He introduced himself as Joe Cobham, so I knew him to be one of our family's rivals from a neighbouring ward. There was little to do but sit back and enjoy the bright white lights generated as the sprites of Abasi Usen danced upon the crystal clear waters.

Before long we dismounted from the small fishing-canoe and clambered up the bank. The forest loomed ahead of us.

"If Mma discovers this, there will be moons of affliction to pay," said Inyene. I laughed, for I could well picture her wrath. Linking arms with my half-sister, we walked, two earthen-coloured tinkling things, strolling up the creolised coast, arm-in-arm.

A line of ants cut across our path. Blood red, their backs shone like the bright poisoned berries that were ground into a paste for the purpose of divining obubit ifot – sorcery of the harmful type. They marched as if to the sound of invisible drums. I stared at Inyene as her eyes glazed over.

"What did you see?"

"People. Many people. Bound strangers marched from town to town."

"You must speak with my mother," I said as the ants passed.

Soon, Inyene began to pick out landmarks from her dream. She led us past long-deserted houses, past many intricately carved rocks. We clambered over broken shards and large boulders that blocked the path through the empty town. It was evident the place had once been inhabited by masons, makers who had crafted in stone. Their legacy stretched firmly into the present day, with strange markings whose meanings had long been forgotten, everywhere decorating the mysterious landscape.

It was said that the masons were descendants of the Sky People, for it was in the skies of distant Abasi Ubong Obot, the mount said to be the mouthpiece of the Great God, that they had learnt their craft. So the place we sought was known colloquially as the Circle of Sky Stone. The story goes that Abasi Enyong, the Mother of Heaven herself, planted the stones in a circle as a gateway through which she could pass between realms. The fable cast a shadow of awe upon the hearts of all creek dwellers.

We happened upon the place quite suddenly. The heart of the bad part of the bush. The place rumoured to be the location of a once-prosperous town, picked up and swept away by nearby ocean waves: thr entire town, complete with the secrets of ekpe, deposited together in a faraway place, on a large, fertile island, across the veil. Said to be the work of Kwarafan and Portuguese traders, the loss was lamented up and down the coast, for the Obong was a secret keeper and his wives famed oracles; and they took with them a portion of the memory of the country, which was feared would never be returned.

$\mathcal{W}$e emerged into a clearing that once stood as town square. The boys had buried their treasure in the mouth of a derelict tree, a thing which in its prime would have been without doubt a wonder, for even its carcass was impressive, its ruinous roots bedded deep within the earth. The ancient stump was located just off a circular clearing, in which stood, dead centre, an arrangement of stones that were undoubtedly more ancient than the stump itself. The monolithic stones rose like giants from the rust-hued earth, casting imposing shadows upon the clearing. That we stood within a sacred place was evident to us, and the shadows seemed lower as the sun slotted into its noonday place. But as the searing sun banished all traces of cloud, we forgot our fears as we excavated the haul.

It was Inyene's idea to construct the watchtower, from which we would plan new ways to protect our newly claimed territory from the gaze of the towering, phallic boulders, with their stern, yet jovial faces. The gigantic images comforted us, yet made the fine hairs on our necks stand to attention.

*A*ll of that occurred the week before last. Since that time we had returned daily to Ikot Nta, ferried by the silken-haired Cobham boy; and little by little, we had constructed our fortress. We built directly atop the flattened stump of the dead tree, erecting rough walls around the base that served as a platform of sorts. On the fourth day of the week, Ekpiri Offiong, Ntiero and Efiom chanced upon us and begged to assist us, which Inyene and I permitted after moments of careful deliberation.

Inside the tall, crooked room, we placed a small chest, two brass candelabra, and a broken chintz-patterned chamber pot, which Efiom turned upside down before placing atop it the damaged antelope skull he had found at the fizzing brook. Beside that we placed an ivory tusk and the badly rusted blunderbuss rescued from Ekirikok Cove. In noonday light, skull, perch, ivory and gun fused into one, casting an eerie shadow which rose, streaked, into the air. The strange shrine called to mind a holy fire arising from the crown of an unknown, unseen deity, so we stood, the four of us, transfixed for a moment. It was the call of inuen ekpo breaking the silence that brought us back to our senses.

"We should say a prayer," said Inyene, "we need to consecrate the space."

"Why? What did you see?" asked Efiom, who had retrieved two large, once-sodden rugs – Persian pieces from across the veil that we dried in the sun to serve as sleeping mats.

"I saw nothing," said Inyene, looking fearful, "but we ought to pray anyway."

"You should pray," I said.

"Why?"

"Because I am perpetually dragging you from Mma and the other diviners. 'Tis doubtful any of us can pray as well as you. Besides, this watchtower was your idea. You must set the words for the watch."

So we closed our eyes and Inyene began. She started with a song well known by all our mothers, all one hundred and forty-four of them; a song which invoked the names of the High Gods, discarded in this part of the country before our family resettled Atakpa Creek. Inyene said our mothers had returned the names to their rightful places, which is why Ikot Atakpa now prospered. As we joined the staccato melody, she spoke.

"On Akwa Offiong, this sixth market day, I, Inyene eyen Okoho, invoke the Gods of my forbears." Her back straightened as her small voice filled the room. "I, daughter of priests, of diviners, of seers and dream-catchers, I who tread between worlds in my sleep, I hereby call upon the Abasi Udung Oyong, the Great Ones, stewards and protectors of our people, who bless each morning with the breaking of the yolk that brings light to the creatures of day. Hear me now, o ye illustrious guardians whose hearts even the most illumined human minds cannot read. May you guide us in times of trouble, may you turn the pellets of our enemies astray, may you be our stronghold and watchtower, turn our feet from peril and keep Ekpo Nyoho at bay."

As my sister spoke we trembled, her voice reaching like fingers into the clearing beyond our fortress.

"May we have the protection of Ekpe and Asabo, may the young Leopard and the Python scatter all before our feet. May you girdle us beneath your great shadows." Inyene rounded off her prayer and Efiom left the tower, killed a small bird and sprinkled its blood on the stones.

"Why did you do that?" she asked, angrily. He laughed and threw the carcass into a nearby bush.

"To consecrate the place."

"Yet you yourself are not consecrated," she scolded him.

At that moment thunder clapped, and we froze. We had arrived at noon, but now the day had lengthened. I felt a creeping fear, not for the first time.

"We should leave," I said. Inyene agreed.

"Wait!" said Ntiero, who came running over with a brass plaque, engraved with foreign characters.

"What do you have there?" asked Efiom.

"The name of our fortress," he replied. The structure was tall enough to enclose a tattered rope ladder, which we used as a stairway to lead to the battered crow's nest, the only intact part of the enormous oceanic structure not to have been swallowed by cruel spirit waves. Our tower was a sight to behold. At the entrance we placed a chintz sheet, which served as a door of sorts, and Ntiero placed his sign beside it, before reading out loud.

"*The Scouse Stranger.*"

"What manner of name is that for a watchtower?" asked Efiom.

"The type that will keep Scouse strangers at bay," he replied.

We laughed. Standing back, we beamed with pride.

Our fortress sat beneath the eaves of the sacred forest where the wandering spirits of the newly departed were said to roam. Inyene's mother had warned us repeatedly, particularly the boys, from straying too close to those parts of the bush where the dead things walk, identifiable by the invisible border which haunts all freeborn children of the creeks. But boys being boys, they ignored her warnings and made a beeline for the profane wood, while Inyene and I waded in the shallows, searching for more treasures with which to furnish our ramshackle creation.

*T*hat happened yestereve, when Inyene found a golden key, turned almost blue-green, like the swollen leg of the sailor Uncle Edidem had carried into Mma's work parlour one bright afternoon. It had turned out to be one of the rare occasions when my mother was unable to save the unfortunate creature, whose entire leg she had been forced to remove with a sharp cutlass. His rotting skin had smelled so bad that we had later been forced to smoke out the room with a mixture of pungent herbs, before rubbing all the surfaces down with salt and throwing the burnt herbs, leftover salt and butchered body into the bad part of the bush.

While the boys roamed the wood, we continued to splash in the shallows. Our bell skirts chiming like the call of swallows. I happened upon a dense patch of weed, like a mound of tangled thread, as a fish sent a jolt through my calf. I investigated further, and glimpsed a case.

"Inyene. Come and see."

We dragged the water-laden box, which was surprisingly light and small, onto the bank, gently clearing the weeds from its body.

"Don't open it," she said. I stepped back in fear: her voice was shrill.

"Why not? It might have anything in it."

"Precisely because it might have anything in it."

"Such as?"

"Eka Kufre said the trunk she purchased on her last trip to Ikot Ekpene was filled with a wicked spirit-pox."

Shrugging, I examined our latest find. It was empty but for two folios. Leather-bound things containing dried white leaves, cut into perfect rectangles.

"Beautiful," I said, remembering that Ntiero had promised to teach me the letters of the pale-faced foreigners. But Ntiero being Ntiero, he was always distracted by his multiple pursuits, so I had resigned myself to the fact that I would have to find another to teach me.

At the sight of my half-brother producing the brass plaque, I remembered the folios. I had placed them the day before in the chasm below the entrance to our fortress for safekeeping. Now I retrieved the oracles of bound leaves.

"What do they say?" I asked Ntiero, handing over the folios.

"I can't make it out. The ink has run. Wait. It looks like a journal."

Studying the pages carefully, he began to read.

"The nineteenth day of June, this year of our Lord, seventeen fifty eight and a half."

"What does that even mean?" asked Inyene.

"'Tis the name of a year. 'Tis the name of this year," he said.

"What a ridiculous notion. Who would think to name a year for a number?" she scoffed.

"The traders from across the veil," said Efiom.

"Well, what does it say?" I asked. "Does it give the engraver's name?"

"No." he said, "but it lists other names."

"Names of whom?" asked Inyene.

"Of places. Of people. It looks like a ledger of sorts."

"Well, tell us what it says." I was growing impatient.

"From the Fante coast." he read. "I cannot make out many of the names. They are in a dialect that is strange to me. Nevertheless, I shall try. Gold: the engraver writes of several ounces of gold. He mentions grain. And people. One Kruman, one Frimpong, twelve Gurunsi, three named Agyeman."

"What does it mean?" I asked.

"I don't know," he said, continuing. "From Bonny," his face became stern. "One hundred pieces of ivory, four hundred yams, thirty persons. It lists their names. Ten Ebele, seven Ododo, three Oyi, nine Adesuwa, one Ivie."

"What is this?" I asked.

"From the Agbishere towns, ten pounds of salt, twenty of palm fruit and fifteen persons. Three Affiong, five Udo, seven Inemesit."

"Stop. Please. Let us leave. I begin to feel afraid," said I.

But my half-brother would not stop reading. He called out so many names, scores of them, many familiar, yet many more foreign names, and at the sound, my heart flinched in inexplicable pain.

Evidently, Efiom and Inyene felt the same, and as I began walking to the waterway, they followed. We left Ntiero's deepening voice trailing behind us. But as we approached the spot where the Cobham boy had dropped us off, he and his small fishing canoe were nowhere to be seen. Only his paddle remained. We assumed he had returned, somehow, paddle-less, back up the creek. As night fell, the realisation that we were stranded dawned upon us, so we made our way fearfully back to the centre of the deserted town. As we approached the clearing, we heard the call of inuen ekpo. That the ghost-gull cried at night was an omen of encroaching death. Ntiero had lit a small fire, but was now nowhere to be seen.

"Where is he?" asked Inyene. "Nsunam iwot!" she added as

an afterthought, cursing the sense missing from his head. We had no food, but Efiom felt brave enough to pick a few wild guavas and pineapples. After apportioning the sweet flesh, he said, "I am going to find Ntiero. You should wait here. It's not safe for him out there alone."

Inyene began to cry. Her soul was sensitive and she was fretful for our brother. We entered our fortress and replaced the flimsy door, hugging each other to alleviate our fears about the beyond. Efiom could be heard calling "Ntiero!" into the night. I was afraid.

Soon my sister began to shake violently. I had glimpsed such a thing just once before, when we were but infants. Inyene had gone into a shaking frenzy in the yard of Iban Isong. Luckily for her, my mother was present and was well equipped in dealing with nkposop, the dreaded spirit sickness. My heart lodged in my mouth as Inyene starting spitting foam from hers. She spoke, muttering: "Ekpo Nyoho, Ekpo Nyoho," over and over and over again. Her eyes rolled back in her head as a chill descended upon me. A long shadow loomed in front of the dying flames as Ntiero entered the fortress.

"Where is Efiom?"

"He went searching for you," I said, as a mask of fear settled upon my brother's face.

"And Inyene?"

"Spirit sickness."

"Go and fetch some water," he said.

I grabbed a gourd and ran into the night, tears streaming down my face as I thought of our predicament. My mothers would hold me accountable should any ill befall my siblings, and rightfully so, for the entire escapade was my idea. We were in a part of Creek Country in which our rivals, the Cobhams and Robin Johns, were known to roam. It was safe for no one.

As I ran blindly, I muttered Inyene's invocation for protection until I thought I would have no words left. Soon I heard the familiar tinkle of running water and filled my calabash at the fizzing brook. Balancing the calabash on my crown, I moved slowly to our newly constructed refuge. The light from the fire illumined my steps, and I managed to approach the looming stones without spilling a drop of water.

It was as I approached the fortress that I heard it. A song chorded in minor that summoned me by name.

"Ayanti, Ayanti," it sang, "eyen Ikwo, will you remember me?"

The voice grew into a faint chorus of an unseen choir. Voices at once solitary and that of a multitude.

> *As the dusk turns my footprints to shadows,*
> *And the gulls lament the passing of my name,*
> *Will you recognise my laughter in the morning?*
> *Forget the sparkle of my eyes; to numb your pain?*
> *Ayanti, Ayanti, eyen Ikwo, will you remember me?*

I wondered who it was that called my name and strung out its meaning, as the question *will you remember me* draped about my neck. Wondered who it was that called out the name of my mother. Wondered where the bodies, from whence came the sound.

A movement drew my gaze. It was a creature with a human skull for a head and long black feathers at its nape. Ekpo Nyoho, rising from the darkness, part-vulture, part-giant, part-deceased human. The creature stood before me, chief deity of Vulcan City itself, no mere figment of my imagination, but a real city in the realm of the unfortunate dead. The home of those who had died, not as aged, illustrious personages; but of a bad death. Those who, like the bluish-green bloated sailor, had been tossed into the bad part of the bush.

The creature towered above me but I looked it in the eye and remained in my place, taking a small step to the side to allow it to pass. I still consider it to be a thing of wonder that no harm befell me, but Mma would later inform me that women should have no fear of the wandering spirit; that because I spilled no water from my gourd, I could now call the spirit to my aid.

*A*s for Efiom, his strange fortune had been otherwise decreed. We would never again lay eyes on our brother, never again hear the sound of his mischievous, raucous laughter. We would never learn of his capture by the spectral horde that passed through the sacred clearing that night. We would only see footprints the following morning, the earth pounded as though by a great multitude.

From the hinterland they came, from Akpabuyo, from the towns beyond Oban, from Okoyong, Uwet and Owi, from towns as far afield as Aro Country, Afikpo, Nsukka, Ugep. Weavers, dyers, bronze-casters, miners, griots, poets, metal-workers; artisans of all kinds, those who held within their tongues the memories of the land. Diviners, sorcerers, dreamers, visionaries and spirit-casters of foreign hinterland towns; thieves; prostitutes; freeborn children of conquered chiefs; bought with children sold in perpetuity as Osu for ancestral crimes.

We would never see them marching in their tens upon tens of thousands, dead things walking, fallen children of Abasi Ibom Isong, from slave town to slave town, through bountiful forest, beyond sparkling rivers, in a bid to reach our coastal wards. That once in Obio Oko, Afaha Obutong and Ikot Atakpa, towns of the Bight that would come to be known as Biafra, they were destined to be crudely ferried to ports named Jamestown and Georgetown and New Town.

That they would be drawn upon great winged vessels built on docks in cities with names as confusing as Liverpool, as Bristol, as London; freeborn and generational ritual-slave alike, shackled by metals wrought in Birmingham, shipped alongside ivories cut down like their owners: gentle forest guardians, who roamed the sacred hinterland woods not knowing that the protection afforded them by Abasi Akai, their living Mother, was fast approaching decline.

That the greatest crime would be perpetrated upon our very soil; and that we, children of the creolised harbour towns and coastal creek coves, apportioned the spoils, which in time we would cease to acknowledge.

Yet, the knowledge would haunt us regardless, for the greater part of their number were destined to fall and rot where they trod. Driven to premature deaths by hunger, by thirst, by the fists of their wily Kwarafan capturers, pushed beyond the brink by cruel whips belonging to Jukun mounted on tall, neighing steeds.

We would never learn their names, which would be whispered thereafter only by pockets of memory that floated in the wind; would never learn of their varied, torturous migrations, never realise that their remains lay scattered beneath our feet, that our homes had been constructed on the bones of their carcasses, nor that it was their rising, wandering spirits which roamed the expanding forests of Ekpo Nyoho.

We would never learn of the fate of our brother, who, though not eyeneka, was our brother nonetheless; never learn of how he had stumbled into the centre of the stones and was seized by a group of shrouded, mounted horsemen, to a town named Ikot Ekpo, where he was marked to be sold. We would never know that for seven days he would work for his masters, but that on the night of the eighth day of the week, he would remember the prayer uttered by his half-sister, the dreamer, and being roused as he slept: would escape, feet led as though drawn by some unseen whisper, silently, past rival raiders, who would spray his masters with bullets from blunderbusses bought from across the veil.

We would never know that he would be led past creek, bight and cove, unseen, as though girdled by a benevolent shadow, back towards the Circle of Sky Stone; that he would discover the plaque that read *The Scouse Stranger* was now a sign by a brand-new road.

We would never learn that he would discover, upon enquiring of an oddly dressed stranger, where he could find: "The home of Ntiero the scribe, Inyene the dreamer and Ayanti the weaver, children of the principal family of Duke," for the new road was confusing and "had not been there but eight market days before."

We would never discover that our brother would learn: "The wealthy, literate, part-creole slaver and Obong of New Town, Anterra Duke, and his famed oracle sisters, were long dead and buried," that the year was now named "nineteen fifty-eight," and in the passing of eight market days in a spectral town named Ikot Ekpo, two hundred of our years had in fact passed.

Instead we would leave the ramshackle fortress to be reclaimed by the stone ruins, and return, weeping, to our compound; to be met by the sound of wailing and wretched lamentation, by a voice refusing consolation, a voice belonging to Eka Efiom: for now, all of her children were deemed no more.

Bleed

Gamu Chamisa

*I*n the end, all my brother left behind was a rubbled world. In his aftermath – mother and father looking on with ghost eyes, three sisters with only grief to hold. His outline crept back from the burial, his last Elsewhere, and settled in corners to watch, to tug at the hems of clothes. He sits in the house's old shadows, breathing so softly you have to strain to hear, and holding time still.

It was years ago, but it is raw still, it aches somewhere, the guilt. The last few years have been a heavy weight pulling me into the deep. I thrash about in the water, refusing to let go. Holding on.

I am twenty-five, and I am here. Australia. Adrift, alone. Spewing secrets into toilet bowls and singing myself to sleep, and keeping the lights on when I shut my eyes so I don't dream.

The walls of this small life, of its boredoms, are starting to close in. So I keep moving. Melbourne, Sydney, Brisbane. It's all the same, a blur. Work days are just hours of scribbling my name while I long for the night. I don't feel so lucky anymore. There is milk here, and there is honey, but that is not enough. This foreign land – *oh, you can make a home anywhere,* I am told – the sea winds make my blood cool and my bones salty-brittle.

It was supposed to be different for the economic refugee daughter of two freedom fighters. A familiar refrain in our household. Parents shouldn't bury their children; it was supposed to be different. Daughters should follow the plan, cling onto Baba's dreams and Mama's hopes, conscience moulding them into their likenesses – *what would Mum think, what will Dad say?* So don't jump. Think of them. Yeah, we owe them only goodness.

But that didn't stop Munya. It was supposed to be different. Sisters shouldn't kill brothers.

"We'll make it, hey. It's in God's hands, whatever happens," Mama said to Ana, to all of us, on the way to The Avenues to see our boy. Dad was a maniac on the road, tears sat in Mama's eyes, and Tana was bravest of all of us, locked into her gaming console. I sat next to her, eating the last of my silence. All of us selfish in our grief already. It was his second overdose, about six months before Dad lost patience with him.

Eight months before I killed Munya.

$\int$o then, anyway, leaving home. The place that grew you
up, your milk teeth cast on the roof of the old house, your
umbilical cord buried in the warm soil of its backyard. Like
everyone else you knew lucky enough to build a life in Jo'burg
or Winnipeg or Kuala Lumpur or London or somewhere-in-
America. Then come back with framed degrees, reasonable jobs,
"fat" wallets, hybrid accents, new laughter and new eyes, or
failed dreams, backs bent a little, deportation stamps in that green
passport, broken-hearted,still with something shiny to prove we
sat there where the grass was indeed greener, or where snow falls
and Christmas is white, where you call your elders by their first
name like it's nothing. Not much to stay for in poor Zimbabwe,
and not much to come back to. Unless your daddy's rich and your
ma ain't never looking.

Didn't realise then how big a thing it is to leave your family.
Leave your mother and father at age eighteen. Never been on
a plane before. To OR Tambo, then Kingsford Smith, then
Tullamarine and Melbourne city, whose heart is big but whose
skies are fickle. In Harare I left my love standing under blinking
airport lights. Four of them instead of five. Not much choice in the
matter. They drown to hold us up, we owe them only goodness.

I left my family in Harare, parents, sisters, baby MJ. Harare,
where people work their fingers to the bone and have little to
show for it except blood that keeps on pumping and laughter
dredged from somewhere deep that stays hopeful. According to
Mama, according to cousins and old friends who stayed behind.
Somehow livings are made, existence eked out. Can't read the
articles about home online, because I am small, and shame makes
me feel sticky. What right have I, sitting comfy on the other side,
to complain?

But now, running towards that place again, towards family.
Back to where it begins. Because I haven't cried in years. It churns
in my belly, this thing I cannot tell Mama, the thing I did not tell

her those years ago, it gnaws and swells and feels slimy at the back of my throat. So I put my fingers in my mouth and try to heave it out. The relief is impermanent. I haven't held down a dinner in months. I am skin and bone. And in my veins a panic courses; the noise is quieting around me, it's getting quiet in my head, and when the silence is complete, I know I will jump. I cannot out-scream this thing, I can't run from it any longer. I need my mother's arms around me. I can't breathe here anymore.

And now, going back, tickets are purchased, presents bought, bags packed.

"Call me when you get there," says my man. It's a soft thing here. He has kind eyes, and comfort.

"I will." Heart half-here, half-there. Goodbye to friends with booze and laughter, a goodbye kiss at the departure gates, and then I leave.

Leave the lover who still cannot say my name right. He holds me as if I am a dream, he looks at me as if I am enough; but I cannot stop, cannot sit, cannot stay. It's a war, this place. Being pushed away, being pulled home again.

So I leave. Leave the hands that ask for too much. Old ladies at work who stroke my dark skin and call it particularly lovely and my teeth especially white when I smile. Leave strangers who plunge hands into my kinky afro hair, let loose or wrangled into a puff, without asking, always believing they have rights to my body. Leave strangers who still call it Rhodesia, or who met a Nigerian lady called Abigail whom you surely must know, or who want you to defend Moogahbee's politics, or who ask after the welfare of those poor babies in the World Vision ads. Leave colleagues who ask, just being nice, just being friendly, exactly how many more of your relatives you've brought over to live here. Leave this place where people tell you in the streets, or on the internet, or in parliament, to go back to where you came from. And stop stealing their jobs. And stop having so many goddamn children to drain Centrelink. Are all you blacks the same? Leave when they start calling it reverse racism when you stand up for yourself. *Why can't I say the n-word, why can't I touch your hair, is it true what they say about black girls, is it true what they say about fucking black men? Did you come here by boat?*

*A*n eighteen-hour flight. Eighteen hours suspended in black hurtling through a sky without stars, over an ocean that doesn't care about your plans and will swallow you and hold you under until all three hundred passengers are dead. Even after a few wines, even with Miles Davis swirling in my head, I cannot sleep. I sit for a while trying to work through expectations and tally my fears. I give up because thinking too deeply nauseates me. I stay awake and watch the colours flash on the mini screen in front of me.

Harare International Airport, at last.

I watch my suitcases come by on the luggage carousel. The colours are obscene. Playful. Coral and yellow. My head hurts, something heavy sits in my stomach. I look up to the viewing deck where people are waving to their arrivals. I can't make out a familiar face. The man at the immigration desk is friendly enough. He stamps my blue passport happily after enquiring how long I intend to stay. He smiles as he scribbles down my finite claim to this country, to this place I was born, and where my grandparents' bones lie. Three weeks, I tell him. They don't really want us over there either, I want to add, but I don't say anything. Instead I smile at him wider, and hope the Shona leaves my mouth dancing true, how I see and hear it in my head.

I haul my bags onto the trolley. All around me other arrivals wear their thoughts on their faces – anxious, happy, exhausted. The attendant at customs scans my luggage, takes down my details, and lets me through with a slip that informs me ZIMRA could be in touch at some point. Too many new clothes packed in there, sister, and they'll be wanting their import duty.

I see Dad first. For a breath, I imagine that one of the young men standing next to him in blue jeans and a football jersey is our brother. My heart jumps, a foolish thing, and then it stops. My welcome party is here. Dad is smiling, and Mama squeezing me tightly, and Tana takes my back-pack from me. Baby, little MJ, Ana's son, is squashed between Mama and I. He's bigger than in the latest photos Mama sent me, gap-toothed and giggly. Tana hugs me next, and then Dad and I do our awkward dance. Half-embrace, half-handshake handhold. Father and daughter at their warmest. The days of sitting on Daddy's lap have long been over.

Time is a heartbreaker. Dad looks greyer, and his bones look like they sit differently, the weight on them shifted. The rings look loose on Mum's fingers; she doesn't tower like she does in my memories. A little less beautiful. Tana is a young adult already, carries a woman's body, holds a mouth full of braces, looks at me with a little indifference sitting in her eyes. And MJ's. The baby, well he's no longer little at all, I was prepared for that, but it stabs me somewhere soft that none of his memories include me. When I left he was barely one.

Dad drives us into the city from the airport, past the monument arching over the road that proudly proclaims national sovereignty – ZIMBABWE 1980 INDEPENDENCE. We drive past a sign that beams "The City of Harare Welcomes You, Welcome to the Sunshine City." Another extols China as this country's true friend in the East, as a partner in rebuilding the erstwhile breadbasket of Africa. The paint is peeling a little, the rust creeping, but never mind that. Look at the colour, look at that sunshine, look at the sky.

Dad speaks with his new laugh eager in his voice – to your right is Cranborne Park, further down that way is Braeside where Aunty Stella used to live – it is easy to forget, heh, Chido, these places where you come from? He laughs again. He splits my heart open and he doesn't even realise.

MJ saves us from the awkward lull after the Australia talk has been exhausted. He asks if I have any sweets for him, and Mama pretends to chide him and we all laugh at his poor manners. MJ likes my accent and so we chat away, and I'm lost in his happy telling of everything he knows – numbers and shapes and letters in English, Shona, and French. He's got plenty to say about Ben

10. He bounces in his seat, not belted down, and tells me it's down with spinach and carrots and his piano teacher and (his finger pointed at Mama) it's down with Gogo who only lets him watch three cartoons a day. Mama laughs and Dad remarks, with feigned exasperation, that MJ is just too clever for his age. The magic of a grandchild.

It was difficult at first when Ana came home from Maryland at twenty with a two-month-old son no one knew about. MJ's might have had a vanishing father, but now he is my parents' world. Already MJ has told me twice that he'll be on an aeroplane too one of these days, flying high up, when Mummy Ana buys him a ticket. He's being a good boy and listening to his Gogo and Sekuru. Ana hasn't been back since she left him as a baby, still waiting for her residency to come through. MJ is eight now. She sends money though, so he can have the best of everything.

The streets that take us home are the still the same. The same as when I drove us home, cousins, brother and me, the only sober one, after a night out. The same as when Munya drove me home from school, having picked me up three hours late even though he'd dropped out of university by then, and fetching me from St Cath's was his sole responsibility. The same as when Mama or Dad drove me home from sports practice or extra lessons shouting at me for not telling them Munya's plans, and look what's happened now. Where is your brother? The same as when we drove home from Borrowdale Police Station the time Munya went missing for four days. Mama cried when the police found him, high out of his mind, and held him close, and took two weeks leave from work to take care of him and organise his stay with family in South Africa for a few weeks. The streets of home are the same as when Dad rushed me back from the trauma centre when I was sixteen, absolutely livid that I'd fractured my wrist playing basketball, reminding me that these were preventable costs, that I needed to be more careful, that I wasn't a child anymore.

Walking into the house winds me. Little is different. Just the colour, faded a bit. A sneaky chip in the odd wall, a small water stain on the living-room ceiling. Mama's decor is unchanged – potted plants in each corner of the living room, even the cushions arranged just *so* on the couches. Everything is where it should be, where it's always been. Frozen, as if the house is waiting for all its children to come home from school and push tables around and rearrange cushions and couch covers so they can play their childish games and cry wolf on rainy evenings. The smell, the particular smell of this house, surrounds me in a hug. Welcome home, my sweet baby.

*I*t's dark when we get back from dinner out, another power cut, so candles are lit and the ghosts of the house retreat to their place at the edge of the light. I pull out the rechargeable torch I brought with me and set it up on my desk. I kick off my shoes and fumble for my pyjamas and my vial of melatonin. I am still a fraud, I am still a lie, hiding behind the noise of busy days here, laughing loudly and seeing family and old friends, but clutching tightly to the quiet thing I must tell them if I ever want peace.

I wash my face in the bathroom, force down two tablets with shaky hands. I see Munya in my face sometimes, if I smile and hold my head a certain way. There he is. Haunting me in the way my teeth are shaped. Tonight, as I have since I've been back, I will put my headphones on and blast music into my head until the tablets kick in. I will lock my door, because I don't want Munya's ghost to come into my room. Sometimes, I sleep until I sense him standing over me, and I open my eyes and choke on a scream, my heart pounding against the bones of my chest.

I don't want to do it again – forcing him to drink glasses of water, sitting on my bedroom floor and talking to him so he wouldn't fall asleep, a bucket at the ready. He made me feel so guilty, every time I told Mama or Dad what was going on with him. He made me feel like his best friend when he needed me to lie for him, or to take care of him, or to give him my pocket money, or to give him my mobile phone to sell off to settle a debt. Then one night, it was a thud at my door that woke me.

Munya was jerking on the floor, limbs stiff, only the whites of his eyes showing, vomit down his shirt. I screamed, woke the whole house up. Got him on his side, put a pillow under his head. The ambulance couldn't come, no fuel, so we sped off to A&E in Mama's truck.

The nurses asked if he was epileptic. He wasn't. In different tones, a slight shift in their expressions, they asked if he'd taken anything. If it was *intentional*. Mama and Dad didn't know. So I answered. I knew. And that was unforgivable. Mama looked at me bewildered, hurt in her eyes, Dad sighed and went back to filling in forms. Tana looked at me with fire. I knew it wasn't just alcohol. He wasn't just doing it for the thrill of it. It was bigger than that, it was more than that. One of the nurses, her back turned to us, muttered something about how Munya could do with a few months kumusha to teach him that life is harder than private school English and overseas vacations, that he should be grateful.

"We all know this is not normal behaviour. He needs help," I pleaded.

"Don't say that about your brother." Dad was furious.

"We all see this, don't we? We have to talk about this! Mama?"

"Listen to your father, Chido. Don't make a scene in front of people." Mama's voice was soft.

Sisi Melissa has already cleaned the house by the time I wake up. She's started on the breakfast of tea, homemade bread, porridge (for Dad) and boiled eggs. Again ZESA has decided on early morning "load-shedding". My head hurts and my face feels swollen. My stomach is already in knots.

"Can you believe that this is Harare?" Dad says as he comes into the kitchen where I sit with a cup of tea, my brooding sister and effervescent nephew. "Haaa, vakomana," he laughs, "no electricity, no running water, rows of maize in backyards, the crowing of roosters early in the morning? It sounds like rural life to anyone, but they tell us this is our capital city." He shakes his head. Standing in the kitchen, my unshaven father, an emperor of a nothing land in his pyjamas and robe and slippers, holding a red plastic bucket and waiting for his steaming bathwater.

After dinner that evening, we watch the South African soapies together. Tana and I have washed the dishes and tidied the kitchen and made tea for everyone. MJ is asleep on the couch with his head in Tana's lap. Perfectly normal. It is quiet in my head; my heart feels like it's beating slower.

"I can't breathe anymore," I announce. The lady on the television is talking about her hair-care routine as a busy mum. "I am so sorry." My voice is shaking. For a while no one speaks, I can't look at their faces.

"I killed him."

"Stop this right now," Tana says. "Please."

"I can't think straight any more, I can't sit with it any more." I am crying. I taste blood in my mouth. "I knew what he was going to do and I didn't stop him."

"Accidents happen, my child, we have accepted God's will," Mama says.

"I knew where he hid his pills and I didn't do anything."

"Get out right now." When Dad is angry he doesn't raise his voice. His tone is measured. I can't look at their faces.

There is a knock at my door. Tana is standing there, her eyes bloodshot from crying too. "You are so incredibly selfish, Chido," she says.

"I jus—"

"This one's not about you. Don't do that to my mother."

"I was there too. I found him."

"But you weren't here to pick up the pieces. You don't know what it was like to live every day mourning him. You weren't here to grind out a way to keep this family together with me, Mama, Dad and MJ. You're just as selfish as he was."

She is shaking. I reach out to her and she lets me hold her.

"I'm here now," I say. Freer than I've felt in years. "And I'm sorry."

*M*y sister squeezes into my single bed with me and pushes her spine against my belly. Inside we lie and cry and cry and cry into the darkness of my room. Tears for years and years and years. Outside is the night pushing against the window. I hear a dog barking somewhere. I lie still, listening to Tana breathe, and will sleep to come.

This Bus Is Not Full!

Fred Khumalo

*V*usi is on a bus home after doing some shopping in Watertown. Though the bus appears to be packed, with some people standing right next to the driver, there's still a lot of standing room at the back. Under pressure from people who want to get on board, glaring at him from the ground, the bus driver gets up and starts shouting, "Move back please! There's room at the back…"

Then some public-spirited people join in, one guy's voice rising above the din: "Motherfuckers blocking the way, this ain't yo mama's living room. Move the shit back!"

An elderly gentleman interjects, "Please be patient. People are moving!"

"Who asked you, fucking cracker? Mind yo fuckin' business."

Vusi is not used to this kind of language. Yes, he sees scenes such as these in Tyler Perry movies. Or classic Spike Lee flicks. Or David Chappelle shows where the f-word is punctuation, the oxygen that gives life to phrases and sentences being uttered. But it's not the kind of language that would be tolerated at Harvard, where he's a graduate student. At Harvard, you step on someone's toes by mistake, and he goes, "Oops, pardon me, my shoe was in your way. My profuse apologies, sir."

Vusi is getting excited: this is the America they've been hiding from him! He must make more frequent use of bus transportation in his peregrinations around the city and its environs, he decides there and then. On past occasions he has relied on charitable fellow Harvardians for transport to the shopping mall in Watertown, which is out of the way from the subway train grid.

Now he is looking at the guy who's just called the elderly man a cracker. He wishes he could, as they do in the movies, say to the brother: "Come on, nigga, pull out your piece and show the cracker whatchu made of!" He's hoping for a scene he can cherish, a scene he will engrave in his memory so he can relate it to his friends back home. Come on, you Americans, Vusi can't go back to Africa without witnessing a single fight. What will he tell the people back home? He can already hear his younger brother booming with laughter: "Man, you're a loser! Two full years in America and you don't even contrive to be featured in one of their plentiful reality shows – or create your own show, something like: *In the Abundance of Water the Fool is Thirsty: The Miserable, Celibate Life of an African Geek In America.* Yes, a complete loser, that's what you are."

In his ears, his best friend joins the fun at his expense: "The fool lives in Boston, yet not once does he get a chance to date Tracy Chapman, who hails from one of the Bostonian ghettos. Loser!"

Another friend of his is saying soothingly in his ear, "Okay, if you're too tongue-tied to date Tracy or any other American, if you're too unimaginative to even appear on their TV, couldn't you at least, at the very least, capture on your cellphone a real-life, fully fledged street fight or, better still, a real shooting on an American street? Capture the thing, put it on YouTube and prove you were indeed in America! Come on, stop lying to us. You were not in America! Anyone can buy a Harvard T-shirt. Go to a Chinese shop in downtown Jo'burg, and they can organise you a Harvard T-shirt and hoodie chop-chop. No magic in a Harvard T-shirt!"

Back on the bus. Vusi is salivating. His heart is thudding. His eyes are wide open. As big as saucers. He's not going to miss a heartbeat of the action.

It's coming.

He's from Africa. The hunter's instinct runs in his veins. The hunter knows when it's time to stand still in the bush, and when to pounce. It's all about timing. About anticipation. And he can feel the timing is right. A black brother is about to pounce. He can feel it.

It's coming.

Those doubting Thomases back home are in for a surprise. The action he's about to capture on his phone is going to go viral on the net, thus landing him a reality TV deal with one of the networks. *From Lecture Room To Da Streetz: The Intellectual With Afritude.* That would be a great name for a reality show. *His* reality show.

He's clutching his phone now, ready to put it to good use once the action starts. How do they say in the movies? Camera rolling! Yes, the camera is ready to start rolling.

It's coming.

Like someone watching a fast game of tennis, his eyes are moving from speaker to speaker – not wanting to miss a word, not wanting to miss the slightest piece of action. They are speaking so fast, these Americans.

"Hey," one man shouts, "you crazy-ass-cracker, whatchu lookin' at? Move to the fuckin' back of the bus 'fore I show you your mother." The speaker has a face that reminds Vusi of a maggot. If maggots could grow this big. Come to think of it, he doesn't really know what a maggot's face looks like. If it has a face. Maybe it's one of those animals whose face is also its backside? Like an earthworm, which has faces on both ends. At least that's what he thinks they said in biology class. He never concentrated much in biology class. He knew from the onset that he wanted to be a money man when he finished school. He's at Harvard not on the strength of his knowledge of earthworms and maggots, whether these creatures have faces or not. He is studying High Finance. No profit in memorising facts about maggots. Therefore, the long and short of it, he doesn't know if a maggot has a face or not. But, still, this man's face shouts *maggot* – that's how creepy it is. "I'm not gonna say it again: move the fuck back! There's people wanna get on the bus! This bus ain't full."

Four people climb in. One of them is a woman pushing a baby in a pram – or a stroller, as they call this contraption in the US of A. The woman needs help to get her pram on board. But her friends ignore her. To get their attention, she says, "Shiit! Can't a bitch get some help get a baby on board a bus?"

Somebody – not one of her friends – finally comes to her rescue. Once on board, the grateful lady says to the good Samaritan: "What the fuck you lookin' at? You ain't seen a black bitch carrying a baby? Whatchu lookin' at?"

The good Samaritan is an Asian man who shrinks into himself at the unexpected onslaught from a woman he's just helped.

Finally on board, these happy citizens of America continue to talk – in voices that pose a threat to the average ear-drum – about what they intend doing when they get home. It's Christmas Eve, after all. Some last-minute preparations still need to be attended to. For the Big Day, you see. Their narrative, as an observant reader would have surmised, is peppered with short words that start with "f" or "s", as if these are the only words that matter in the dictionary, or the entire lexicon of civilised humanity.

Some gentleman then opines that, perhaps, just perhaps, it would be preferable to eschew what he terms "profane and impolite speech" in the presence of young children.

To which one of the pilgrims explodes: "Now I can see why they lock black people up. I know exactly why. Black people be talkin' among themselves, know what I'm sayin', mindin' their own bidness, and some cracker be tellin' them, *teachin'* them how to talk. Cracker, I don't wanna be arrested. So don't pro-voke me! You been pro-voking me the whole year. The year's almost ovuh. Is Chrismas tomorrow. And baby Jesus gettin' born tomorrow. And I ain't need no pro-*vo*-cation on Chrismas Eve. Hear what I said? I said: 'Nuf pro-vocation! Get the fuck outta my bidness!"

The scene Vusi will take back home to Johannesburg, the scene that he will post on YouTube, the scene that will land him a reality TV slot, the scene that will gain him street cred back home, is just around the corner now. He can feel it.

It's coming.

"Imma crack a cracker's skull ri' now!" another man booms. "So help me God, I'm a crack me a cracker's skull ri' now an' baby Jesus gonna wash mah sins tomaraw!"

A woman jumps right in: "I know them crackers be phoning the po-lice right now, tellin' po-po we be disturbin' the peace and shit. No, we ain't done nothin' here. And I been recordin' this shit here on my fuckin' iPad. So, brother, please don't go crackin' no cracker's skull 'cos I'm recording everything. Shoh, you can crack a cracker's skull if he try to crack yo skull, thas for shoh. But right now, as shoh as it is Chrismas Eve, no motherfucker be tellin' lies about black folk. Sayin' niggas started the shit. I ain't puttin' my ass in jail for no shit round Chrismas, no way!"

This pacifist dampens Vusi's spirit. No fight on the horizon. The man who'd just promised to crack a skull has gone all sulky. The bus shudders to a stop. The door opens. A grey-haired man in a tweed jacket takes his time climbing in.

"Driver," one of the brothers shouts, "Get the fuckin' bus going. Whatchu waitin' for?"

"We got families to look forward to, nigga."

"We ain't losers like you, drivin' a bus on Chrismas Eve. Shee-it!"

Curses fly around like confetti at a wedding party.

It soon becomes clear that the gentleman who's just climbed in is perturbed by the exchange of insalubrious words (the gentleman is of such a demeanour as to trigger the words *perturbed*, *insalubrious*, in Vusi's college mind). The gentleman is whipping his head this and that way, scowling at these citizens who are speaking – no, *shouting* – as if there were no tomorrow. Clearly a decisive man, a man of conscience and high morals, a man of good breeding, a man of authority, a man who knows no fear, the gentleman does the civilised thing: in a firm, direct voice, he addresses one of the speakers, enunciating each word distinctly: "Sir, there are young children here. Please. Mind. Your. Language. Mind. Your. Language!"

To which one of the women cries triumphantly: "Ah, this here cracker's got a Canadian accent! True, he got a accent. Speak up again, sir. What'd you say? I'm tellin' y'all, he got a Canadian accent…"

To which someone responds: "What a Canadian accent gotta do with gettin' on the bus?"

Now, the ice that had taken possession of the entire bus begins to thaw. The people start laughing. Shyly at first. Then in huge, bubbly gales. Then the laughter comes like avalanches hurtling down the tallest mountains. Wuuu-yoooo-wwweeee-hhhaaaa-ghhhhrrrr!

"But, hey," says one of the speakers, "the white people in Canada, do we also call them crackers? Or we have a diff'rent name for 'em?"

"I guess they be crackers too," the woman with the baby says. "They be cool Canadian crackers. On account of all the snow over there. And those Canadian crackers don't have no beef with niggers, far as I know anyway. So they be cool Canadian crackers!"

Yooooo-hahahahaha-weeee!

Vusi can't help but laugh out loud. Really loud. COOL. CANADIAN. CRACKERS! These Negroes are cracking me up, Vusi is saying this in his heart, trying to sound American to himself. They're cracking me up, these Negroes. COOL. CANADIAN. CRACKERS. Yoooo-hhhaaa-ghhrrrrrrr!

The woman with the baby frowns, throws piercing eyes at Vusi. "Nigga, you laugh funny."

From where she's sitting – Vusi is standing in the aisle – she sizes him up, a tiny smile on her face. "Yeah, nigga, you creepy. You laugh funny and you wearing funny glasses, and yo hair funny. Where you from, nigga?"

"South Africa."

She's smiling broadly now. "Aha, I knew it! You a Mandela nigga!"

Vusi notices that the lady is a scruffier version of Tyra Banks. She's got a complexion the colour of the yellow cling peaches that are popular back home. A better hairdo, a change of clothes would do the trick – make her a Tyra Banks look-alike.

But his assessment of Not Tyra Banks gets disturbed, by Not Tyra Banks herself: "Hey, lissen up y'all: today is full of wonders. There's a Canadian cracker ovuh there, and now a Mandela nigga ovuh here!"

Vusi smiles, internally thanking Saint Mandela for saving him from ridicule, or worse.

"Oh, African nigga," a woman's voice croons from behind where Vusi is standing, "I'll have myself a African nigga anytime, baby. *Any*time."

Vusi turns to see a woman with very unique features. Her face, chin and neck are all fused together. But she has beautiful teeth and kissable lips. She's not done talking: "All my friends call me African Queen, I guess on account of my generous lips and overly generous booty. Pity you cain't see my booty 'cos I'm sittin' down."

The laughter that follows is so loud, Vusi is scared the lady might just get up – to prove to all and sundry that she indeed is bootylicious. Vusi is not in a hurry to see the booty, if the face-chin-neck fusion is anything to go by. But he suspects that the reigning president in his home country would probably love to see her booty – and add her to his collection. The president of his country has been collecting wives as if each one were a talisman that would help him run the country more efficiently.

But someone is muttering, clearly referring to Vusi, "He don't look starving, for a African."

Not Tyra Banks comes to Vusi's defence, "He ain't from just anywhere-Africa. He from Mandela Africa. They got elevators there, they got McDonald's, and big highways too. Saw it on History Channel."

Vusi is swelling with pride. What the Americans have taught him since he got here is: *don't be modest, you ain't famous.* He must say something now. He can't suppress the need to educate these Americans right now. Those Americans at Harvard pretend they know all about Africa, so he never bothers to tell them about his country. Half Tyra Banks is very observant, indeed. She can tell South Africans from the other Africans. Vusi must take her mobile number. So they can stay in touch. Hit two birds with one stone: get an American who will listen with star-struck admiration to his African tales of conquest and civilisation, and also get an American lady who will date him, a lady he can brag about once he gets home. Vusi has been highly inspired by Half Tyra Banks' intervention on his behalf. When he finishes his studies, he will take Almost Tyra Banks back home to Africa – and tell his brothers she, indeed, is the real Tyra Banks' sister. Yes, he must talk to this woman who can differentiate Mandela's country from the rest of the continent.

He clears his throat now, puffs out his chest, ready to tell his more ignorant fellow passengers that the land of Mandela is not about lions and giraffes and starving babies and cannibals and people living in trees and Ebola. Mandela's land produces the likes of him, intellectuals of his stature. Thinkers who can converse at the highest level with the citizens of the world, cosmopolitan connoisseurs who buy their food and clothes at Watertown, not Chinatown, intellectuals who carry themselves with pride as they walk under the shadow of John Harvard. He is proud to have been anointed by Mandela to go out into the world and...

"Hey," one of the black brothers breaks into Vusi's thoughts, "Let me guess: you a Harvard nigga? Or is it MIT?"

Vusi doesn't care for the word "nigga" – black Americans will never cease to amaze him; why have they decided to embrace what used to be a racial slur? – but the inclusion of Harvard in the man's enquiry somehow cushions the blow of the n-word.

"Answer me, nigga. You Harvard or MIT?"

This is taking an interesting turn. A pleasant turn. He had taken these people to be ruffians, you know, the detritus from the pavements of Roxbury and Dorchester, the ghettoes of Boston. But for them to recognise him as a Harvard man, for them to realise that he is a Master of the Universe in the making! That's something. It counts in their favour.

Before Vusi can confirm to the man who asked the question that he indeed is a proud Harvardian, another man shouts from the back, "You one of them African niggas living large at Harvard on mah tax dollar when I cain't even afford mah next meal!"

The speaker shoots up from his seat. Now he is fighting his way forward, pushing past the people standing in the aisle. "Outta my way, y'all, outa my fucking way!"

His big arms are like oars wading through a resistant body of water.

"Outa my way, y'all. Don't you hear me, outa my way."

Foaming at the mouth, the rhino on the rampage is bellowing. He cries again, "I wanna get to that African nigga shit. Living large on mah tax dollar. You cain't get away now, conceited piece-a-shit. I'ma whup yo ass so bad you regret being born. It wasn't enough that you motherfuckers from Africa sold our forefathers into slavery, now you living large on our sweat..."

Vusi's African gods are on his side. The bus has arrived at Central Square where he has to get off anyway. He shoots out of the bus like an arrow that has got something on its mind.

Of Fire

Mignotte Mekuria

I – ASLEEP

*S*he awakens into her dreams, bathed in milk and blood. For an instant she trembles between worlds, neither here nor there, blind and deaf in a fog of gold dust and coffee grounds. Her being reconstitutes itself slowly, deliberately, skin unfurling over vibrating atoms, eyes opening inwards.

The first of her three names tumbles from the shadows. It strikes like a hammer on glass and the world begins to shatter, littering the ground beneath her with shards of remembrance.

A sun rises and banks on the horizon, sieving its rays through the woven walls of her once and future home, skittering over her flesh, settling over the sparse furniture and amidst the folds of the intricately worked thatched roof.

"You should not have come here again." The voice drifts to her, carried on a breeze pregnant with once-beloved scents. Frankincense and injera, bougainvillea and berbere spice the air and hold her firm.

"I have nowhere else to go." She whispers to the person she cannot yet see. "Please, Amakelech, let me in."

A moment of uncertainty passes and she begins to drown, from the inside out, her lungs compressing with each breath, her heart contracting, and her sanity unravelling across the sun-speckled space.

"Please… please!" It is her ghost that speaks; already she is beginning to drift, helpless against the sucking tides, the crush and retreat of time and place.

"Addisalem."

The second of her three names calls her back from the precipice, expands her lungs, reassembles her mind, fills her heart, and for an instant, she is whole again.

The sensation is unfamiliar, even after all this time, after all these forays back and forth between worlds.

The scene solidifies, and Addisalem knows that her galaxies have steadied, stopped erupting into life and death for this moment at least.

Tap, BUMP. Tap, BUMP. Tap, BUMP.

Her sister sits on a stool, bent low over a wooden mortar and pestle, one arm rising and falling to the cadence of her own internal music. The roasted coffee beans burst and powder to the steady rhythm, their heady scent exploding into the cool air.

"You knew I would come." Addisalem's eyes devour the sight before her, knowing it would fade.

Up and down, her sister's arm does not pause or hesitate in its ritual strike and retreat.

"Amakelech...?"

"You always come," her sister's low voice dances among the dust motes, "trailing your agony behind you like a cloak. Leaving our treasures behind. Tracking your bloody footprints across my floor. You always come."

Tap, BUMP. Tap, BUMP. Tap, BUMP.

Her left hand holds the pestle steady, while the right continues to labour alone.

"This is my home—"

Amakelech looks up, and the sun seems to vanish behind her, disappearing into the halo of her perfectly rounded afro. Her eyes, at once severe and pitying, meet and hold those of her younger sister. "This *was* your home. It is no longer, no matter how you cling or fling yourself backwards to regain it."

"Then tell me how to break free of this place, how to pull away from you! I should have been here with you. This is the only home I know. How can I fathom another?" The words pour from Addisalem's lips. They dislodge the calm, like sediment kicked up by rapid movement. Her sister blurs briefly before her eyes, the bright colours of her dress fading into sepia, the luxurious thickness of her starling hair fluttering into dandelion pieces. She fights for equilibrium.

"The fire needs tending." Amakelech is watching her with steady eyes, her right hand gone still, the black circles and crosses of her tattoo stark against her golden-brown skin.

Addisalem takes a step and falters. Something is amiss. It is there in the slant of her sister's shoulders, in her blurred edges and undefined smile.

"But where are the flames?" Addisalem's voice sounds indistinct; it bubbles and pops and bursts into the ether.

"Do you hear me, Addis? The fire needs tending."

She shakes her head, watching her sister begin to dissolve.

"Amakelech... Amakelech! Keep me here."

But the die has been cast. Her sister's throat has lifted the sound, her lips have formed the word, and Addisalem's third name has rent the air between them, and she is melting like wax, crumbling to the earth in a heap of smouldering fabric and gusting ash.

II – AWAKE

"Addisalem? Addisalem?" Her niece's tearful voice jerked her back into herself, so that she was reinhabiting her body. Once again feeling the laden weight of her limbs, the greedy drag and pull of her lungs, the weight of her soul being pressed to the earth by gravity.

Her nostrils filled once again with the metallic tang of blood. Her tongue was coated with it, thick and coagulated, curdled with milk and honey. A lake rippled outwards and she lay, the island at its epicentre, still fragmented, too hastily reassembled.

The little girl beside her was crying, great sobs that wracked her scrawny frame and sent her trio of thick braids bobbing about her neck.

Addisalem turned from the girl and pushed slowly to her feet. She staggered to the edge of the clearing, her footprints imprinting the wet earth, crunching over the spilt qolo and the crumbled remains of her earthenware jug. The heavy mantle of night pressed down upon her like a living thing, welcoming her back.

She heard the girl tripping behind her in echo of her own long strides, felt the slide of cool thin arms around her waist, the press of a wet face against her back. Her own hand, when she lowered it, swallowed the little ones clasped over her stomach. For a moment Addisalem stood, feeling the girl's tears soaking through the thin fabric at her back, swallowing against the lump in her own throat, the burn in her own eyes.

They stood, two creatures, alone under the twinkle of a million stars, each surrendering to the emotions that twisted their insides and settled within their hearts.

"Addisalem?" The little girl's voice hiccupped, planting itself in the little corner where Addisalem bottled away her deepest regrets. "Where do you go when you sleep?"

"To my yesterdays."

"Am I there?"

Addisalem disentangled herself from the little girl's grasp and turned to face her. Her eyes skimmed over the delicate tear-stained features.

"No, Isatay," she replied gently. "You live here, in my todays."

The girl dropped her gaze to the crushed grass and trampled flowers beneath her sandal-clad feet, her fingers twining and twisting. Her lips trembled with questions she did not dare to ask. She raised her eyes back to the woman who stood before her as unspoken words charged the air.

What do you see when you are there in your yesterdays? Why must you travel there so often? Why do you leave me here when you go?

The questions withered on Isatay's tongue as her eyes took in the formidable woman before her. It had always been like this, as though they stood on opposite banks of a turbulent sea, their words and intentions stolen and garbled by gusting winds.

Addisalem towered above Isatay, muscles spread taut over bone, the sparse moonlight casting her half in shadow and dyeing the blood on her chin a mercurial silver. The slant of her deep-set eyes, the slash and hollow of her cheekbones, the hard line of her shoulders and the scarred planes of her hands were forbidding. She was formed in echo of the jagged peaks and scooped out gorges of her homeland, a human landscape to repel invaders and quash rebellion.

And so Isatay said nothing, only watched as the woman changed her clothes with quick economical movements, rushed to obey when told to fetch Addisalem's horse from where the woman had secured it beyond the clearing, where the tall thin trees grew in a thick tangle of crooked limbs.

She swallowed her words as she swayed with the movement of the beast beneath her, her arms stretched once again around the warm body in the saddle in front of her, her cheek pressed against the sculpted muscles of Addisalem's back, the rounded ridges of her spine. Cocooned within the woven folds of the netelah that Addisalem had stretched over them both, Isatay closed her eyes and counted the beats of the horse's hooves, the bass of her heart, the swirl of time around them – anything to calm the panic building in her throat. She counted to keep from succumbing to madness, to keep from screaming until the horrors were past, until the world was over and she with it, and all was calm again.

She knew they had arrived by the way the warm flesh against her cheek turned into a column of steel. She knew by the stuttering gait of the horse and the stillness in the air. She pulled herself free from the entanglement of cloth and fear, and out into the cool air of the dawn.

Isatay gasped, even though she had braced herself for the vista unrolling before them. They had arrived at last. She knew this landscape: the cobblestone paths and the thatched homes cluttered in the valley below, the rumble of the distant falls, and the scorched earth gaping like a wound in the distance. All of it etched into her memory as indelibly as the carvings upon the stone obelisks of the north.

In the year that she had not seen this place, she and Addisalem had travelled far, her aunt setting a punishing pace. But here they were, back at the place that painted Isatay's nightmares with blood and flame, scented it with smoke and charred flesh, drowning her in sorrow.

They had returned home.

III – THE DEAD

*I*n her dreams, Isatay was whole again. The fragments of her life, the remains of her heart – all stitched up.

She wondered what Addisalem saw when she slept. When she lay shuddering and gasping for breath amongst the shattered fragments of the earthenware jug, with its mixture of blood, milk, and honey staining her out-flung arms and twitching fingers. Isatay would watch her aunt convulsing, her eyes rolling back in their sockets and flashing white in the moonlight. The fevered mumbling of Addisalem's lips, the brittle crack of the woman's body, would meld with the gust and flare of the fire, the heavy presence of the night. And Isatay would sit with fear as her only companion, her eyes on the writhing woman.

There was so little left of her past, so little holding her to this world; she felt the fragility of her existence like a living thing. So much had been lost, and yet more could be taken from her still. She could lose this woman too. This last link to who she could have been.

Isatay imagined herself without Addisalem. Without the woman's heavy silences and gaunt frame. She saw herself severed from all her yesterdays, floating away amongst the stars, suspended in time with no future, her present lost. She struggled to breathe as the vision seized her heart and squeezed her sanity until it bulged – a leather pouch threatening to burst.

It was a horrible sensation, but one she already knew. It had overcome her a year before, as roaring flames had singed her eyebrows and sooted her face with the remains of all those she held dear. She had been alone then too, crouched like a wild thing among the enset leaves. Shivering so violently that essential parts of her were pried loose and fluttered away, leaving her unable to hold herself on the earth, and her body rising above the crackling fire, the eddies of ash, and the guttural screams.

It was Addisalem who had dragged her back. Addisalem's voice, inhuman and agonised, that had hauled her to earth, the painful grip of the woman's blistered hands that had pulled her clear of the void. She had opened her eyes and met those of this woman who was both like her mother and not. Even then, she was a pale echo of all that Isatay had known before. A faded replica of the mother she had adored.

It was Addisalem who had yanked her free. They had been floating away together ever since, dangling over chasms and clinging to cliff-faces. The horse's hooves had rung over great distances, skidding and sliding on pebbles that tumbled into the gorges below, crunching over sun-baked vegetation and wading through grasses so tall that Isatay felt they would pluck her from the animal's back.

They had spoken little to each other in those first few weeks, watching the mountain ranges rise and fall, the terrain gaining and leaching colour, the sun blazing then sinking to make way for its pale and humble twin. The peaks and valleys of their homeland had flattened as the distances they travelled stretched, and every night Addisalem had gone further still, leaving her body behind, abandoning Isatay to the darkness that bound her to her past.

And the little girl would sit and extend her eyes beyond the prostrate body of her aunt, to the trees that ringed them and seemed to dance and blur and take on the shape of her mother. The thick cloud of hair, the kind gaze, the outstretched hand, the black ink etched on her chocolate skin: a cross encircled by a sun, with two further crosses climbing up the length of one long finger. And she would watch as her mother burst into flames and contorted with agony, and know that she had made this thing happen and feel the terror tightening its fingers around her throat.

Isatay would watch her mother blaze and burn into a gnarled heap of charred wood and black leaves, and flee the horrors of her mind to fall at her aunt's feet, kneeling in the spilt blood and upon the shards of the broken jar. Her voice and hands would pull her aunt from the other worlds she travelled, dragging the woman back as the woman had once dragged her. She would clutch Addisalem's hand, and feel the scars that had their origin in her folly.

She would clench the hand and see once again that fateful moment. At its centre was Addisalem, who had crouched beneath the emerald leaves of the sheltering enset plant and held out her hand to Isatay, the glow of the flames behind her framing her silhouette. The woman had clawed through flames to reach her. Isatay had watched her smouldering amidst the wreckage that her recklessness had wrought. She had watched Addisalem's clothing catch alight, had observed her aunt's hair go up in flame, and had said nothing. She had watched her aunt searching desperately for her amongst the charred remains and had stayed quiet, cowering and weeping, ignoring the woman's hoarse cries. It was as though she had swallowed the fire into herself, her insides giving way to a roaring emptiness where no will and no words remained.

Addisalem's hand, when the woman had thrust it through the leaves towards her, had been a mess of puckered skin. The remains of the markings that twinned those of her mother only just visible on the abused appendage. She had been afraid to take that hand, afraid that the skin would fall loose and leave her clutching at meat, afraid of what leaving with the woman and leaving behind the ashes of her past would mean, afraid of those black eyes even as she followed their silent command to come forward from her hiding place.

They had travelled far since that first unhappy meeting and yet, in the truest sense, they had gone nowhere at all. Isatay gazed at her homeland and understood that this had always been their destination. She and Addisalem had both dreamed of this place, leaving it knowing that they circled back to it.

IV – THE LIVING

*T*ap, BUMP. Tap, BUMP. Tap, BUMP.

Addisalem swayed with the upward lift and downward plunge of her arm. The early morning sun was cool and uncertain, adding a golden shimmer to the breeze. Her afro bent and reshaped itself with the more savage gusts, and the loose dress she wore buffeted against her long, angular shape, tracing newly acquired flesh.

Her lips were parted as she worked, and the breath that came from her lungs sang with the rhythm of mortar against pestle.

Ama. Kelech. Ama. Kelech. Ama. Kelech.

The name and the action became one and dispersed into the world around her, and the world echoed the sound until everything thrummed in time with her thoughts. The charred soil just beginning to sprout tufts of grass beneath her, the woven walls and the thatched roof of the little house behind her, the rustling of the enset trees beside her, and the undulating mountain peaks before her. And all around the flurry of rushing feet and laughter as Isatay raced, breathless and bright-eyed, away from the baby goat that pursued her with butting head.

Addisalem felt the stretch and sear of her heart as it widened, and she contracted it back to size with practiced care. Still cautious. All that she could see had once so easily succumbed to flame, and she with it. She was waiting still. Would wait always for the roar of fire to burn away all that she had gained. To force her to grow anew.

She watched with eyes that looked beyond what was before her as Isatay tripped and fell, blood welling quick and bright from her elbows and knees. She did not pause in her work but watched the child dispassionately as she whispered her sister's name.

It was a strange bond they shared. The blood that ran through Addisalem's veins now ran from the little girl's grazed skin. The memories that haunted one, taunted the other. Their pasts intertwined like strands within the woven straw baskets that hung on the smooth mud walls of their shared abode. They had lost everything together and regained it together, and yet there were distances between them that both were hesitant to bridge.

Ama. Kelech. Ama. Kelech. Ama. Kelech.

Isatay sat up to smear the blood dry, tinting the golden-brown skin of her legs and arms. The baby goat watched her from its perch on top of a leafy tree, its cheeks puffed with vegetation, their game forgotten. Isatay in her turn watched Addisalem as she overturned the pestle into the narrow mouth of the jebena, stood, and ducked into the darkness of their hut. The shadows of their home seemed to leap out and swallow the woman, dragging her out of the blue-tinged morning air, and Isatay felt her heart squeeze in panic.

She pushed to her feet and followed her aunt, dashing the pebbles embedded in her palm against her dress as she ran, hearing her little goat bleat in response to her sudden departure and rustle down the tree after her. Then she too was swallowed by the darkness and in the instant it took her eyes to adjust to the shaded interior of their home, she heard the gentle exhale of her aunt's breath, the rustle of coals, the tap of wood, the snap and pop that signalled the birth of flame.

The rising glow revealed the planes and hollows of Addisalem's lean features, making a mockery of the months they had passed here and of the changes it had wrought in them both. Because the face that the fire revealed was that of the woman Isatay had known before. The shadows skittered over high-flung cheekbones and concave cheeks, rimming deep-set eyes. Then the image dispersed as the fire grew, and there was only her aunt, sitting on a stool before the flames, her scarred hand balancing the jebena gently over the heat. The woman of blood and milk and honey dissipated with the swirling smoke, and Isatay felt the pressure in her chest ease.

It was Addisalem who had brought her to this place, who had forced them both back from the brink – and Isatay knew that immense will had been exercised on her behalf. She was safer with this woman than she would be anywhere else on earth, and even as she felt the guilt wash over her at that thought, she had to acknowledge that it had been she who had tangled their paths together in a single moment of carelessness.

She had been staring into the budding flames, but that last thought jerked her back to awareness. She pulled her eyes from contemplation of the fire and met the gaze of the woman sitting across from her. Isatay watched the flames dance within the midnight depths and recalled a time when they had rolled milky-white.

"You look just like your mother."

Isatay started at the quietly spoken words. She could not understand why they struck her so, until she realized with amazement that they had never spoken of the woman whose presence hovered around them like an elusive perfume. The shock of the realisation burned in Isatay's throat and ran down her cheeks in hot, silent tears.

The flames flickered and threatened to die, and behind them a little girl wept without sound. Addisalem sat and breathed and awakened from her dreams. Her being reconstituted itself slowly, deliberately, skin unfurling over vibrating atoms, eyes opening inwards.

She watched with eyes that looked beyond what was before her and spoke with a voice that was hers but that also entwined itself with one from their mutual past, from the yesterdays of the lonely girl and the reassembled woman.

"Isatay… The fire needs tending."

My Sister's Husband

Nyarsipi Odeph

"*H*ave you greeted Onindo?"

It is impossible for Akello not to smile. How often does your auntie try to matchmake you with someone you might be related to a few hours before you bury your sister?

Auntie's voice is scratchy, the hallmark of a professional mourner. Twenty minutes earlier she had been prostrate on the ground next to the wooden coffin in front of my mother's house, asking me why I had left all the cooking to my living sister. Thirty minutes ago, Auntie had been running beside the hearse from the top of the hill almost five kilometres away, her voice piercing the air and Akello's ears with the clarity of a debtor's fury.

Akello is fluent in four languages; none as proficient as that of grief. She knows that grief is a suffocating spouse. One who comes fully stocked with corrosive acid that incinerates your nervous system, and words are insufficient when confronted by his bride. Once grief has stained the fabric of your soul, you are never rid of it. You are his bride for eternity.

She's toying with grief's ring around her throat now, her lungs constricting as she remembers placing my obituary. The angry eyebrowed sales rep telling her that it was cheaper in black and white and if you used less words. The shame as she summarised my life in one short, glum paragraph. The endless committee meetings trying to raise money for my funeral. The faces and voices that spoke to her through the blur. Her new phone vibrating incessantly.

You see, when you die, your loved ones have to switch from smartphones to mulika mwizis for their longer battery life because *everyone* is calling. It's a curious affair, the price of amnesia. People don't know how to handle grief's bride. So they pretend. They assume that red-rimmed eyes are the result of a lighting defect in the room, rather than the bleeding of the soul. There are awkward hugs and notes hastily thrust into grieving hands. Crisp thousand shilling notes, jaded five hundreds. Everyone is God's spokesperson claiming that you have finally returned home, which is all right, because that's where we are all heading. The people who stood on the sidelines as your family imploded want your bereaved to know them by name and amount. Mpesa is alive. Beep after beep. *Let me send something small. She was a good woman. She is with your mother and father now. Be strong.* Watching Akello then and watching her now, floating through these rituals of death and what comes after, with that odd smile, makes me feel wretched.

Akello inhales deeply. The feeling of drowning persists. She's thinking about the fight our uncles had a week ago over my burial. The elders from Father's clan wanted to bury me outside the gate facing... is it north? Because I am unmarried. A terrible affliction for us Luos; a woman being unmarried and having no men or relatives to cook for nor any healthy sons who would have also needed to be cooked for. We take cooking very seriously, you see. They didn't want my unmarriageable spirit corrupting the only living single girl in my father's home.

Things have changed, my uncles argued. We live in the city. The children should be buried in the graveyard their father built. We believe in a benevolent God now. Spirits are powerless against his might.

Akello had sat through the meeting with a mask on her face. The thought of me being buried outside like a castaway had made her vomit in private. Smoke more. Eat less. Hadn't I been enough of a castaway in my lifetime? As the men decided, she remembered her last words to me: two angry sisters screaming at each other about everything except the fact that they were alone and frightened and had just buried their mother.

"You will always be alone," she had said before slamming the door on the way out of our house. Before moving to university in Uganda. We allowed our newly acquired husband, grief, to mute us until I died.

Before everything changed, before the walls in our house were stripped bare of any trace of laughter, before love was suffocated by loss, we had the table. A mahogany marvel cheapened by an odd white finishing. The centrepiece of my mother's life, where important family announcements were made, pre-spanking speeches about the fate of children who shamed their parents were held, and where she placed elaborate dishes before her husband and three children. Father had a knack for returning from his mysterious work trips just in time for mother's special osuga; the greens treated to nightly soaking and boiling in fresh creamy milk for almost two weeks, the catfish fresh from our ageing Dani back in the village, a side of melted ghee for Father in a little metal cup, and the ugali made from bel as brown and as filling as Bamburi cement.

We were seated around the table, polishing off our supper when my brother, Telo, announced his scholarship to New York University. Mother's voice caught a little as she unfolded the letter he handed her.

"What's wrong with Nairobi University?"

"This is better, Mami, there's nothing here for me. I'll just end up lounging in this house waiting to gobble up your aluru if I stay in Kenya," Telo laughed.

His laugh had a magical effect on her; always throwing her off-balance.

"If I go to Nairobi Uni, I will only become a professional stone-thrower like Father," he added.

"That professional stone-thrower will buy your airplane ticket, Jatelo." My brother's full name lumbered out of her throat as if it was hurting her stomach, the way it always was when her crown jewel disappointed her.

"Mami, I am playing, yaye." He reached across the table and folded her hands into his. Akello and I watched silently as he teased her. Marvelled at the potency of his charm. How effortlessly he melted our ferocious mother into a chuckling mound of compliance.

We never understood why he stole her money. She had organised a successful harambee and raised enough money to last him a year, even more if he was practical. The scholarship was going to cover his living costs, too. But this memory reminds me of the force that was Telo. He did it because he could. He existed in a world where you could charm and con the woman who birthed you, and still sleep soundly at night.

It was at this table that Father told us about their separation many years later, after cooking Luo delicacies ceased to be a priority. It was here that he told us that she was sick, and here that he told us she had died. It was at this table that Akello and I decided to sell the Nairobi house after our father died in a car crash, take Telo to rehab, and move to Father's rural home. Where we are now gathered.

I wonder whose idea it was to use this table, still sturdy after decades of neglect, as the base of my coffin. I like their sense of irony.

"Just go and talk to him and see what happens."

"I don't need a husband, Auntie." Akello's voice is placatory.

Auntie clicks, her tongue so abrasive that both Akello and I bristle. "What kind of nonsense is this now, nyara? Every woman worth her salt needs a family."

Akello closes her eyes, trying to control her face. Her wry thoughts ring in my ears.

My sister had a family and she still died alone.

"You need children. What would your mother say if she heard you right now?"

"I think my mother more than anyone would understand my disinterest in wifehood, Auntie."

"Who made you this way?"

Silence. Her languid voice in my head again. Fury laced with frustration.

All of you did.

"Onindo is a good man, jaber. God-fearing."

"I doubt that a God-fearing man would appreciate a wife who smokes."

Out of habit, I hold my breath.

"You smoke?"

"Yes."

Auntie's fingers gnaw into the side of her arm. Her eyes crinkle as she scans the subdued compound. It's almost as if she is worried that the wind will carry Akello's confession across my coffin and into Onindo's waiting ears. He's perched on a rock near the tent he had helped erect for the mourners earlier. Trying and failing to not watch my weary sister and her inappropriate auntie.

"Since when?" A hiss.

"University."

"I knew it was a mistake, letting her children go to other schools in strange lands. Look what it did to you, to your brother."

Silence. That smile.

"Akello, your mother was a good woman who didn't smoke."

"And yet she still died."

"Why are you talking this way?"

"Why don't we mourn one soul before we begin planning the annihilation of another?"

"You need someone to comfort you."

My mother was a married woman. Still. Alone.

In the ensuing quiet, Akello's eyes focus on our brother's thin frame walking towards my coffin. I feel the tightness in her chest. The longing. I feel the heaviness that assaults her tongue, making her swallow. She wants a cigarette now. Needs to add burning to the mess inside her chest. Her fingers twitch and she folds them into shaking fists.

Auntie mistakes Akello's silence for concession.

"I know you must be tired from your trip." A truce.

Akello nods, swallowing the nicotine she cannot have without causing a scandal. Her eyes are still on the figure now standing over my sleeping face. Auntie follows her gaze.

"Have you spoken to Telo since you got here?"

"No."

They haven't spoken in five years. Well, five years, eight months, four days and six hours , if accuracy is the goal here. Not since he was kicked out of the last rehab facility. He used to be my problem.

Telo, the object of Akello's drifting eyes, had always been good at theft. Stole the affections of every pre- and post-adolescent friend we ever had. Stole our mother's favour. Tall and disarming. Stole cigarettes from strange Uncle Tom and smoked them while we watched. He drained my mother's account on the day of his flight to New York. Stole Akello's meagre twelve-year-old savings. Stole her dream of what New York could be. Before he left she had burdened him for hours on end with questions about the college he was about to attend. When she would visit him. The places they would go. But oh, how New York took our entitled brother, chewed him up with ease and spat him back out at us.

I picked him up at the airport the day he was deported. Still tall, all the light in his eyes dissolved into a muddy vagueness. He had faded jeans, a black T-shirt, an oily duffel bag filled with papers, and nothing else. Telo was quiet on the drive back home. Quiet for weeks after, during which my sister and I tiptoed around the edges of his drug withdrawal-induced insanity.

He stole speech from us, first slipping into unfettered whispering, but then eventually abandoning conversation altogether. Every night he frightened us with his incomprehensible interactions with the family cat; the one he skinned alive one day and tried to make us eat. When he was out scoring his next hit, we had to clean his room. It had begun to smell so bad we couldn't be in the house without tearing up.

We found the letters from his school.

"...we regretfully withdraw your scholarship. The university has arrived at this decision based on repeated instances of theft reported by fellow students..."

"...in spite of continued leniency by the Dean..."

One year, four pastors, six clan prayer meetings, one dead cat, my graduation, countless screaming sessions in our three-bedroom bungalow and three rehab stints later, Telo bounded back into the arms of crack cocaine, an expensive habit for a middle-class deportee, a widower, and two college-bound sisters. Father had stopped taking us with him on his trips. I was at university clearing up post-graduation details. And Akello was at home with Telo. He needed money. Broke her arm so she would give up the maintenance money Father had left for us.

He stole mystery from us. When Father came home and saw what he had done to Akello, he decided to curse him, African-style. Stripped down and exposed his genitals. My brother, never one to be outdone and ingloriously high, had stripped too.

Two generous body parts that neither of us needed to see, nor could we forget.

Perhaps the curse took hold. How else could one explain what became of all of us?

"*H*ave you eaten?"
"No."

A lengthy silence.

In Akello's head, a whisper. *We all left at one point or another, and leaving was what ruined us.*

*T*he singing and wailing has stopped. Dusk descends in my father's neglected compound, covering all of us with a shroud of subdued melancholy. There is hollowness to everything even though there seem to be hundreds of feet milling about. In Auntie's raucous laugh, in the barking of the stray dogs that have followed the scent of freshly slaughtered cow, in the breeze fanning the cooking fires. My mother's house, echoingly empty four days ago, is full of strangers who do not remember her children's names.

"You should eat," Auntie says.

"I should."

Akello is smiling again, unnerving me.

People keep trying to feed your loved ones when you die, as if unconsciously trying to plug in the gap you have left with nutrition. Tea. More tea. For every tear your loved ones shed, there is a corresponding thermos flask filled with tea. They flutter around your loved ones, avoiding the vacant stares, the muted responses, the ugly marks of grief. They don't remember that when we, the dead, move to the hereafter, we take our loved ones' taste buds with us for a while. So you can pour in all the salt you want or none at all, but they cannot taste. Each sip and bite is agonisingly bland, a reminder that we are dead and they are not.

Kerosene lamps begin to appear and illuminate the small groups of five or more scattered in and around the tents. Everything is muffled. Everyone glancing at me in my little coffin laid on the table that shaped our lives while on their way to the latrines, on their way to another cup of tea, on their way to Auntie's boisterous laugh in a smoke-filled cooking hut, on their way to find the local brew, just glancing at my sleeping form and my brother's equally impassive face as he stands over my box. The face Akello is still looking at.

"Talk to your brother. You are all he has now." Auntie rises and starts walking towards Akello's would-be suitor.

She doesn't respond. She is thinking about Uganda now. A time when all she had was solitude.

*T*he bus ride into Kampala seemed to stretch into another time zone. She struggled, of course, as she always had when Father moved us around like chess pieces on the path to his goal of success. She never did well with change. When she was ten and we moved to Kisumu from Nairobi, she had been a nightmare; unable to bear the thunderstorms, screaming through them. When our estranged mother died, Akello moved back home and did not utter a word for almost a month. Father feared she had lost her mind.

Shortly after entering Uganda, she had been stunned to find that chicken could be sold on a stick by the roadside like maize, but had bought and ate one with relish. She had gone to get breakfast the next day, and had almost wept upon discovering that matoke was considered breakfast while tea and bread were seen as peculiar. Their ugali was known as posho, made of maize flour too fine and too white; the texture on her tongue made her feel like she was betraying the entire Luo empire from here to the Kano plains.

She learned not to hate Kenya Power too much when she discovered that load-shedding was a normal part of life. It took her a while not to openly gawk at the women who would kneel in greeting at the feet of senior men no matter where they were in the city, how muddy it was, or who was watching.

It warmed her skin the way Ugandans spoke to each other, always attaching an affectionate "bambe" or "mukwano" at the beginning of their sentences. How the language had a malleable manner of making words more tender even in moments of anger or annoyance. She found it charming how consonants did not stand a chance in the musical fluidity of Luganda. How vowels appeared where they had never existed, so that rolex, her staple food for most of her stay, was always rolexi. But she loved that meal and the vendor with his jiko and egg crates, his peppers and tomatoes and cabbages. She loved his smile. How he existed in a constant blur of motion, flipping the omelettes into her chapati while whistling a Juliana Kanyamozi song. Always a Juliana song. She envied the obvious calm he possessed in his chaotic little bubble.

Akello stood out in the quiet rural Kavule area, which was littered with hostels and students attending Makerere University. The plump shopkeeper was always calling her the Kenyanise girl, always speaking to her in Luganda, making her miserable in her Nilotic inadequacy.

But Kavule was magical to her because in her visibility, Akello felt invisible. She loved that she could depend on the rolexi master for all three meals, sit at his feet, and just focus on being unseen. She discovered the allure of solitude in Kavule's unpaved hilly pathways, always choosing to fade into shadowy corners even in social spaces where she communed in peace with her loneliness. She discovered cigarettes during those seasons of solitude. When the smoke burned in her chest, she felt in those moments like she could live through anything.

Transition has always been an agonising matter for the members of my clan. My father never recovered from the discovery that my mother, disillusioned with her marriage, slept with another man, and later ran off with him. He who had three other secret wives.

We don't do well with big moves. Akello had been there when my father chased my mother's lover with a blunt machete.

The scene plays itself before me. My mother in a torn blouse on her knees, begging for leniency. Eight-year-old Akello standing in her checked blue school uniform undetected. They had forgotten to pick her up from school so she had walked the short distance home. I wonder if I will see them soon; Father and Mother? Whether they are on speaking terms now that they are dead.

I can taste the salt in my sister's unshed tears. I can feel her pulse. I don't understand why I am still here. Why am I coursing through her thoughts and whizzing through her memories like an unwilling but riveted passenger? Tethered to her, I have been oscillating between feelings of pain, amusement, and the fear that I may never leave.

*P*yok! Pyok! Pyok!

It is pitch black now. Midnight came and drifted into the wee hours. In the cooking huts, wood has turned into ash. Feet no longer move. Voices have become slumberous sighs. The air is even more condensed than it was during the day. It's cold, but the gravediggers are all shirtless and suitably intoxicated, as is the custom.

Akello is sitting by the fence of the graveyard, watching them dig. Slabs of cement from older graves sit stoically in a row next to the fresh hole. My father and my mother. He never divorced her, and wept for weeks after he buried her in this very compound, even though they had not spoken in ten years.

The bushes look like an extension of Akello's form; leaves entwined into her afro, the black cotton soil melding with her canvas shoes. They haven't even noticed she is there, and has been since they started working. The earth seems resistant to their attempts to prepare my final resting place. They have been digging for hours. She lights another cigarette, presses it into her mouth.

Closes her eyes. Inhales. She hasn't slept in days. It's cold but she isn't shivering as she watches the gravediggers prepare my final resting place.

I cannot feel or hear Akello anymore.
Something is confining me to my coffin. Daylight has been broken long enough for fires and feet to resume their daily duties.

Someone is singing as they congregate around me. Midday has passed and the burial is set for two o'clock. That person's voice is haunting. Is it time to go, I wonder?

Remb Nyarombo ma nonegi, Obedo gi teko
Mar pwodho jogo magene, Ni kik giketh kendo.

They are singing about the blood of the lamb saving us all from guilty sin.

They are looking for my brother, the oldest male, so he can begin the burial formalities. No one knows where he is. People are confused, looking to my uncles and aunties for answers. When was he last seen? And where is Akello?

T here are special kinds of screams that life may or may not let you experience. Like my mother's scream on the day she gave birth to me. There's the scream that burst from her dried lips the day she discovered her beloved son, whom she trusted with everything that was hers, was not above betrayal, when she went to pay a bill with a debit card linked to an empty bank account. There's the sound my father made when he found his favourite wife writhing beneath a stranger. A choking, like blood curdling in the throat. What heartbreak sounds like.

There are other screams you can only see, if you look keenly. Like those of a college student in a hospital room quietly saying no thank you to the nurse offering her tea, after telling her that her sister has died. Her lips behind a puff of smoke, always smiling, but whose eyes have no light.

But long after today's sun has set, people in this rural county will be talking about the screams that came from my inappropriate auntie. They will talk about how her feet had no shoes when she emerged from the abandoned hut in the farthest corner of the compound. How she ran round and round and round like a chicken that refused to accept its destiny to fill someone's plate and later stroke their full stomach. How she screamed my mother's name. How the stones cut her feet and how she kept going, faster and faster, as the crowd stood immobile and entranced. How the screams iced their blood. How in the sounds she made, you could hear the birth of a woman who had just inherited life-long insomnia. They will describe the matutas on her head, which no one had seen before because she had been wearing a wig, but had yanked it off in her frenzy. They will talk about the blood... all the blood on her kitenge dress.

*T*he force tying me down, lifts, and here I stand in front of Akello again. The crowd in the compound joins my auntie in wailing, but we are alone and uninterrupted in this hut where we used to play as children, when Dani was alive.

She is looking *at me*. No longer through me. The burning intensity in her eyes is so potent that I, forgetting that I am already dead, step back in fear. There stands her husband, Grief, his hold creating a glow around her form. Her lips move.

"None of us will ever leave now. We are all together as we should always have been."

I look down at the floor where she is pointing.

My brother's mutilated body. And beside him, with a smile as simple as the cuts on her wrists, lies my sister's body.

The Castle

Arja Salafranca

Cape Town, 2011

*T*hey walk through the doors of the five-pointed castle, and into the grounds. For July it is a temperate day, and thin jackets are enough to keep them warm. The grass is green, well-mown, looked after. The mountain rears over the city, a grey-granite presence, and the sky is perfectly blue. The sun is harsh though, even in winter.

It is like walking back into time: the thick grey walls shut out the noise of the growing city of Cape Town, enclosing them all in another world. And yet, in a way, not. Children run around, shrieking, as children do, shattering the atmosphere, although the expanse of grass is so big, their voices rise, and are carried away by the winds.

Kiara brought it up first, while checking her cellphone for emails, idly remarking that it must have been terrible, relying on months-old letters for news of loved ones from home. Imagine sailing out here, enduring a long sea voyage, with just memories and words to sustain you. Carrying pictures in your memory, in a time before photography had been invented. The ultimate form of torture, she thinks, now, to have only your mind's eye to rely on.

Tomorrow she flies back home to Johannesburg. This trip is yet another interlude in her life. On these short breaks, time assumes weight, reality. Days are remembered as they are not when you are in the midst of routine. It's partly why she loves travelling.

She is with two friends who live here now. They are a couple, the women in front of her, Suzy and Annie, both shorter than she is. She is tall, for a woman. Sometimes, when walking with women only, she feels like a giant, and yet she knows she is anything but.

Her friends are holding hands, then the younger one, Suzy, lets go, skips toward a bell. She wants to ring it, but there are stern warnings not to. Instead they stand looking up at the bell, cast in 1697 in Amsterdam, and shipped out to the Cape. The past rubs up against the present: her friends stand silhouetted against the bell, Kiara raises the camera she's carrying, snaps them against the morning light. Suzy's looking at Annie in the photos, Annie smiling behind her big dark glasses. They have been together for almost two years. Suzy younger by almost fifteen years, yet more prepared to settle down, have a child, than Annie ever was – or Kiara, for that matter.

Their hands touch again briefly, they turn, skip ahead again, leaving Kiara to bring up the rear, watching them walk away, drop hands, if you look quickly, you might think they are friends. Look again, and you realise they are walking too close together for that.

Now Kiara walks behind her friends alongside the wall, lifts her camera again and again, storing memories on her camera's card.

Cape Colony, 1834

*I*t takes months for letters to arrive at the Cape Colony. News is old when it arrives. We knew that when I left, and we knew too that there were some things we wouldn't say. Even sealed letters have a habit of spilling their contents.

But this letter isn't for you, my love. I will never send it, and you will never receive it. But it helps if I address it to you, as though you will one day reach out, read it, know me again.

I sometimes wish I had cut off more locks of your hair, you'd never miss them among your tangle of red hair. Instead I have just the one single curling lock, which I hold often. I hold up the dry hair to my nostrils, but there's scant scent of you in there. There's nothing left, even after just a few short months, just the hair, almost brittle. I keep it safely away, and away from the sun. The sun fades things, especially here, you wouldn't believe how harsh it is. It warms you, then it rapidly starts to burn and blister you, there's no protection here. At first I enjoyed the rays of heat and would raise my face to the sun, bonnet off, but I burn easily and the mistress of the house warned me against making my face black like the slaves here. Chasing me inside, admonishing me, warning me. I was scared soon enough, and then I too retreated indoors into the cool of this large house I now live in. But yes, you'd love the heat, it seeps through you until you almost forget our cold, icy northern days.

You're in the thick of things there, I presume, getting ready for the dead of winter, storing and making Christmas puddings, preserving food for the long nights ahead. I'm indolent and idle here, indulged. I don't have to work or help in the kitchen, and my days are endlessly long while I wait. There is a household of help behind the spotless interior. At times I am bored. I read. I play with the children, and the mistress is expecting another, and wearied from it, so I help a little with her brood. I sew, as I always have, and my needlepoint is admired. I'm sewing an image of Table Mountain at the moment. I may send you that, just that, without a letter, without explanation, and I think you'd understand, wouldn't you?

I am, of course, still painting.

I miss you, fiercely at times, at other moments I can remember my anger, and I can almost forget, and accept what had to be. It's strange being between these two emotions, longing to hear your voice, or to run my hands through your thick red curly hair; and yet, I know, that the only way to peace lies in forgetting, in letting your face warp and dissolve away until all that I have left is that single curling strand of your hair. It will fade in time, I know it, even though I keep it hidden, in the dark; it will fade, as all things do.

And how is Paws? Does he now lie on your bed and purr loudly? His green eyes closed, disappearing into the black of his fur, he always looked so innocent, didn't he? Licking his white paws clean, only to muddy them again in the dirt outside the next day.

There's so much to tell you about here: the bright sunlight, so different from anything we ever knew, the way the mountain looms over this place, the shadows that seem to move and plunge the place into moods that the people then wear as cloaks. About the sea which thrashes wildly at the shore here, violent, violently African as I have come to see it. It's beautiful: despite the circumstances, there's a wild wonderful wicked beauty to this place. Even though I want to hate it, I find I cannot. I already love the capriciousness and hardness of this land, it has edges that ensnare you.

Mind you, I will not remain here, and already I feel the pang of that separation – when I have been separated from so much already. But I have been assured that I may return often, I won't be stuck on the farm forever, and can come into town at least once a month. I've been promised.

I haven't seen the farmhouse yet. It's a few days journey away by ox-wagon, and I haven't yet met Peter. He's away. They say he will return for the Christmas holiday. Already it's warm here, late in November.

I think of you, staring from the frosty window, the ice already thick in the mornings. How you'd love it here, with your hatred of the cold and the dark.

2011

They walk through the archway. Suzy is holding the information booklet they bought when purchasing their tickets. There's a cross to the right, made of wood from the forest at Delville, erected in memory of the South African soldiers who lost their lives in the First World War. They pass through silently.

The dungeons are grim, as dungeons usually are, since prisoners were tortured there. The place is dark, seems to hold memories, pain, and they leave the small rooms quickly. There's an upside-down horseshoe on the door.

Climbing stairs, they find themselves walking along the top of Block E according to the map Suzy is holding. The wind blows up here. It's eerily silent. Kiara dimly remembers having visited the castle as a twelve-year-old as part of a school trip to Cape Town. But she doesn't remember the dungeon or torture chamber. She remembers something altogether grander.

"I remember climbing through tiny tunnels into dark rooms,"

says Suzy, shaking her head, puzzled, "but there's nothing like that here. Maybe that was it, maybe things seems bigger when you're smaller."

They come to small prison rooms. Dank, even though they've been open for years. When shut in, a man would have scant room to move, the darkness all enveloping, Kiara imagines. She mentions having visited Alcatraz a few years previously. In some ways these small rooms of pain and despair remind her of that more gigantic prison.

They move on quickly, chased by their imaginings.

1834

*H*e arrived last night. Everything is coming to an end, my dear. The slaves are packing up my belongings and we are getting ready for the days-long journey to the farm. I feel like I am going into the wilderness. Staying here would mean safety, I said as much. I told him how much I had come to love the mountain and the bay. The mistress also seems reluctant to let me go, and I tried to enlist her help in letting me stay. But it's no use, is it? A wife's place is with her husband, and, yes, he has already made me his wife: that part was clear from the beginning.

The farm is isolated, I have been told, as though he were punishing me somehow, yet what does he know, how much does he know? I haven't said anything, I doubt you did? And the master and mistress of this house know so little, Mama and Papa wouldn't have said, I know they didn't. But he's determined. The man has a streak of something – I don't know what, I don't know him well enough. He is not a nasty person, that is certain, everyone talks kindly of him, but there's a determination in him. A determination to take what's his. I have nothing else to offer, nothing else to give. I had those long months at sea to think, to reflect. Have you? Do you understand, have you accepted?

I remember those last few nights before we were found, fumbling in the dark, hurrying as footsteps came nearer.

"Nothing good will ever come of this," you said. Do you

remember saying that? Your face so close to mine, your breath hot and close, saying these words, pushing me away with words while you always let me come near with my mouth, my breath, my own lust.

1835

*I*t was so strange to celebrate Christmas with the sun shining, the sun's glare is wrong somehow. And yet, you know me, I relish the unfamiliar. Perhaps a life at home in England would not have satisfied me after all.

These February days are airless though, the heat rises and we gasp through the hottest hours of the day. I can't recall knowing this kind of heat at all, it's deathly, it's impossible. I feel hourly as though I were being attacked. Your body boils in the heat. And I am also expecting.

Yes, I am at the big manor home in town. Peter was called away at the beginning of January. I'm not told much. And not in my condition. He hasn't returned to the farm, but has been called away to lend support to the fighting at the frontier. As I said, there's something in him, some wildness. This is a man who will not be caged; perhaps we will make a good match, despite everything. Perhaps Mama and Papa knew what they were doing?

How is Paws? I wish you could write, tell me that he lies on your bed, sleeping in the middle of the day, as cats do and always will, readying themselves for the hunt at night. Do you give him a piece of cheese in the mornings as I asked? He's the only tom I've ever had who adores cheese. Perhaps you give him a tiny bit and think of me when you do so?

2011

*T*hey've come to the end of the tour, they're hungry. Kiara visits the toilets, set back through more dank-like tunnels. She still has her dark glasses on, it makes the place gloomier. When she emerges Suzy and Annie are sitting on a bench, waiting for her, holding hands as they stare at the clouds tabling the mountain.

They've been discussing lunch plans: there's a hotel along the Atlantic coast with views straight to the South Pole. It does good calamari. Would she like to go? She eagerly agrees.

Still, they sit for a while, there's something strangely compelling about this place. A peace not found outside. The castle was first built between 1666 and 1679. The time is so far away, Kiara imagines darkly lit streets of the centuries past, it is almost, but not quite, incomprehensible. But it's time to move on.

"You seem so happy, so good together," Kiara says when they are seated at the restaurant.

Annie smiles, non-committal. The sun slants down lazily and the sea smiles in the distance. Kiara was given a seat with the view of the ocean from the terrace, Kiara who lives land-locked all year round, starved of the sea. It is implicitly understood that she will get the view, it is only fair. And, yes, there is some pity in this, for those who live so far away from the sea. The undercurrent runs through.

Suzy is fetching a jacket from the car when Kiara says this to Annie, and Annie smiles back enigmatically. The history lies between them: they remember the woman before Suzy, the woman who was responsible for Annie moving down here in the first place. She'd got a job here, and so Annie had to move. But once she had done so, her girlfriend turned around, said she was sorry, but she had fallen out of love. Annie's picked up the pieces, the past implied in the way she never refers to the ex by name but only as "the ex". She has a new life, a new home, is building something else with the woman who is bounding back across the parking lot with her red jacket.

As they negotiate traffic back home to Sea Point, Kiara brings up the subject of children. Annie is trying to get pregnant through a sperm donor.

"How does it work?"' she asks, "will Suzy then adopt the child?"

"Not if we're married," Suzy replies.

"I don't want to get married," Annie says, "I never have."

There's a crack of silence. Kiara rushes into fill it, "Neither have I," she says, "I totally understand what you mean, Annie."

Beyond the car's windows, the ocean pounds at the beaches and the rocks of Llandudno Bay. The sun is cold, hanging low in the sky.

1835

*I*t was the slave woman who helped me. Up until then, I had barely noticed her presence. Did I mention to you that slaves were freed last year? But there's a clause that they must work a further four years as apprentices before they are fully freed. This is the lot of Marta. I have no precise idea how old she is. She was taken at the age of nine or ten, she thinks, and has been here ever since. Old enough to remember her mother and family and yet young enough to forget, mercifully. She comes from Java, she says, and remembers a long dank ocean voyage. I once said we had both endured long voyages away from home, but Marta looked at me, and I shut my mouth. We both know how different our circumstances are.

I bled the child away, and I regret to say I'm not sorry. I didn't want his child, not now, not when I am so new to this land.

"The first one is always the worst," the mistress said, "best you get on with it." But there was nothing to be done, the child was determined not to grow within me. I wasn't far along, three months. Marta knew what to do, washing my forehead with ice cold water, the only thing that helped that long, cramping night, and when it was over she took away the bloody mess in a battered wooden bucket. I asked her to throw away the bucket, or to bury it, I said it was bad luck otherwise. I don't know if she did that. I could never ask.

She has a quiet presence, Marta. I've never known such peace to radiate from a person. She's old, as I've explained, and made older still by the life she's led. She has hooded brown eyes, crinkled by time, and yet they are soft and gentle, and her nose is small and straight, sitting pretty on her face. She covers her head with a kerchief, and I have never seen her hair.

I have asked the mistress for details about Marta, but she shrugs wearily at my questions and says that Marta has just always been around, from the time she was born. Marta, I take it was a kind of nanny, but she's old now, and tired. She was given kitchen duties years ago, and cooks for the family. I suspect she is happier in the kitchen. It's quieter, and she can work according to her own rhythms instead of having the children rush around her.

It's been months since I saw Peter. It's winter here now. Summer there, I know. Are you well, are you content? How is my darling Paws? I received letters last week from Mama and the eldest children, but no one mentioned Paws, or you, obviously. I must infer from their silence that all is well, that everything is right with you, or surely they would have told me?

I wrote back at once. But I didn't mention your name, I didn't ask after you and once I hadn't asked after you, I couldn't ask after Paws, of course. He's four years old this year, do you know that? I know you can't celebrate a cat's birthday, but it was four years ago that you brought him to me, saying he was a birthday present, a present for my sixteenth year.

2011

They talk about the paintings they saw on show at the Castle. In some, Table Mountain looked strangely squashed and small, and grossly out of proportion. Kiara and Annie had looked at each other and laughed.

"Maybe people in the past saw things differently," Annie had ventured, doubtfully.

"The mountain couldn't have changed," Kiara had added, also doubtfully.

It was only when Kiara was buying postcards of some of the paintings that the explanation was offered. The woman at the till had explained with a smile that the painter, Samuel Scott, had never actually been to the Cape or seen Table Mountain. "People described the landscape and the mountain to him and he painted from descriptions, and that's why the mountain looks so strange and out of shape."

"Aha," they had exclaimed. Now they tell Suzy, who had missed this exchange, about the painter and his strange-looking rendering of the mountain.

Kiara gets out the postcards to show her, passes them to the front of the car, and recalls how suddenly, after hearing the explanation, she'd remembered hearing the same thing at the age of twelve, and had looked at the oddly squashed mountain with the same kind of puzzlement. Another crack opens, she thinks to herself, wonders whether it's worth mentioning this slight remembrance to Suzy and Annie, but Annie is pulling up the handbrake , they've arrived.

She wants to show the other postcards she bought, by an unknown female painter: Sophie Owen. Annie had wandered off to find Suzy at that point, and Kiara had been about to turn away when she'd rifled through some other postcards at the till. Dark, intimate female figures. The woman had said these had only recently been found, the painter was unknown. There were only five, but the beauty in each was apparent. They were an invaluable documentation of Cape life in the early 1800s.

"I'll take those too," Kiara had said, glancing at them, she knew Annie and Suzy were waiting, and there was something in the rough, almost harsh brush strokes, she'd look more closely later. At the moment, something in the figures caught her eye. The milky peach skin almost luminescent in the dark of the paintings; the darker woman almost fading into the brown background. In one, a milky hand lay against the dark skin: that was all, blackness framed the cheek, the hand, the features blurred. In another the darker face was lit by something, a candle in the background: it was painted in such tender tones, you felt as though you were gazing on a moment that wasn't meant to be seen. In another the implication was clearer, the strokes bolder, there was less blurring, less subterfuge. In it, the two figures lay side by side, unclothed. The picture was almost shocking in its nakedness, and all that it implied.

There was one painting in which there were no figures, just an old wooden bucket, with a cloth draped over the side. It was lit from the side, and, a chair stood nearby. The painting gave her the shivers, to be honest. But she'd bought them all; there was something compelling in this unknown painter's vision.

1835

I was invited to dine at the castle! It was such a grand affair, eating in a long room, with that huge long table. There were easily over one hundred of us. The atmosphere was so gay, I have been missing dancing and being around people my own age! There were so many courses, and such witty conversation. There was a gentleman from London talking about a play he had seen there, the name escapes me, about a man pretending to be someone else much younger than he is … oh, what comedy.

I missed you then, though, my love. I thought of you. You would have so enjoyed his bright comely conversation, the talk of London. Your face would have lit up, you would have looked pretty again.

I admit I should stop writing to you; but this keeps you alive, and I still need to keep you close, present. I am not ready to let you go. At times this place is so far away, it's a blessing, I will never see you again, I know; but at other times I stare out at the Atlantic Ocean, such a heaving churning mass of water, and it's stronger and more powerful than any prison.

2011

*W*alking along the Sea Point promenade, Kiara watches as Annie and Suzy lean into each other. They hold hands again. Kiara notices. She wishes she didn't, but wonders how to stop. She'd hate to admit to jealousy; in fact she doesn't know what she feels. She strides along, the camera as ever looped around her shoulder, her long blonde wispy hair blowing in the wind. The blocks of flats all face seaward toward the ocean. Their shutters are down against the setting sun. She imagines living in a flat here, at the end of the continent, facing the sea view every day, rolling down the shutters every late afternoon. An idle dream though; she is as landlocked as ever, her life tied up neatly in the city she still calls home.

"I just moved," Annie says, "I just decided, you know. Sold my home, followed the ex, and despite everything, you know, I still feel like I'm on holiday."

Kiara sometimes feels like there are chains binding her to Johannesburg, wonders whether Cape Town will always be the place where she is on holiday, freed, unfettered, but never home.

She catches an unguarded moment between Annie and Suzy. The sinking sun highlights the auburn in Annie's hair, and bathes them both in an otherworldly golden glow. She presses the shutter. Annie and Suzy pause, look toward her, no longer unguarded or as intimate.

She still cannot describe her feelings. She still doesn't have an answer.

"Maybe there is no answer," Annie had written to her months before. But Kiara needs an answer, whatever that answer is, suspects it lies there naked before her as she looks at Annie and Suzy walking ahead, waiting for her.

1835

*I*t would hurt you if I said much more. You know that as well as I. I cannot describe it, I cannot even put that in my diary. That's how I was caught the last time. Never again.

Peter returns tomorrow. We sent word ages ago about the baby. A boy. I'm sure it was a boy. Marta reassures me that there was something was wrong with the child, and that's why my body couldn't hold him. But that I am young and strong and that the next one will take, and the next, and the one after.

She has been a great source of strength and comfort, my dear. It is hard for me to say so, as she's a slave, and not of our own kind. But I've learned so much since leaving you, since leaving

England. It is all too much to express. Try to imagine what I have painted, these small rectangular paintings. It's dark in here at night, and so I paint in dark, sombre colours. That gift hasn't left me at least. I suspect it never will, and I suspect that it will always remain stronger and better than my ill facility with words.

Five paintings: of necessity they are small, easy enough to wrap in these pages. It's all I'm sending, among some blank pages and these marginal thoughts. I beg your forgiveness if I hurt you, but I also know that you will understand. You will perhaps feel the need to forgive, but that perhaps there is also some comfort in these images.

Dear Síne, I remain your adoring Sophie.

2011

They walk along the promenade. The sun sets. Middle-aged lovers sit side by side, not talking, looking out at the ocean. The gulls circle through the sky, calling. Teenage girls run past in jogging gear. An elderly woman and her friend walk a pair of white poodles.

They are now following the path of a series of dragonfly sculptures, walking from one to the next, reading the plaques. "He is a creature of the sky, and cannot be caught."

Suzy's shivering now, she's left her jacket in the car again. Another step: "The little girl watches in despair as the dragonfly disappears into the heights of the sky, walking on air and leaving her far behind, unable to follow.'"

Another: "Heartbroken, the little girl realises her loss. A dream has come so close, an offer, an invitation to fly together was made so freely, all now seems lost.'"

The sculptures stretch out into the distance. Kiara reads the rest of the text: "But wait! Could it be? Out of the sky a winged creature is approaching. The dragonfly is flying so low, it looks as though he is going to land, right next to her."

They walk back to the car. The wind is cold, biting now, but her thick grey parka protects her against the frigid winter air coming in. She can follow the rest of the story online. It's not the most romantic way to do it, but back in the warm fug of the car, she plugs the web address into her phone, pleased to be in the warmth, away from the elements.

The little girl carries on looking toward the sky as they pass, blurring as the car gains speed. Kiara presses the preview button on the camera, the grey granite-like face stares innocently out at her, the expression imploring, hopeful. She's satisfied she's captured that, at least.

Teii mom, win rekk lah

Francis Aubee

"*T*eii mom, win rekk lah" – these were the words of the coach as the team gathered together ahead of its first match. *As for today, winning is the only thing that matters.*

In the soaring heat one Saturday afternoon in July, our local team Bantaba was setting out to play their opening game in the local summer tournament called "Nawettan" – rainy-season football. The whole team had gathered round beforehand to camp at the house of the second-most influential player in the team, Kaalo. Kaalo's compound had a full fence on three sides with an "official gate", while the fence on the fourth side was broken in places due to a heavy rain that had destroyed it the previous year. This was the meeting place for the players and supporters alike. Young boys with bare feet ran up and down and around the compound, while the older boys and a few girls hung around the team. The coach, Ala, a thirty-something man with an unconnected beard paced back and forth, emphasising his point.

"Teii mom, win rekk lah."

There was a great sense of anticipation. The journey towards the tournament had not been a smooth one. It was the very first time that our street had managed to put a team together, finding sufficient donations and funds to join the Nawettan competition. Previously, players from our street had played in the tournament, but for other teams. Now, there was a feeling of collectiveness.

Ben 10 sat at the corner putting his shin pads together, while two young boys of about seven or eight played with his football boots. He could hear shouting from the supporters. "Bazuu! Bazuu! Bazuu!" the people chanted as the man of the moment walked towards a half-broken fence. Bazuu, short for Bazuuka, was the hero of the team, their leader, an all-rounder. Still a teenager, he was fearless; he had the resilience of someone who had fought multiple wars and was still standing strong. A midfielder, he had the skills of Ronaldinho and the brashness of Cristiano Ronaldo. He was as tough as Genaro Gattusso, yet calm as Xavi. The complete package.

Bazuu had played for Young Guns two years running, and in the last tournament he took them to the final, where he won the MVP award, even though his team had lost in the end. His superstardom translated into huge crowds whenever Young Guns played. The local field was always full, not because we liked Young Guns, but because Bazuu was playing. We wanted to see one of our own shine. The Young Guns coach even wanted to make Bazuu – a mercenary – the captain, but this decision did not go down well with the other players. Bazuu wasn't disturbed either way: all he wanted was to play football.

Our street, Zanga, was more or less a small community, a friendly place, where we all knew each other. A government minister lived right down the street from a UN worker and a WHO expatriate. Civil servants, farmers, artisans and petty traders also lived there. As it was, the entire community spanned a much larger area than just one street. For Bazuu and most young adults in Zanga, football was a way of life. Finally, it seemed as though this way of life was going to be improved with the participation of Bantaba in the tournament. The team had begun seeking for funds months ahead, knowing that once they had the funds, things would go smoothly from there on. Previous attempts to get funds had often failed because the team depended on contributions by its members. But now everything seemed to be working in Bantaba's favour. The UN and WHO workers promised to fund the team and provide twenty-three jerseys for the team. Bantaba was set.

"Saul, Bamba, Commander, Ben 10, Bazuu, Kaalo, Becks, Messi, Mangalo, Boy Boy and James. These are the eleven players who will bring victory today," Ala, the coach, said. The players knew what was needed from them: they had been training for two months, preparing for this big day. The game was scheduled to start at 5 p.m., so at 3:45 p.m., we – all the players and all the supporters – gathered in a circle to say the final prayers before leaving. Bazuu then gave a two-minute talk on behaviour, character, and passion. The young boys who had been running around now carried ice coolers filled with bottled water, juice and other refreshments. Bazuu gave a final rallying call – "Aleeee Bantaba!" Come on Bantaba!

The players stayed back while their supporters set out on the ten-minute walk to the field. It seemed as though we were going to war, with more supporters outside Kaalo's compound waiting for the team. It was like a swarm of bees going to find honey.

"Teii mom, win rekk lah!"

As the crowd marched on, people from other streets looked surprised to see such a large crowd. A group of young boys sitting on a fence – whom we knew very well – looked at us. "They'll go and disgrace themselves," they said among themselves. They were members of the team from the next street. Their team had existed for a decade or more, and it roused their sense of rivalry that our street had finally been able to put up a decent team together, worthy of competing against them. It was the old guard versus the new guard. Manchester United versus Manchester City.

One right turn, two left turns, and there we were, approaching the field like a wounded battalion coming for revenge. The field had no seats, so getting some space on the fence that surrounded it on one side was a privilege. Our players finally arrived at 4:05 p.m., fifty-five minutes before kick-off, as was the norm.

Warm up, pre-match rituals and formalities all concluded, it was time for the action to start. Peep! The game was underway; we were attacking from left to right. A quick counter-attack and Ben 10 was fouled in a dangerous area. Bazuu took the first free kick, close to the left-hand side of the opponents' eighteen-yard box. This was Bazuu territory. Chest out, feet wide apart, a focused look, this was Cristiano-esque. Next stop, the ball was in the back of the net as Bazuu wheeled away in celebration. Some of our supporters ran onto the pitch to celebrate with our players.

By half-time, everything had gone according to script. Ala kept rallying his players. Ten minutes into the second half, Bazuu scored again, assisted by Kaalo. Five minutes later it was the reverse. Three-nil – this was too good to be true. As the game approached the dying stages, three-nil up, Ala substituted his star players, Bazuu and Kaalo. They received a standing ovation, quite literally: even those on the fence were now on their feet.

The match was done and dusted: this was the perfect start to our fairytale story. Going back home was the best ten minutes' walk I had ever witnessed. Singing, jumping and shouting, one would think we had conquered Mount Kilimanjaro. As the sun set, the crowd dispersed gradually, but even then a sizable amount of the supporters were still outside on the street. Slowly it started to dawn upon us what a day we had all just witnessed.

A few days later, my family and I were about to leave our home, our country, relocating due to a diplomatic job in Nigeria. The thought of relocating had bothered me for a while. I was just fifteen. Leaving my friends and Bantaba behind was tough, but there was no choice. By the time Bantaba were due to play their second match, we were already in Abuja. By the time we got to our final destination, we were exhausted, but the Bantaba game was still on my mind. I called my pal Sully on his cell phone to let him know we had arrived safely, then went straight to asking him about the Bantaba game. He told me we had won the game, albeit a tight affair – 4-3. Bazuu scored a hat-trick and got sent off, while our defender, Commander, scored the fourth goal. Bazuu was suspended for the last group game. Regardless, we were through to the next round with a game to spare.

Three weeks later, the tournament was over. Bantaba had made it all the way to the semi-final. Bazuu's performances somehow got even better – he had scored in all the knock-out games. Becks had scored four goals in one game. Saul was excellent in goal. The quarter-final, as Sully told me, was between Bantaba and our arch-rivals, Suku FC. It was a fiery encounter, with four players sent off, two from each side before Bazuu scored the only goal from the spot. A fight ensued between the players, as well as some of the supporters. Sanity was restored when three elders spoke to both teams a day later.

Once the dust settled, it was clear that Bantaba had accomplished a great feat. As semi-finalists, they received a handsome sum of prize money and some football materials. Bazuu was the MVP again, Saul was the goalkeeper of the tournament, and Ala was highly praised. Sully said Ala's players told him that maybe he could finally cut his unconnected beard, to huge laughter, at the party organised for the team by the minister. A professional team in the local league were keeping tabs on Bazuu, and they wanted him to join them for three weeks' trial in the capital. (Ironically, Young Guns eventually won the tournament without Bazuu after the previous year's disappointment.)

After feeling homesick for some time in Nigeria, I started acclimatising to the Nigerian environment. I made friends at school, mostly because we all loved football. My friends and I would spend fifteen to twenty minutes every morning before classes started, discussing and arguing about matches that had been played. By my third year, I already had a grasp of Hausa, which helped me make more friends, both in and out of school. But during my fourth summer in Nigeria, I received the best news possible: my dad told us that we would be going back home for a holiday the following summer.

*F*ive years after that wonderful match, I was home. Back to a community where football was more than just a game. I was so excited that I could not resist telling Sully about my return, even though I told him to keep it a secret.

I was optimistic, looking forward to meeting my friends – but Zanga was not the same. The street was muddy – because it was the rainy season. But it was dull and quiet, too. Could it be that I had been gone for such a long time?

The next day I paid Sully a visit at his bungalow, which had been my second home, a place I would often go to relax and sometimes complain about life. Upon greeting each other, we did a little trick with our legs, something that was synonymous with us. I was then ushered into his little parlour, where I made myself at home. In a short while, I was served some attaya. As I waited for Sully to close his back door and join me, I noticed that the rain, which had just started, was already making its way into the parlour through a hole in the thatched roof. Sully rushed to get a bucket on the spot so that the raindrops could fall in there.

Finally, he joined me as we shared our hot attaya while talking about the rainy season. He started the conversation by telling me how he had been dealing with his poor roof. I consoled him and promised to do something about it before I returned to Nigeria. With that out of the way, I attempted to ask questions about the changes my eyes had seen on arrival, but Sully would not let me proceed: he wanted me to know that he had paid a carpenter to renovate his roof months before the rainy season. However, the unscrupulous carpenter had used Sully's money to fund a trip that he called "backway". I did not understand what that meant, but did not ask him in case my old pal thought I was stupid.

Sully, almost swearing at the carpenter as if he was present, looked at me and said that the carpenter was not even the major issue. He spent a while articulating what I would I later understand to be the effects of climate change. He explained that in the past few years, farming had become less productive; his harvest had declined and thus his source of livelihood was not guaranteed anymore. I shook my head in dismay while occasionally sipping my attaya. After realising that he had been talking for a while, Sully caught himself and stopped for a bit before continuing.

"Life has always been hard on us," he said. "The only reason why it was never obvious before was that the people of Zanga always assisted each other through hard times."

At this point, I asked if that had ceased to exist. He nodded in affirmation. By now my body at this point was shaking, as I feared the worst. Noticing my state, Sully offered me a torn blanket, which I took without hesitation.

Once I felt a little bit more stable, I commenced my round of questions. I started by asking about the youths of the community, mentioning names such as Ben 10, Bazuu, Kaalo, Commander, and the rest. Sully excused himself to get more charcoal, and I seized the opportunity to stretch my legs and check on the bucket, which was accommodating yet more rainwater.

As I returned to my seat, I picked up a pile of pictures that I had been eyeing as I sat in the parlour. "It seems like yesterday when we took these pictures," Sully commented as he returned. I laughed as I saw the good times flash in front of my eyes. I stumbled across a picture of our team, and started asking about the same folks I had mentioned earlier. Before Sully answered my question, he served me another glass of hot attaya. Then he braced himself to tell the story.

Two years ago, a phenomenon termed "backway" ushered its way into our community, he began. "Back-*what*?" I asked, finally – it was the second time Sully had used this word, and the term did not sound too pleasing.

Sully, leaning forward, tapped me on the shoulder twice. "Boy, this journey makes climbing Mount Kilimanjaro seem like a day's job!" he said, his voice cracking. "It was a matter of life or death – only the brave and courageous got to live another day."

It had all started when a human smuggler named Langboy promised to take them, the youths, to Europe if they paid him "a small fee" – ten thousand ropopo.

"On hearing of this offer, most of us got excited and sad at the same time," Sully said. Basically, it was the cheapest way to go to Europe – but still expensive, considering our conditions. Homes were thrown into turmoil as most of the youths, including Bazuu, Kaalo, and Bamba started demanding and threatening their parents for the required sum. In the case of the lucky ones, their parents had to borrow, sell family lands and even lease some very rare and precious jewellery that had been passed on across generations to secure the funds.

"You and I both know that playing football in Europe was the main goal for us," Sully reminded me. "At least for the talented ones."

After getting the necessary funds, the boys promised their parents that once they made it into Europe, life at home would improve. The story of a guy who had gone to Europe illegally and somehow made it was floating around. He built a big mansion for his parents, and everyone thought they could emulate him. His story served as an inspiration for both parents and the youths who bought into backway.

"Boy," Sully recounted, "this is how it started."

One windy night that November five years ago, Bazuu, Kaalo and Bamba stopped at Sully's place to inform him of their departure. By midnight, their small wooden canoe had left from The Gambia for Dakar, where they were expected to join the mother ship on their way to Europe. On arrival, they met people from other parts of Africa, all eager for a taste of the good life.

The captain of the ship, smallish in stature, made sure that everyone was on board before he commenced what seemed like a presidential campaign speech. "This journey is not for the weak," he began, "nor is it for the fainthearted. Trust me to take you to your destiny, as I have been in this business for a long time. But once you all make it into Europe," he said, "your lives will not remain the same."

This was followed by an announcement on the route of the trip: a stop each in Mauritania and Algeria, then on to Libya, before finally proceeding to Italy. This did not go down well with the rest of the people on board, who had believed theirs was a straight trip into Europe. Bazuu, confused and uncertain of his decision, reached out to Kaalo and questioned the legitimacy of the trip. Kaalo assured him that many people had tried and succeeded, so they were surely going to do so as well.

As calming as that was, the seas made it even better. They sailed for several hours without any problems, until a massive wave tilted the ship, causing everyone to start chanting prayers. A woman with a child started vomiting, but eventually she calmed down. After a few torrid hours, the ship made it to Mauritania, where they spent a day before continuing the journey towards Algeria.

Bamba was still in high spirits then. "This will all become history when we start playing football in Europe," he told Bazuu, who managed a smile.

Ten minutes later, Bamba was no more. He had been attacked

by what the captain described as a sea spirit. He had started behaving strangely and could not be tamed, so the captain ordered for him to be thrown into the high seas. Bazuu's toughness broke for the first time. He cried for hours. With Kaalo's intervention, he calmed down at last, but would not talk to anyone until they arrived in Libya.

There they were arrested and charged as mercenary soldiers. After two days, they were released and allowed into the country. Their ship was nowhere to be found, and the others with whom they travelled were also out of sight. Kaalo and Bazuu were stranded in no-man's-land. They had to survive, and worked as bricklayers for almost nine months in harsh conditions to amass sufficient funds to continue their journey. They got in touch with a smuggler, who finalised their travel plans, and they were off.

The Mediterranean was not merciful. First there were huge waves amid heavy downpours of rain. When these subsided, they had to deal with patrol boats. After all these ordeals, hope was restored once the passengers could see from afar what seemed like a European port on the horizon. Cheers erupted as the eager men and women on board came a step closer to their dreams.

But the tumult was not over. The ship started to sink. Those who could swim floated for a while, while the rest saw their destiny disappear in the distance. It was there that Bazuu and Kaalo struggled to keep themselves and their dreams alive.

By this point in the story, Sully and I were both struggling not to weep. The room was tranquil; the only sound that could be heard was that of the raindrops. We both looked at the coal pot that powered our attaya, and saw the fire within burning out slowly.

"Did they survive the trip?" I asked.

"I only know because someone did," Sully said. Some years later, Sully recounted, Kaalo returned from Europe. He was at last able to give a full account of all that had happened to the three teammates, starting from that cold November night when they bid the Gambia farewell. He went on to explain everything in detail, from the ship on the high seas to the dreadful nine months in Libya.

"Kaalo said Bazuu tried and tried," Sully said, "just like the fearsome guy we knew. But he did not make it. The sea claimed him, right in front of our helpless friend."

I finally started weeping then, thinking of Kaalo. I imagined the sadness in his heart. I imagined that cold ocean, with only one voice calling out this great man's name, calling it out as he watched his friend drown: "Bazuu, Bazuu, Bazuu!"

A Door Ajar

Sibongile Fisher

WINNER OF THE 2016 SHORT STORY DAY AFRICA PRIZE

"There are a thousand ways to kneel and kiss the ground;
there are a thousand ways to go home again."
– Rumi

She grabbed the wailing infant and threw it against the wall. The newborn died instantly. It was the third one. She needed to find a suitable successor, but it seemed like fate had dealt her the wrong hand. Again.

Sela watched in horrified wonder as the infant lay still on the vinyl-tiled floor. Something moved inside her – a storm far off on the horizon. She looked at her mother, MmaLeru, who was cleaning her up, handling her vulva as though it were a damaged chest of useless memories. MmaLeru, paying no attention to her daughter, moved from thighs to floor like routine, cleaning up the mess as though nothing happened.

MmaLeru had blue-black smooth skin that looked like the finest mineral or coffee. Yes, coffee. The perfect morning fix after a long night. She had thick, hard dreadlocks that kissed her waist, the kind that warriors wore. Her pupils were a calm brown that turned to black when dilated. They had a blue ring around them, and when she gazed into a distance, they looked like cosmic bonfires. She had a small face and a petite body, but her demeanour made her seem larger. Her quick tongue lashed out like lightning, which is how she got her name, but it was her nose that made her seem scary. She had that big fat flat nose shaped like something smelled off.

"I'll do it! I'll do it!" Sela exclaimed. MmaLeru swiftly turned to examine her daughter. "I'll be your successor..." she sighed.

"You foolish girl, do you think we would be going through all of this if you were worthy?" MmaLeru examined the dead infant roughly for parts that she could use.

It is said that the tradition can only be continued by those who survive the wall. In our small mining town, every second girl child is meant to be part of the tradition. It is said that this bloodshed in the thickness of the night is offered to the one who is not named.

It is said that when her thirst is quenched, she will bring back the gold and the mines, and the mines will bring back the town's livelihood, and the livelihood will bring back the men.

When MmaLeru was born, her mother, Sefako, threw MmaLeru against the wall, and she survived. It is through her that this secret tradition is kept, but no baby girl born to our generation has ever survived.

MmaLeru grabbed a black plastic bag and threw the baby, umbilical cord, and placenta into it before neatly tying it up. With the plastic bag in one hand and a pair of rusted scissors in the other, she looked like a woman who just had stepped out of a war zone. Her black doek was coming undone, covering her forehead. This made her stagger as she left the room.

Sela struggled into a seated position, resting her back against the wall. Her pink continental pillow, which smelled like wet wood, swallowed her back, and for a moment it felt like she'd just dipped her swollen feet in a cool pool. Something inside of her moved again. She studied the drying blood spatters across the wall, the new artwork. It was high art, to watch your child's blood dry, and do nothing, say nothing. The wall was light yellow and fresh blood in colour. She pulled her bright 1970s-inspired coloured duvet cover over her head and kept still. She didn't hear her mother come back in.

"Hela, get up! And sit on that bucket!" MmaLeru placed a black bucket in the corner of the bedroom, near the window. Inside it was a solution of hot water, sea salt and aloe.

"I'm not feeling well."

"Mosadi, woman, I only have six weeks before we can try again."

"But MmaLeru, I don't think I want to do this."

"Watseba, you know, I should have let Sefefo kill you."

"Eng, what?"

"Get up! Skatana, filth!"

Feeling faint, Sela slowly rose and made her way to the bucket, unaware that she had passed out and that her mother had been gone for hours. The tingly feeling of the rising steam crept up her thighs and vagina, reminding her of the first time it happened.

That night, MmaLeru had come home with a man who used to work for the mines. She helped him to rape Sela, who had rejected the invitation to sleep with him when her mother proposed it.

Nine months later, the wall was full of blood, and a dead newborn lay on the floor. Sela neither ate nor spoke for three weeks afterwards. Then she called me and told me all about it. It was the first time we had spoken for longer than a minute on the phone. First time we had spoken since Sefefo's funeral.

At the other end of the bedroom, between a rustic 1980s dressing table that Sefefo passed down to her and a three-legged coffee table, held up by a set of old bricks, she watched her mother burn the sun-dried umbilical cord. MmaLeru whispered what seemed to be a prayer. She got up and went to her daughter.

"Close!" She slapped Sela's thighs.

"It burns!"

"It should burn. That useless hell-hole should burn!"

There was a heavy silence in the room. Above the bed was a small print of Leonardo da Vinci's "The Last Supper", the only feature on the wall apart from the blood. It was given to MmaLeru by a Catholic lover; after the man left unannounced for Spain, she gave it to Sela.

Sela got to her feet, banging against the wall. Her body, a lighter shade than her mother's, and more frail, looked like an empty island waiting to be claimed, with dead fish at its shores. MmaLeru flung her daughter across the room. They were now both on the floor, their wilted bodies spread across the bloody site where no more than five hours ago, an infant, the last of three, met her death. After an unchoreographed wrestling match, the women lay, one against the foot of the bed, the other on the floor, like laundry wrung dry. They broke into a disturbing and robust laughter that lasted a long time.

Afterwards, MmaLeru helped her daughter up and sat her on the edge of the bed. She used the water solution in the bucket to bathe

Sela. Then left and came back with a plate of pap and cabbage. Sela ate in silence as her mother cleansed the floor.

*T*he two women were in the backyard. It had not changed much over the years, and this always brought about a feeling of nostalgia. Sela was sitting on the small stoep that led to the outside tap. MmaLeru was kneeling over a tin basin of wet clothes balanced on top of an old beer crate. A concrete slab covered most of the backyard; it used to be the floor of a shack.

"I could have been in Spain you know—" MmaLeru paused and coughed, "playing wife to a man whose heart belongs to a white God." She burst into laughter.

"Then what happened?"

"Then—"

"Then what, MmaLeru?"

MmaLeru ignored her daughter and continued to hang up their laundry.

Sela got up and fetched a wash basin. She was wearing black tights and an oversized T-shirt, one of those that are worth your vote. She must have gotten it from a political rally somewhere. She loved politics. She was twenty-six years old, but looked thirty-five; poverty has a way of taking its toll on a human body. She slanted the basin underneath the tap. In the corner near her bedroom window, ash and burnt wood. She knelt on the ground. The last three years of her life had been something straight out of a horror movie, the kind that plays around ten at night on SABC. She doodled with her finger in the ash. MmaLeru pulled her up and pushed her. Sela had no fight in her. She helped her mother find her balance, and the two women took down the laundry and went inside the house.

*M*maLeru's health had been deteriorating over the past three weeks. Last night, Sela found her lying like a wet dog outside the front door; she was shivering and her words made no sense. MmaLeru didn't believe in doctors and refused to go see one. What they didn't know, and what I found out from her eyes a few weeks later, was that she had pneumonia.

Every Wednesday and Saturday night, part of the secret tradition, the women gathered to skinny-dip in the river that ran through the town. It was the winter solstice and the frost had worked its way inland. Sela wondered how she did it, MmaLeru. How did she go on like nothing ever happened? Like the evil didn't exist.

She missed her grandmother. Sefefo was an old woman with a bent back, who always mocked her own stature: "I grow old like a tree, hell-bound. Instead of upright to heaven, I am on my way to kissing the ground." Something about her kept the neighbours away. Many called her a witch, but besides her suspicious rituals, she was as normal as the African sun. Well to Sela and I, that is, until the week before her death.

That week, a sandstorm of great weight had hit our township, covering everything in dust. Sefefo was in a feverish state of dementia: she kept talking about flying, shadow men, and pacts. She was in and out of earth, throwing toddler tantrums, growing newborn. Sela and I were passionate teens, too young to understand. Besides, Alzheimer's does not visit this kind of town. No one here has ever heard of it, and no one cares much about it. The township folk say if a black person goes mad, then witchcraft is the cause.

Unlike MmaLeru, who was jealous of Jesus and swore off Christianity, calling it "the devil's tool to keep lovers apart", Sefefo loved the Bible. That whole week, Sela read it to her like an avid reader reading a sweet-lipped novel.

On the day of the funeral, the sandstorm worsened. The dust nearly buried the township. Everything was brown and dry. Only three people besides the Apostolic priest, myself, Sela and MmaLeru, attended the funeral. Pule, the drunkard from across the street, who attends every funeral in the township, was wearing his infamous baggy suit. Partly sober, he sang out of tune, swallowing all the other voices in the tent. Maseloane, their neighbour, was present, but later confessed to other neighbours that she only attended to make sure that the old witch was dead. There was also a woman whose identity is still not known to this day. She wore ropes around her ankles and hands, the same kind that Sefefo used to wear. She began every hymn and sang like a morning bird until Pule's voice took over. At the gravesite after the sermon, she spat around Sefefo's grave before disappearing into the distance. She didn't go back to the house for food and other pleasantries.

It was only on the Sunday that people gathered in our back yard to drink bojwala ba Sesotho and motoho o ritetsweng. The ants and dust made their way into the leftover food, making it inedible. MmaLeru had to throw it all away. It was Sefefo's vengeance on the vultures who had the audacity to miss her funeral but crave her food. This broke MmaLeru's heart. That Sunday night she decided to cut ties with the township folk.

I didn't stay long either. I arrived the day that Sefefo died and did not wish to stay a day longer than I had to. The clouds had gathered. It was about to rain, that thick, dark, hard rain which stings when you dance in it. Something about the rain, thunder, and lightning seemed to calm Mma-Leru. On the day of her tsosetso, an awakening by young girls into womanhood usually held between the ages of twenty-five and thirty, it rained so hard and fast that it flooded the small mining town.

Home had formed a lump in my throat. It had become a faraway noose, a suicide note always written for tomorrow. It was now a twisted secret gathering dust in the back of my mind. I hadn't been there in nine years. The last time I was there, it was to bid my grandmother farewell. After Sefefo's funeral, I went back to my "home", the City.

This city has fallen to its knees at the sight of my beauty. There is no building I have not had sex in, besides the office parks with prudish security guards.

I'm watching him lay like an island off the grid, dead fish at his shores. Last night was great, and I think I like him. I don't bother to take a shower. I smell of alcohol, cigarettes, and good sex. I slip into yesterday's clothes and quietly search his pockets. I find a couple of hundreds in his wallet and a few coins on the coffee table. This is a refined antique, nothing like the one that Sela owns, a modernised version intended to exist in this new millennium. On it, there is a pile of books; one is titled *Eight Days in September* by Frank Chikane, and another *Dinner with Mugabe* by Heidi Holland. There are others that read like a revolution always coming or long gone, like home. This man is a politician of some sort. Beneath the box of cigarettes there is a well-handled Quran that hasn't been opened in months; you can tell by the light dust that has gathered on its cover.

I honestly thought that this man was Christian: there is a cross hanging on the wall above his bed, for Christ's sake, and a palm cross on the door. There is something about men who seek Christ that warms my blood. Sometimes before the sex, I make them recite the Hail Mary or the Apostles' Creed.

At one end of his bachelor flat, there are remnants of a burnt bundle of sage. I am wearing my leather boots, and the one seems to not fit me as well as it did yesterday. I light a cigarette and watch over him like a Madonna. I've only known him for a night, but I have a feeling we will meet again. I should have been out by now, but I'm stalling. I don't want to go home. I'd rather nurse this hangover right here, between the wretched sheets of this stranger, but I promised Sela I would come.

She sent me a Whatsapp telling me that death was imminent: MmaLeru was fading rapidly. I feel nothing, but a promise is a promise. I stuff a sandwich into my already full handbag and leave the door slightly open. He will wake up soon and realise that I am gone. I hope he doesn't come after me. I might wish it, but they never do anyway.

Outside the block of flats is a Palestinian shop and pavement vendors with all kinds of fruits and veggies. I make my way to the taxi rank. The taxis there are tired horses that loathe their owners. It's the way the doors keep falling off that gives the feeling we are not welcomed.

"San'bonani." I greet the people in the taxi, expecting the silence that has become tradition. I find a seat in the first row in the corner behind the driver and pass out.

We are halfway across the country when I wake up. There is a child crying, and another stuffing his face with an overripe banana. Their mother wears the tired face of an underappreciated priest. The taxi driver is lost in translation. We go on for a while, and I start running out of things to think of.

I feel like an immigrant being forced to leave home and go "home". It's happened before: I am a darker shade of blue-black, silver-black, and it is this attention-seeking complexion of mine that always gives me away. We were visiting a friend in a township near the city when we were approached by a group of men determined to send all amakwerekwere back to where they came from. They were pulling at me like a parcel while my friend was helplessly fighting them off, four men all wanting me at the same time, ready to courier me "home". Luckily I had my ID that day; when you live in the city, you carry your ID with you everywhere you go. It is your pass book, your entry into buildings and apartments.

I can feel time unwind as we enter our hometown. On my left, there is a big welcome sign about to fall down; it hangs against a backdrop of a sea of sunflowers stretching as far as the eye can see. Something moves inside me – a storm far off on the horizon.

The children beside me are now fast asleep, one on their mother's lap and the other safely squashed between us. I stare at the mother for a while and realise that we could be the same age. She must be in her late twenties, old enough to pass off as an adult and young enough to still eat at the sun. She must have recently had her tsosetso. I hope they named her Lerwele; she is sun dust and more. Her face is wrinkling before time but its grace is stark, hard to ignore. She reminds me of a young Sefefo.

Earlier, she had insisted the man seated next to her to open the window, and since then, there has been a mixture of fresh air and something stale. It must be the smell of yesterday's alcohol on my skin, fermenting in the sun. "It smells like rubbish," she whispered to the man, who seemed like he was forced to be in this taxi, going home.

Home – here, men are the ones who always leave, never the women and that is why we never call them by their names. We call them by their roles, and if you don't know, you always refer to him as monna, which simply means man. The women are never called by their roles. Every woman who undergoes tsosetso is called by her name. This is what makes her stay, her real name. It is said that the town in which you are named is where you will be bound by spirit to live out the rest of your days. When a girl child is born, she is named after her most prominent feature, and it is only after she undergoes tsosetso that her real name is chosen, by her and those who know her.

My mother's name Tselane came as a result of her big feet. She left for the city a week after I was born. Sefefo used to joke that I had my mother's road-like heart, and that one day I would follow her. She came to visit us once, and it is true, she had big feet. I remember wearing her yellow heels and parading around the house the way she did.

My mother was beautiful. She had dark skin a lighter shade than mine, Sela's shade, and plump lips that let secrets slip with a honeyed voice that surely swallowed all the men in the city and our hometown. A tall woman with wide hips and a small waist, she was the total opposite of MmaLeru, and it was her body that was the source of their sibling rivalry. The day she left, I stood by the gate and smiled. Everyone was surprised that I wasn't pulling at her pencil skirt or tugging at her ankles, crying, asking her to stay.

*W*e reach the taxi rank at our destination, and the driver, still lost in translation, begins to come alive. There are vendors selling everything they bought in the city as though it was manufactured in their own houses, in a back room of magic.

I watch the woman struggle with the two children before offering to help. We are going in the same direction. I later find out that she is an old childhood friend of mine, Mela, now named Tsebo. I wonder if I still smell like rubbish now that she knows we grew up together. I light a cigarette. The children are in awe of a woman smoking, as though it's forbidden.

We reach a fork in the dirt road and go our separate ways. On the left, there is an old butchery that is only open because faith allows it. And on the right, a Methodist church is kept alive by the few who still believe in Christ. Only the main roads are made of tar. When the mines closed, we watched the town's livelihood fade, one day at a time into myth. The men left and never came back, and those who stayed are always in the pits of a beer bottle somewhere.

I look around and take a deep breath. I'm surrounded by a community of forgotten people wasting away in mundane poverty. I hate this place. I pass a group of women playing cards on the stoep of one house, then a group of boys playing soccer in the dirt. I can see home draw nearer with every stride. There is a chorus of whispers and dancing curtains. I can feel the eyes watching me strut my stuff. I am home. The fence is about to fall over. I choke.

Sela is hanging laundry in the back. She turns around and screams. I think she is happy to see me. She gives me a long-awaited hug, and pulls the boat to shore. I'm home. The weather changes, and I help her take the laundry inside.

I have been home for a few days and the rain has not stopped. It is evening, and the wind is saying something. We are in MmaLeru's bedroom, which reads like an occult cathedral; the curtains are a deep blue that gives the walls their shadowy shade at noon. The vinyl tile flooring is a mockery of wooden flooring.

Her single bed is in the corner facing west, just like the graves. She rearranged it a week before her untimely sickness kicked in. It's been six weeks. She was supposed to be searching for a suitable lover to father Sela's fourth child. But here she lies, in sickness and disgust, with the threat of the tradition ending here, with her.

At one end of the room, there is a small table with bags

underneath it. There is no other furniture in the room, just the words "Die already" racing in our minds. We sit by her bedside and watch her fade. We are happy that she is dying: Sela, because she will no longer fuck for the love of superstition and I because I will no longer be haunted by my first lover.

That is how I came to leave home. I was twelve when we started, but fifteen when we got caught. My lover and I. He was older, in his thirties, I think. He was also MmaLeru's lover and she was jealous of our Bible study sessions. Over the years, they had become more frequent, and he started ignoring her.

On the night it happened, she found my lover and me at the feet of Christ. I was on top of him and he was lying there, just right. Sefefo was still alive then. She protected me from MmaLeru's rage. The lover moved to Spain, and on countless nights afterwards, she tried to kill me. I decided to leave home. To go searching for my mother in the city, but when I got there I found something better: city men who love Christ.

I still think about her – my mother. Watching MmaLeru fade, I wish she was present to bid her sister farewell. Sela and I are sisters, fathered by the same man. Sefefo said that my mother had slept with MmaLeru's first lover, days after Sela was conceived, and that is how I came to be. Because it was unspoken of then, for women to wed men in beds spoken for, Sefefo asked my mother to leave town after giving birth to me.

She feared for my mother's life. She had slept with many men in our hometown, and when MmaLeru waged war against her, the other women were ready to light their torches and burn her. And that is how she came to leave. My mother, like me, is at sea –but what really broke MmaLeru's heart was that Sefefo hadn't a care in the world. "He is going to leave anyway," she said.

I want to tell Sela about all of this. It's as though MmaLeru is reading my mind. "You are sisters. Your father is her father." The words escape her mouth. I expect Sela to throw a fit, but instead she smiles. "I know," she whispers.

It is raining a baptism of demons outside. We can hear the

water rise. There is thunder and lightning and the lightbulb keeps flickering.

"Please fetch me that bag." MmaLeru's crooked fingers point to the table. Reluctantly, I fetch it.

"Open it and break off a piece of the wood. Chew it every night and spit on your pillow before you sleep."

"Why?"

"Because you are carrying my successor."

"I'm not pregnant."

"You are. A couple of days only, but you're definitely carrying a girl child."

"You are sick. You don't know what you are talking about."

"Chew the wood. When she is born, throw her against the wall. I'll be waiting for her on the other end."

"No. I won't. This girl will live."

I think of her father, the man in the city, whose name I don't know. Who probably won't want to see me again. I think of his body, a remote island with dead fish at its shores. I think of the money I stole, of the dusty Quran and the palm cross. I think of the political books on his antique coffee table. I think of the door ajar and why I left it open, why I wished he'd follow me. I am stalling again.

MmaLeru fades. Just like that, she is no more. The rain hardens, then starts to calm. Sela stares at her mother in contempt. I am at sea again. My witchcraft is between my thighs, in the city.

Sela knows she has to come with me. She has to leave home. I am with child. I am child.

We leave MmaLeru's eyes open and start to burn everything in the room. There isn't much, but the vinyl tiles catch fire quickly and the flames spread. The storm inside of us calms. We are moved. We are warm. We are outside in the soft rain, smoke escaping from the window. We sit on the concrete slab where once, a shack rested and my lover and I nested. There my sister and I watch home burn, and before the people of the town gather, my sister and I promise each other never to speak of home again.

Farang
ฝรั่ง

Megan Ross

SECOND RUNNER-UP FOR THE 2016 SHORT STORY DAY AFRICA PRIZE

NÈUNG

*A*cross the road from my childhood home is a stretch of ordinary veld. Red-hot pokers push through the thick grasses like babies' heads, the lick and curl of the Indian Ocean only a breath away. I wish you could see it: the way the sky shines like polished silver; the gulls descending on unsuspecting shad. There is something freeing about this place, in a breathing, thinking kind of way. It's where you'll find my wanton mind, in all those moments you don't know where I've gone. Here, in this place of remembering and forgetting, is where my spirit rests. On humid nights like this one, when that stench of raw sewage and fried duck mingles with orange blossom, when even the air conditioner cannot cool our damp thighs, this is where I go.

If I were to tell you the truth about me, I would need to bring you here. I would have to guide you along this embryonic path back to South Africa. Back to the belly of my mother, her twisted insides, those parts of her that knitted together the tissues of my soul. But I won't go that far back.

SŎNG

*W*e kissed within two hours of meeting, in a cramped dive bar smaller than my apartment, to which I wore platform heels and too much makeup. A woman with black nails and iceberg skin approached me to say I had great hair, and something about the way she said this made me feel further from home than I ever had been, a gaze turned inside out. I was the only foreigner, and because I didn't know anyone there I felt weightless and free, spinning around the room as thin and bright as candy floss, in a tiny, shiny dress that crept right up my thighs. I danced too wildly and drank too much, and all the while I felt you staring from behind the bar, where you served cheap margaritas without the salt, in a T-shirt that said FUCK YOU.

It didn't take long for us to get back to mine – a studio of maps and little coin towers of baht and rand – a room owned by an elderly Japanese man who called me Miss Becca. Just out of the lift, I lost my underwear. Moments later, you lost yours too. Something was caught between your body and mine, something alive, and moving, strung between us like a strip of lights. I think that's when the condom must have broken, or slipped off, or done something to negate its purpose. A flood of unwelcome swimmers crossed the channel, cleaving to my insides, little saboteurs bounding towards their prize.

Had we known, you might have laughed and made a shitty joke about Thai condoms, and we could have made that awkward visit to the chemist the next morning, even maybe got a coffee afterwards. Except we didn't know, and so instead of swallowing two pills at opposite ends of the clock, two cells met, and the inevitable happened. When I think back to that moment, the split second that caught us unawares, I imagine a flash of light. I see the world splitting into water and air, night and day.

Inhale, exhale.

I'd booked my ticket on a whim.

I quit my job, left my wretched digs in Woodstock, and decided to explore the world. It was a big dream with a small budget, and I never knew it would involve love. I never knew what any of it would involve.

Sǎam

You wanted to teach me Thai. We'd start with numbers, so that I could bargain in the markets and direct a cab driver late at night, two things I'd never manage without being able to count to ten. You were adamant I learn immediately, so we set aside an afternoon for you to tutor me, which was also a good ruse for a date. When that Tuesday came we decided to meet at the river, so I took the Skytrain to Saphan Taksin station and scrambled down to find you on the platform. We sat cross-legged beside a replica of the Leaning Buddha, the sounds of the city quietening to a synchronous roar on the waters. Long-tail boats carved cerise and turquoise paths through the Chao Phraya, its murky brown teeming with monstrous fish.

We shared coconut ice-cream, and you peeled numbers from your fingers like hangnails, counting slowly on your hand so I could mimic you in turn. One two three four, nèung, sŏng, săam, sèe, five six seven eight, hâa, hòk, jèt, bpàet. I discovered the lyrical quality in Thai: its alternating high and low sounds, a song that jars and soothes. You asked my age and when I told you I was twenty-five, you blushed and said you were younger than me. I only minded when you made me work out how much yêesìp-sèe is, but I finally worked out that you were twenty-four.

You taught me the number of my building, the amount of change I'd need when buying fruit, the correct way to pronounce my address. Once I'd memorised each number, I repeated their sounds until they tolled like bells in my mouth. Until it felt like I'd split numbers right from their centre, chewing and spitting them like snuff. Nèung, sŏng, săam, sèe – one, two, three, four.

Nèung, sŏng, săam, sèe.

Sèe

*W*e went to a cat café on our second date.

You'd asked if I liked cats and I'd stupidly kept quiet about my allergy, replying that yes, I did like them, very much. We sat in this pink, face-brick restaurant eating Belgian waffles with sweetened cream, while Persian and Siamese felines rubbed themselves all over my legs, stopping only to sniff the camel leather of my handbag or each other. By the end of the date, my eyes were slits. I was sneezing dreadfully. I must have looked quite ill because when the waiter brought us the bill, you asked if I was okay in this concerned tone. Only then did I admit to being allergic, and in urgent need of an antihistamine. But then you laughed. You didn't know what an antihistamine was, and I burst into tears, thinking that you were being callous. I didn't know then that Thai people laugh to diffuse tension. But you called a motorbike taxi anyway, which we both hopped on to, and instructed him to take us to that Chinese pharmacist on Naradhiwas Road.

You clung to me on that motorbike drive, incidentally, my first. Only afterwards, over drawn-out tea breaks with my American expat colleagues (whole hours dedicated to dissecting our love lives), did I realise that whether I liked it or not, this thing between us was more than a fling.

HÂA

Your English wasn't very good and my Thai was shocking, so in the beginning it was with our bodies that we spoke. One evening in those first weeks together, before we knew, you told me that your name meant *from the south*. Thaksin, a name for an island boy, for a body filled with the Andaman Sea that curls around the south of Thailand and ripples out to India and beyond. A name given by proud parents and prouder grandparents who'd found their way to Bangkok in the space and strength of a generation. My own body held the Indian Ocean, my blood being that of surfers and fishermen tucking their daughters into boats at dawn. In your eyes, I felt myself returning to this liquid, to the saltwater quietly lapping at our shores, as if by merely willing it, I could bridge the oceans between us, wave by undulating wave.

As we lay together, I made an index of our bodies, noting the places where our limbs slotted together, their perfect assembly like that of continental plates, a configuration to be read, and sung. I gazed at your body, which had grown steadily familiar to me by then: bronzed limbs, sallow stretches where the sun hadn't yet reached; a purplish birthmark on your lower back. From your neck hung gold amulets for protection passed on by your grandmother, to ward off evil spirits. Around mine I wore the Saint Christopher that once belonged to my mother, a misplaced icon for a patron saint who had never intended to guide travellers. You started saying something then, and although I listened to you with the kind of focus one has when newly in love, it wasn't your words I heard, but the timbre of your voice, a babbling brook with flat spells that ebbed into the softest silence. From this swelled all the stories you would never tell, translated from unspoken word into flesh, into the hands with which you always spoke. Your hands. Hands with songs. Beautiful as rain. Slender fingers, deep coloured and soft as baby's skin. The things you taught me with them, the things I showed you in return. Whole worlds, constellations. And in your palms, something eternal as planets orbiting the earth.

We broke apart our mother tongues to share like loaves of bread. We fed them to each other in hungry mouthfuls, piece by piece, as if we were starving and they were all we had. We consumed the flesh of our words like our lusty last meals – furiously.

You attempted the English of my mother, but the Afrikaans of my father was locked inside my teeth, rattling around like keys. You said "lekker" and "kiff", imitating me, and I returned with the kind of Thai I later found out is spoken by the lower classes, women of the night, gang members on the outskirts of the city. I stripped to nothing, my bare skin against yours, the history and potential of us wrapping itself around our bodies, like soot and salt and smog. And even though I let you have it all, deep down I knew I would refuse every diamond you gave me until the earth spat out its last one.

HÒK

You bought me mangosteen and farang, a great waxen fist of unripened guava sealed like dead flesh in clear plastic. It was cool and icy from the fruit man's cart, the colour of pallid skin and rain clouds. The fruit itself was as smooth as the elephant tusks in your grandfather's house, tooth-white and sticky like wads of wet tissue. The centre pips were a milky, frangipani sap, reminding me of the blossoms in my mother's garden and the prehistoric-looking trees dotted around my condo. That fruit was at once dead and alive, as if in another time, parallel to this, it still clung to a spindly branch, in a field somewhere, or a garden. With each mouthful, I fixated on the deep-set eyes of that blind man who played his harpsichord on the corner of Soi Saint Louis and Sathorn, and how he shook his tin pleadingly at passers-by, the coins ching-chinging like the rains in monsoon season.

The fruit man laughed and pointed to me as he passed you the bag. It was an old joke, a silly one because farang means both guava and foreigner. He found it hilarious all the same. You dismissed him and we ambled along the road, stopping so I could throw up in a steel drum I left wet with my sick. I wiped my spitty chin and my snotty nose, and then we bought that pregnancy test from 7-Eleven that said I was going to be a mother.

I told you about South Africa whenever I could. I think all the Saffa expats do this. I told you about the elephants and giraffes of the Wild Coast. Of the thick, impenetrable bush circling the Eastern Cape and those berries near the river that gave my little town its name, Gqunube. I told you about the Point and the surf and the Great Whites that swallowed people whole. About the sand dunes rising up from the earth, the sky so blue it hurt. Yet despite seeing it more clearly than I ever had, with eyes washed clean by distance, home came out in broken fragments. No matter how hard I tried, I couldn't scrape together enough to feed that part of you that wanted to know me, and understand my point of view. In these romanticised morsels I starved you of the truth, and I began to sound like a caricature of myself; strangely garbled in my efforts to convey my sense of everything to the man I loved. But you listened all the same. There are eleven official national languages in South Africa, I said. It was early evening, that curious hour when Bangkok wakes up and turns neon, and we were drinking craft beer in Thong Lo. Sìpèt, I said. Eleven whole ways to say, "I love you", to say "I'm hurting", to say, "Please stop". We'd moved beyond the intrepid politeness of our initial conversations, those first weeks of dancing around anything that could possibly be construed as contentious (politics, the King, my being Methodist while teaching at a Catholic school). Although neither of us were fluent in each other's languages, we had arrived at that lovely meatiness that either exists between lovers, or doesn't (the latter usually a sign that a quick end is in sight). It had become okay to probe: to forget caution, and stride right into each other's beliefs or childhood.

There was some confusion about my home languages, about there being two, and you asked me about these mother tongues, about Afrikaans and English. *Do you speak English at all times? When do you speak this Afrikaans you've mentioned? And you say you have servants. Do they also speak Afrikaans?*

JÈT

*M*y mother put me on the pill when I was eighteen. She'd told me it was for my skin, but we both knew that wasn't its purpose. Seven years later we chatted about Asian men and mixed-race babies over Skype. She had joked about me getting pregnant at East London's small, dingy airport only moments before I boarded the plane for Johannesburg. I don't want coloured grandchildren, she'd said in that old language, the one still spoken in yellow tongues behind closed doors.

If only she knew.

They say that there are options but in my case, there was only ever one. And it's hardly a choice, after all.

BPÀET

*Y*ou were supportive, yet I can't help remembering your reticence. You'd asked if I was sure, in a voice that was barely a whisper. We were walking out of the hospital, hand in hand, hurrying because the rains were about to begin, and we hadn't called a taxi. I had a scrap of paper in my pocket, a doctor's note with the number of a man who'd be willing to do it for me. At a cost, of course. Nothing was free.

I'll never forget your face when I made the call. Unmoored, conflicted. Lost in that sea we'd been cast into when we saw those two magenta lines. You kept your hand on my leg the entire conversation, only stopping to wipe a tear when I put down the phone. We fought over who would pay. I wanted to cover the cost myself since I had savings back home but you insisted that we at least go halvies. We argued over this until late that night, until you boiled green tea in matching cups and sat down beside me on the balcony.

"I'm sorry," you said, in English, looking at me with this expression I'd never seen before, a look that said you'd both grown overnight and shrunk back into yourself with fear. You said something then that I didn't quite catch, something in Thai, venom filling your throat.

"I'm sorry," you repeated. "I'm so sorry."

I first took the morning-after pill in the Marie Stopes clinic in Bree Street. I swallowed it with flat Appletiser in my lunch hour, and then set my alarm to take the second pill twelve hours later. The nurse told me I was damaging my insides, and that I'd probably never be able to have babies. In that darkened clinic that smelled like mercurochrome and menstruation, I wept and prayed I'd one day fall pregnant.

That was a year before I bought my ticket out of South Africa.

GÀO

I didn't move. The clinic gown was too small, so it caught at my hips, and I could feel the little knot where it tied in my back, like a pea, or a dagger. Across the alley, a Philippine band sung Nirvana covers at an Australian bar. *A denial, a denial.* I was terrified, but I hummed along to "Smells Like Teen Spirit", until the doctor told me to take a deep breath and be still. He was firm, but not unkind. I could tell by his tone that he was trying to tell me a joke but I couldn't understand him through the thickness of his surgical mask. The nurse however, was swift; an automaton on platform pumps the colour and consistency of paracetamol. Her hands too, were slight and pale from whitening lotion, and they flittered over me in this half-dance, which I watched with detached fascination. Thai nurses always reminded me of china dolls, something about their uniforms, a throwback to the 1950s, and the rosy full-moons they drew onto their cheeks.

I counted the injections in Thai: nèung, sŏng.

I felt a tugging, then a sharp pain.

The doctor asked if I was okay. My silence hung between us until I realised he was expecting a reply. I tried to say something, but the words caught in my throat like fish bones, and instead of answering in Thai, I let out a garbled "dankie", then "thank you". My head was abruptly filled with the Afrikaans lullabies of my childhood. Wieg nou my baba tussen takkies so sag. There was a strange sound, like the one the Kreepy Krauly makes when it's out the pool, a grotesque mangling of water and air. The doctor made another joke. Kyk wat gebeur as die takkies waai. We were almost done.

Met baba en al sal die wiegie draai.

A few moments later, he left the room. I was completely empty, a waned moon invited to rise up and re-enter the sky. I struggled to swallow, and began to think of my mother, when a second nurse whisked me away to a room where the only decoration was a viridian orchid and a poster of two Thai women with perfect skin and teeth. I sat next to a teenager whose nose was held in place by plasters and tape, who gnawed at her fingernails until she drew blood. One times abortion, I remember thinking, one times rhinoplasty. I remember thinking how bizarre it was that I could terminate my pregnancy while in the adjacent room, a cosmetic surgeon chiseled away at septum and bone.

The room had a sweet, chemical smell, like perfume, and anesthesia. I felt very little except for a dull ache, and the painkillers began to numb even that. I remember looking down at my abdomen and worrying that maybe that was how I'd always feel, aware of a lack, or this indeterminable absence. Perhaps that moment was the first inkling that relief would never come. That in my haste to make it all go away I'd somehow misjudged things and done something I shouldn't have. I wondered what I'd done to my body, to us. There was sadness, but it was less my own and more a thing that orbited me, begging to be felt. I clasped my hands together on my lap, as one did for class photographs during primary school, and realised I felt none of the guilt my friends had warned me about.

When my waiting period was over and I stood up to leave the clinic, the receptionist surprised me by bowing. I didn't think that she would treat me so respectfully; Thailand was Buddhist after all, and despite its availability, the procedure was still illegal. No matter how much it cost you.

You wanted to be there, but I convinced you I would do it on my own. This was my procedure, after all, my choice. I'd thought all that but while taking the Skytrain home, I found myself regretting my earlier decision, wishing that I could insert you into the past three hours of my life. You were probably leaving work, stepping on to the metro, travelling west to my building in the business district. When I got home that evening, you were waiting outside with flowers. At the time I was pleased, and kissed you, quickly, on the mouth. I didn't think it was odd to arrange the long stems in a tall blue vase, to find the perfect alcove for their serene blossoms. In that moment, flowers were not the domain of congratulations, or the property of children born.

Sìp

The Saturday after the procedure, we took a mid-morning walk down Silom Road. It should only have taken us twenty minutes to reach the bridge, but because we were so busy watching the life of the street unfold around us (uprooted melon trees being drawn on carts, nests of soi dogs coiled around palm trees, and this all set to the score of Bangkok's unmistakable hum), it took us a full hour before we reached the Hindu temple.

You bought two garlands of marigold and orange blossom from an Indian woman outside the temple. We slipped off our shoes at the entrance and stepped inside, to light a candle before the statue of Shakti. When we walked outside, you asked me if I knew why there were no bins in the street, and I interrupted you with a kiss –

– I still wonder why there are no bins in that street.

I swam every day for a month, laps of breaststroke and freestyle, in the rectangular pool on the eleventh floor. I was usually met by the same faces: a Nigerian woman and her infant son, a Japanese couple in their late fifties, a set of fraternal twins I guessed were from China, or Taiwan. We all swam beneath this reinforced concrete ceiling, a monstrous slab set with a rusted watermark that looked a little like Jesus.

I stared up at rusty Jesus, this urban messiah who held up pillars, and listened for the sounds of hadedas and ocean waves and trucks driving by. They weren't there of course, but I pretended a lot in those days.

I think I had to.

SÌPÈT

*O*n my last day in South Africa, before my big departure for Southeast Asia, I found myself in my mother's garden. She and I walked around the small square, the edges rounded with stocks and mint and rosemary, clumps of pennyroyal massed around the hibiscus, discussing the medicinal and cosmetic properties of her plants. We were two women lost in the beauty of a garden, in the quiet simplicity of an afternoon, delighting in the simple pleasures of scent and sight.

What's that one, I'd ask, and she'd tell me, lemon verbena – you can make a lovely ice cream with that – or pennyroyal, not to be trifled with. We carried on this way, me pointing out an oddity or something I thought was beautiful, her labelling and dissecting, until we drew near a small bird bath rising from a mound of purple bells.

What are those, I'd asked, enjoying our game, expecting more of this sweet diatribe.

That, my love, is morning glory, she'd replied. Is it indigenous? I asked, expecting the affirmative. No, I'm afraid not, she replied, a pinched look on her face.

That is a rather noxious weed.

Sìp sǎam

*M*y mother's washing always smelled like the ocean, strung across the garden where the wild fig met the mist off the sea and the sheets hung like damp, salted skins. There I would find the Omo-soaked shirts, the greying socks, the period-stained panties, sorted into darks, colours and whites.

There is one day that sticks out in all this. It was a week after the procedure, a strange, blank seven days in which everything felt altered, as if the universe had tilted further on its axis and I was left suspended at odd angles. You knew I was feeling out of sorts, so after school that day we ate quail pancakes from a street vendor and you showed me how to ride a scooter side-saddle. I was wearing a skirt, as teachers at Thai Catholic schools are required to do, and the fabric swaddled me in the cloying heat, clinging to my legs like a shy child. That afternoon you taught me the Thai names for ice and water, and we slunk down a side alley where little vials of red Fanta were set on trays for tree spirits. I think that was the night you took me through the streets of Silom and the clotted green of Lumphini Park, setting me down beside the Chao Phraya River to kiss me on the mouth.

I knew I was in love with you then.

ONE

*T*he sky is slick as paint, the dark dropping in on the stretch of the train tracks, spilling into the unlit sois of fourteen and twelve. Rooftops are strung with the promise of night, Prudential and Visa and Kasikorn signs bathing my small apartment in a spangled glow. The Skytrain turns its attention east and settles on its course to Chong Nonsi station, cutting through the smog, emptying and refilling itself every five minutes or so. At once foreign and familiar, the sight of this train stirs up the slow sediment of all I've left behind.

I am naked except for panties. The kind that hide at the back of your underwear drawer, waiting for you to menstruate. And yet only weeks ago I was pregnant. A gentle flutter, your hand in mine as the tiny chrysalis appeared on the screen, the silence of the menopausal doctor as frenetic as white noise. Sometimes I experience this moment as if it weren't a memory at all. Instead, it feels then as if it were still happening, always happening, again and again, less a repetition of itself and more a single, timeless current that flows parallel to my life, this instant I will find always find myself returning to. Some days, it feels like this, or like a past life, and yet it is the very same as this one, here, now, where the fan spins dust around the room and the fluorescent bulb flickers lazily. It is still humid. You are still my boyfriend. Despite the sirens outside, the world has not drawn to a dramatic end. Here are the damp, twisted sheets. There is the aircon turned to sixteen degrees. Outside is the city.

I get out of bed, slowly so as not to wake you, and pad to the balcony. The seamless rectangles of a thousand windows burn against the black sky. I slide open the door, and am met by the sounds of fifteen million people.

It's too hot to sleep. I head back inside to fetch a towel from the loo, twist my hair into a messy bun and spoon a mouthful of rice into my mouth. You're sleeping through all the noise I'm making, so I tiptoe over to the bed, to kiss your nose and marvel at how lovely you are. I slip off my underwear.

After my swim, in that watery womb of the building, I climb back into bed. Your body is warm, the air from the fan hitting me in waves. Outside, the sounds of Southeast Asia are a steady hum, like the refrigerator, or a swarm of bees. In Lumphini Park, swan boats circle the pond. Lugubrious monitor lizards slither beneath their ceiling of water, while at the outdoor gym, a terrible, rusted thing, Chinese men huddle in cloistered groups, taking gleeful sips of 60baht whiskey between hasty sit-ups.

I nestle up next to you, the curve of my torso framing your back, and rest my cheek on the cool sheet. I feel the weight of what could have been. Its acrid taste, like green wood burning. A sense of loss, and muffled silence. But then it passes, leaving only its absence behind. No more. No less.

Lymph

Anne Moraa

*W*amũyũ has never seen the city from this high up. It looks upside down, the stars littered on the floor, and above it, hard, dewy ground. There is no moon, no cloud, just dark grey reflection. There are no mountains or hills, no valleys or rivers, no ocean or lake, nothing to break the monotony. The city is flat and spreads out, endless. The tall flags that mark her home are indistinct in the night. Her world from up here is nothing.

"Are you comfortable?" Ng'endo asks.

Wamũyũ nods, and he moves closer to the bed. He carries a tray with his gloved hands. On it, a tall bottle of pale blue liquid, saline solution, cotton balls, a four-centimetre long needle attached to a cannula, empty syringe and plaster.

"Please, lie on your back. It goes in easier this way," he says.

Ng'endo places the tray on a heavy mahogany table, the medical equipment an odd fit in his home.

"May I?" he asks.

"Yes."

He opens the bottle and places the cotton ball on the rim, soaking fragrant spirit through the cotton. He rubs the sodden wool on her breastbone, near the heart. He ensures he remains professional, not once grazing her nipple or gazing with lust. He has none for her. He had none when he bought her. She was as naked then as she is now. Her ribs showed just as much, her brown skin was as translucent, her hair as faint. She winces at the touch of the cold antiseptic.

"Am I hurting you?"

"No."

"It's to numb your skin, so you don't feel pain."

"Oh."

"When the migrations began, we would have had a doctor to help but now… well, here we are. I know how to do it, but I may not be as smooth as a doctor might be. Do you know how this works? How it all began?"

She stays silent.

"Well," he says as he discards the dirtied cotton, "a long time ago a friend of my grandfather, a holy man and priest, discovered there really is another side, a better side. More importantly, he found out how to get there."

With his right hand, he takes the needle as his left hand presses down on her chest.

"This will only pinch slightly. Tell me if it hurts, please."

She barely feels the hand on her chest, and even if she did, it wouldn't matter. She nods again. The needle pierces the thin skin above her ribcage. He moves with a practiced ease, attaching, detaching, pressing, placing, pulling. She watches tubing grow out of her flesh – unexpected, like new branches on a dead tree.

He releases a breath he didn't know he was holding.

"Good. Very good. You can sit up now, just rest on the pillows. Are you sure you're comfortable?"

He attaches the tubing from her chest to a long cable, and that to a machine with large whirling discs. He turns the machine on, a simple switch. A low refrigerator-like hum begins. He monitors the cable sticking out of her chest.

"Back then, soon after that family friend completed his migration, many people left. There was a time when almost everyone who could and dared to believe travelled. Back then you weren't even called vessels. You were called lymphs, for the lymphatic fluid that was drained out of you. Historically, people always thought it was the blood that carried life, but there it was, all the while, the carrier of our souls just floating hidden in the body. Lymph. I always found it amusing – you know nymph, lymph – but…'

A drip-drip sound punctuates the room. A straw-gold fluid is drawing out of her.

"There. It's working. We just have to wait till it's time."

He looks around, searching for imperfection. He has already ensured that the lighting wouldn't overpower her enlarged pupils. There is an injection waiting, ready to dilate her eyes chemically if need be, although he was certain he wouldn't need it. The bed she is on is perfectly placed. Plush pillows, view of the city, enough space on the bed for him to lie beside her when it was time for his journey to begin. As he scans the room, he is attacked by the luxury of the space; the high ceilings and pillars, all the silks and carpets. A cough chokes out of him. The pain radiates. He can't wait to leave.

Ng'endo never fully believed in the idea of travelling through a body to a better world, not even when his father told him, not even after his father took his final journey. Even when the cough began and his body began to fail, Ng'endo had his doubts.

It was desperation, not belief, that led him to his first vessel. The vessel's eyes were wide and blue, sky-blue, true-blue. When he studied her eyes, he finally saw it. A whole world. Oceans, continents, people. His first attempt at a move was thus through an expensive thoroughbred; a direct descendant from the first line of lymphs, or so he was told. Right at the cusp of the ceremony, right when the last drops were being drained and the doorway widening and the new world touchable, right then, the vessel closed its eyes. Kept them closed. Ng'endo tried to pry the lids apart, but the chance to migrate is short and fleeting, a wink and a flutter. He stared at the empty vessel for hours. He couldn't bear to look at the world he was still in. He became a true believer.

His second vessel failed because he was weak. She was a beautiful girl, just beautiful. He kept slipping and saying nymph not lymph and she would smile back. She was so ready. Golden-brown eyes and black skin, otherworldly. She must have come from the other side to ferry just one lucky man back. Even the non-believers, those fools who couldn't see a whole world right in front of them, hesitated when they saw her. When she began emptying and Ng'endo readied himself for his final migration, they kept eye contact. The full hour passed and they never once looked away from each other. She believed. She smiled wider and wider as her body faded. Towards the end, when her vessel was cleanest, her eyes lit up. He stared deep into them and began to move. He heard it first. Waves crashing. There was ocean, fresh and salty. He tasted it, the salt, and felt the spray land on his skin. He felt it and started to cry. It was too much. He closed his eyes. She screamed at him, but he kept his eyes shut. By the time he realised what he had done, it was too late.

He had both vessels painted, eyes closed, after their wasted deaths, and hung them in this very room. Not even the portraits of his father and his father before him hang here. The vessels are more important, reminders not to fail again.

He heard of Wamũyũ, his third, as one does, from the right people. He found her at the site where the movement began.

"See how wide her pupils are," the priest said, shining light into her eyes. "See? They never shrink, not even in the brightest of light." He pulled her left eyelids apart, pressing his palm into her nose.

"Look closer. See there? Can you see the movement? It is slight, yes, translucent, but it's there. It isn't an illusion whatever anyone else says. I mean, you can't expect to see heaven perfectly from here, can you?"

Ng'endo found the priest distasteful, a bastardisation of the priests before him, a symbol of the decomposition of a great religion to its skeleton. Ng'endo knew he was leaving this world, regardless of his opinion of the priest, but he needed to ensure he would go on to a world of his choosing. He let the priest's words wash over him as he studied Wamũyũ's eyes, brown and limpid. He, unlike the priest, had caught a glimpse of heaven once, and he could recognise a doorway in the eyes. He came closer and looked into her eyes through a lens, a camera, carefully assessing the details of her iris. Ng'endo selected her because, unlike his previous, failed vessels, she didn't turn her eyes away. Not once.

He refuses to stare into her eyes now, in his own house. He is saving his strength for the journey.

She must be hungry, he thinks.

He moves to the far left side of the room, where a spread is laid out. Beans in coconut, fresh fish, calf's liver, dates, plums, fermented honey, fresh pear juice. Wamũyũ, lying perfectly still, can't turn around. The cables can't be moved. She focuses on the sounds in the room. The low hum of fluid being drained out of her. Spoon scraping plates and bowls. Plop, plop. A soft mash, perhaps. Step, step. Heavy, careful steps. He moves like a fighter, but old, as if his knees can't take the impact of the ground.

He places the food on a footstool near the bed.

"It's here if you're hungry. They said you could eat."

She shakes her head once, polite.

Instead of eating, she opens her eyes once again to drink in colour. The bed she lies on is covered with cushions, plush and thick, velvet-cased, infinite colours. She is used to the full spectrum of brown. Dirt-brown floors and walls, rough brown skins of vessels like herself, the toffee-brown stained teeth of sellers, the butter-soft browns of buyers, the rotted whorls in collapsing stands, the sharp crinkle brown of money, soft brown dust on hard stone floors in tight spaces. Here instead is a spectrum of greens and blues, yellows and reds. Are there as many colours here as there are shades of brown in the temple? The colours blend with rich purple curtains, carpeted floors, two gilded frames on either side of the wide window, each holding a portrait. Even the sheets she rests on, silk and purple, have a weave of many shades in colours she doesn't know how to name. Her right palm touches the softness in the space he has left for himself.

"Well?" he says.

She looks at him. He must have been handsome in his youth. All the structures of handsomeness remain. Tall. Muscular. Broad-shouldered but belly rounded. Skin like dark stained mahogany. His square jaw filled with full lips. Teeth perfect save for the two incisors on the top row. They are sharp. But his handsomeness is iced over with age and sickness.

"Yes?"

"Are you hungry?"

"No."

"Oh."

"Thank you."

"For?"

"I meant, no, thank you."

"Oh, of course."

She is confused, watching him wringing his hands and tracing maps on the floor with his feet. She expected to be scared. She always thought she would be afraid when the time came. Instead, she has a calm and clarity that surprises her. She can hardly move without disturbing the cables, and all the draining is weakening her body. Yet her heart isn't beating as fiercely as his, and there is no sweat on her brow. Why is he afraid? She asks herself because she cannot ask him. At least he knows where he is going.

He sits beside her, still averting his gaze. She doesn't speak unless spoken to, and even then, nothing more than a mutter or a nod. The silence confounds him. His mouth opens from time to time, the barest hint of a word slipping out before it settles back down and chokes him. He swallows down the coughs as best he can.

She watches him sit beside her feet, avoiding the cables draining out her lymphatic fluid. The subtle hum of the circulator drones on as they dance around each other. She found the attachment of needle to flesh painless, and the winding of cables, like a python, around her left breast and down her wrist, mechanical. But his nervousness is making her itch. She tries to focus elsewhere.

The paintings catch her eye. The first is a man, no, a child, no older than fourteen. A cherub, his cheeks almost comically pink. The second, a lady with rich black skin, an artist's exaggeration. They are perfectly framed and preserved, a couple.

"Who are they?"

"Who?"

"Them. In the paintings."

He wants to tell her about them, he does, but how? He can't document his failures to Wam y of all people. He can't risk another one.

"Nobody, just art."

She doesn't ask again. She learned a long time ago – back when she was sold into the temple, back when she was taught that her destiny was to carry a man to the other side, back when she learned to empty herself like a womb sheds its lining – not to ask questions. She was always told she'd be richly rewarded for the sacrifice, that she should be grateful for the chance to prove her worth. Not many people, the priest said, have the courage to give themselves up for larger cause, to allow themselves to be the ship that carries voyagers home.

Wam y wants to believe it. That this isn't yet another time when stupid men thought they had found a way to outsmart the gods, where sacrifices are made out of their lies. Sometimes, right before she falls asleep, and now as her body dries out, she feels footsteps in her eye, like the strings of her iris are being plucked by some kinder hand. She has never seen the other side for herself, not once. She does, however, know how to use her eyes, the same way one can breathe without seeing their lungs. She knows how to bat her lashes for an extra piece of bread or for the sleeping mat in the corner without the draft. She had long learned how not to swallow back tears, but to keep them pooled, held back in her lower lids. How to pull her lids wide apart and gaze upon a man, make him believe he is the centre of the universe. She does that now. She looks at him, tears pooled, but doesn't speak.

She remembers the paintings she saw as she walked into his home, generations and generations of stately men with wizened beards and dark eyes. They were on full display at the entrance, commemorations of power, a motif echoed everywhere but here. Here, in the room with them, there are only two paintings: a boy and a woman. Their eyes are closed. Whoever they are, he must be terrified of them.

She tries to shift her body, get some blood flowing into her numb thigh but she can't move too much without shifting the cables. She twitches instead.

"I want to thank you," he says.

It is hard to accept thanks when you cannot reject the task.

"It is my duty," she replies.

"Still, I am grateful for your belief."

She tilts her head to look at him. She can't imagine how he

218

believes that they are in this together. That this is some kind of symbiotic, spiritual sojourn before his voyage to the holy land. That his migration from this world to a better next is enough for her. He is an old man now, with children that hate him and a world that doesn't understand him. He bought her so he could escape. My belief, she thinks.

"Yes. Why... do, don't you believe?"

She is thinking out loud. The straw being spun into gold out of her flesh is drawing thinner the veil between mind and mouth.

"Well, don't you?"

"Believe in what?"

"In this! In the chance to go to a better world."

"Does it matter?"

"Of course it does."

"Okay."

"It does."

"Okay."

"No, don't just say okay, say what you mean."

She sighs.

She wants to talk, but cannot decide if it's worth it. Nothing can change the outcome. She knows she will die: her only choice is the value of her death.

"I don't mean anything. I'm here."

He recoils from her words as if they were made of flame. She watches his eyes flit and hands wring as he realises he cannot afford to lose her, not when they are this close.

She doesn't know what it is to be that desperate. He has options. He has a home that he wants to run away from. He has a dream that he wants to run to. He has the means to get there, the fear of failure, the hope of success. She, a mere vessel, has none.

A foggy silence fills the room as she stares at him, expression blank. She knows how he needs her. Empty.

"Are you scared?"

He chokes down another cough. She doesn't blink.

"Scared? No."

She lets the silence be. He shuffles in it, shifting his body to and fro, his foot tracing lines on the ground like a little girl with a crush.

"We are going somewhere better," he says.

Wamũyũ remembers the priest. Once, when he was drunk, she asked him why he wouldn't travel himself. He said that buyers and sellers are the same in every world, and the money here is good. The next morning, like every morning, he preached to her and the other vessels on the honour of service.

"You won't die," she says.

"Yes—"

"You won't die, but I will."

He bites his lip. His fear is exhausting her. The lip biting, the foot tracing; he luxuriates in his fear. She is disgusted by the weakness of it.

"You are doing a great service," he says.

She laughs. The sound is unfamiliar to both of them. A cross between a death gargle and a chirping bird. Rough and soprano. Hearing the sound makes her laugh harder. Gasping air and aching rib laughter. He laughs too, unsure of what else to do. Both their lungs ache.

"Okay, okay," he says.

Tears are running down her face and she feels heavy drops land on her breast. They tickle. She laughs more.

"Okay."

His face is turning to a frown, his vulnerability turning to anger. When he frowns, his lips jut out even more and, with his square jaw, he looks like a carnival mask, carved to entertain. She laughs still more.

"Enough!"

Stop.

Swallow.

She tilts her head down, an acknowledgement, but she doesn't look away from him. There is a surety in being someone's last hope, the last floating piece of wood from a shipwreck. She is even more tempted to refuse him. When the moment comes, he will be staring deep into her eyes, and she into his. No one knows precisely how the journey looks – only those who've made the voyage can tell us – but she always imagined a pier, a rowboat and an endless sea. He will walk along the edge of the pier, bare feet damp from cold sea spray and fog, towards the boat. She, holding a lantern, because all great voyages happen at night, will be standing in the boat. He will walk up to her, passport in hand and eyes shining with hope. She will take it and flip through the pages, inspecting his worth. Then she will rip each page out, one by one, and toss them into the water. She will sit down in the boat and row and row and watch him shrink into the distance.

His cough erupts. It racks through him like her laughter did. He sits on the floor, trying to catch his breath. A few tears escape down his face. She realises tears are still streaming down hers.

What are you doing? he shouts at himself. Keep her comfortable. She can't back away or be scared, she can't. He takes a deep breath and releases it.

"This is important for the both of us."

He sits on the bed, trying to make peace.

"Are you sure you aren't hungry?"

The food is still on the footstool by the bed. She reaches out and takes a small plum. She really doesn't have the taste for food, but it is more important to be open. She takes a small bite and lets the fleshy tang slip over her tongue. She chews it slowly. He watches every grind. She swallows. Places the bitten fruit back on the plate.

"Is it good?"

She nods.

"You can have more."

He can't stop the quiver in his voice.

She shakes her head: no.

Tea

TJ Benson

FIRST RUNNER-UP FOR THE 2016 SHORT STORY DAY AFRICA PRIZE

She is Tiv and knows no English. He is German with familial connections to the Nazis. They are in a hotel room somewhere in Italy. On the bed is an assortment of sex toys. A gruff voice behind the camera orders them to take off their clothes. The girl doesn't understand English, and a heavy-set woman in an orange buba gown whispers the translation into her ear. The boy places his finger on the girl's cheek, testing the texture. She shivers at the touch. Chalked in white on the charcoal placard are the words, *From Italy, with Love.*

They have each taken different paths to get here. He, a small-town boy, has been roaming around Europe on a quest to find himself after killing his co-worker at the textile factory back home. It had been an accident. Involuntary manslaughter. She has been brought here by the woman in the orange buba. It's the old story. Young girl from a small village fed tales of steady employment and a high salary in Europe. No sooner had the plane landed in Sicily than she realised it had all been a hoax.

"No, no, it will be just acting," the woman said, "nobody will tamper with your virginity." If she could just do like fifty thirty-minute videos, the woman said, she could return to Nigeria a queen.

And so, here they are. The boy is staring at the girl. Searching for words to tell her it will be okay, that he won't do anything outside their contract. The director who scouted him last week had informed him that his co-star might not speak English, but that would not affect the script. And he didn't think he would want to say anything, until now, stripped down to his briefs. He thinks of the few English words that he knows. Re-arranging the order of them in his head. Thinks of what he might say to the girl.

The director growls. Yells at the woman in the orange buba. He closes his eyes and focuses on the English words fired from the Italian man to the furious woman. She is saying that what he wants is not in the contract. "That's the point!" he shouts. "The boy. The girl. They are not *supposed* to know." It will make her acting more real, the pain and aftermath of the pleasure more genuine.

The boy doesn't realise how angry he is. He is more stunned than anyone in the room when the bedside lamp leaves his hand and smashes into the director's head. The man crashes to the ground, dragging the tripod and the camera with him. The assistant tries to make a run for it, but the German boy rushes at him with a barrage of punches. He doesn't stop until he hears a gunshot behind him. The madam, her face contorted into a strange expression, falls to the ground. Behind her stands the girl, in white lace underwear, a gun pointed in front of her. She is shaking.

Sense returns to him. He approaches her cautiously. What is her name? Useless question. How do they get out of here?

Two knocks on the door. Brisk, polite knocks. Tap. Tap. He shuts his eyes. Ice cream… balloon… mirror… bicycle… cloud… spaghetti… The random association of words helps him relax. He exhales. Opens his eyes and turns to her, placing a finger over his lips. She nods. The air is raw with tension. The knocking persists. Faster now. Tap-tap-tap. He pushes the bodies into the wardrobe and walks to the door.

The bellboy apologises for the disturbance and informs them that neighbours said they heard gunshots coming from this room. The management has sent him to make sure that everything is all right. Could the boy open the door so he can enter the room and check that everything is all right?

The boy is livid. What sort of management is this? How dare they intrude on his privacy? The young porter, very politely, informs him that if he doesn't open the door, he will have to get help from security. After a few minutes the boy opens the door. The bellboy is astonished to find a white man in black briefs holding a black girl in white lingerie, both wearing masks. He decides he has seen enough when his eyes fall on the sex toys on the bed. He apologises for the intrusion on behalf of the hotel management, but they should please be more discreet, he says, before closing the door.

A giggle escapes the girl's lips when he shuts the door. It's the last thing he expects. He giggles too, and they collapse onto the bed in laughter. It dawns on them when the laughter has ceased that it is the only language they have in common. They lie on the bed for a while, contemplating the colour of each other's skin: light brown and pale white. It's like nothing the other has seen before. The sounds from the morning traffic below float into the room, muted like music from a dream as they study each other on the bed. Then, in his peripheral vision, the boy sees blood dripping from the wardrobe.

We have to get out of here, he thinks, jumping out of bed and cursing himself in German. He has to find a way to talk to her. He gestures to the girl – whose eyes are welling with tears at the sight of blood – to put on her clothes. A red T-shirt and a denim skirt. She heads for the door once she's dressed. No, no, no! He gestures. We can't go out through the entrance. They will see our faces.

He motions her over to the window. The street is just a few storeys down. No wonder they could hear the traffic. He guides her out of the window onto the ledge below. They climb down level after level of the hotel until they get to the last floor and jump into a parked truck laden with sacks of flour. When they turn to see their faces whitened with flour, they both laugh. The laughter is broken by the sudden rheumatic cough of the truck's engine. As they truck begins picking up speed, they reach for each other's hands. That too, is another language they have in common. Touch.

The truck stops at the kitchen of another hotel. On impulse, the boy decides to carry the sacks into the kitchen, and the girl follows his lead. Afterwards, the sous-chef serves them lunch. In the evening, once all the sacks of flour have been packed away in the pantry, the chef pays them each ten euros. Tells them to come back tomorrow.

"Danke," says the boy to the man. "Or tom kuma nja," she says. A worker is worthy of his pay. The boy doesn't know what it means, but he laughs anyway.

They spend that first night together sleeping under a bridge, their bodies wrapped around each for warmth.

After a month of working dead-end jobs, they're able to afford a rundown apartment on the outskirts of the city. The boy's grasp of English is rudimentary, but he knows just enough to know that the police are searching for two young foreigners in connection with the case of a murdered woman. The report he read in the paper said that the woman's body was found in a hotel room and the two foreigners, a boy and a girl, are still at large. If seen, please contact… He balled up the paper and threw it out the window.

*T*he girl is making cocoa and milk. They have argued about whether this beverage should be called tea or not. The boy had wanted to broaden her English by showing her different labels in shop windows – slimming tea, Chinese tea, mint tea… But the girl just sighed. Then she rushed into a shop and seized a canister of chocolate powder and a tin of milk, and screamed with ferocity: "Tea!" She was sick with a cold, so he didn't argue. He just smiled at the Italians staring at them and paid for the goods at the till. But her cold has gotten worse since then, and he is glad he bought the "tea" because it is the only thing that will stay in her stomach.

Even days like this are wonderful. Days when she is too sick to work and neither of them have money for food; they just lie there on the battered sofa in the living room, in each other's arms, enjoying the silence, as time goes by. They don't know that their neighbour, the woman next door who sleeps all day, is a sex worker who receives her clients only at night. They don't know that in the room next to the sex worker is a wiry young Italian painter contemplating suicide because he has realised that he will never be as good as his predecessors. They don't know that on the floor right above them, a thickset detective spends his nights trying to figure out the mystery of the missing German boy and Nigerian girl.

On one such day, he wakes to the gentle burn of the sun on his face, but as he drifts from sleep into consciousness he realises that she's not there with him. No more in his arms. He leaps from the sofa in a panic. He feels a desperate urge to call out her name. He opens his mouth, but nothing comes out. He still doesn't know her name. The realisation moves him to tears. Where could she be? She's still no good at English or Italian, anything could happen. Oranges… duck… Santa Claus… obelisk… rice… leather. As always, the habit of stringing random words together calms him. Returns him to himself. He drags in a lungful of breath and begins searching the apartment. The place is small and it takes him less than a minute to search through all the rooms. She's nowhere to be found.

He curses himself in German as he pulls his shirt on. Why did he take her health for granted? He'd been afraid that the pharmacist would ask questions he wouldn't have answers to. Questions like "Where are your papers?" or "Do you have health insurance?"

*H*e runs from door to door asking if anyone has seen her. A slim black girl who can't speak English or Italian. Nobody has seen her. Again he feels the urge to scream out her name. He flies down the stairs prepared to go out to the world and look for her. He leaps outside into her embrace but he doesn't know this immediately, he thinks he has been caught by the authorities. But the body is soft and familiar, so he looks at the face and yells: "Where the fuck have you been?"

"Show you. I show you," she says, grabbing his hand.

"What?"

"I show you."

He relaxes when the path she leads him becomes familiar, their route to the restaurant.

"It's Sunday," he says, almost jogging to keep up with her, "you know they won't let us work on Sunday."

"No, not work."

She points to the broken-down ice cream truck parked next to the flour truck. The ice-cream van has been parked there ever since they first arrived here.

"Tea," she says.

"What?"

"Tea," she says.

His mind clears and it dawns on him what she means. "No! No way!" he says. They will never have enough money to buy enough cocoa powder and milk to start the "tea" business, and besides, who will buy anyway?

"Them." She points to a black father, mother, and child in matching check shirts crossing the street. "We make them like tea."

*T*he next month they work extra hours at the restaurant so that they can afford to buy the ice-cream van. Gradually, the girl's English improves, and they start to grow apart. He misses the days when they could anticipate each other's wants, those days of silence when there was no language between them, when a million things could be communicated with touch. Now her English is getting better, so no more hand on the shoulder when she needs something.

They take alternate shifts at the restaurant, and they see each now only at night when they're both exhausted. The girl also misses the way things used to be. Sometimes, when she is walking home after a shift, she imagines them rolling on the couch together, their bodies colliding in the heat.

One night she comes back from a late shift ecstatic, but he pays no attention. When he wakes up the next morning and sees her dressing with a big, luminous smile, somehow he knows, even before she says it. "You're leaving."

She doesn't deny it, and that only makes it worse. The police have plastered notices in three languages – Tiv, English and Italian – begging the Nigerian girl who miraculously escaped being forced into pornography to make contact. The notices said her country wanted her back; that the governor of her state would sponsor her trip back home. The only thing she had to do was to turn up at the same hotel she'd escaped from. But all he gets from her long explanation is that she's leaving.

He doesn't ask her stupid questions like what she's going to do when she gets back, or why they didn't ask her to turn up at the police station. He knows they know she is a stranger here and might fall prey to all kinds of people. The only thing he can ask from the sofa is "What of tea?"

"That is for if I stay. I not stay anymore. I want to go home."

She looks down at her lap with a sad smile. Somehow she has grown into a woman over these few months, and even this realisation is painful.

He massages his temple to stay sane. "This..." he says, stabbing the couch with his finger, "this is home!"

"I want to go home." A cry this time, a plea.

He descends the mount of his fury; he can never say no to her. He motions her over to him.

"If I hug you, it will be hard... to go," she says.

"Come here! You can't go home with all that chaos on your head."

She fingers a braid and smiles as he motions her over. "Come, come," he says.

$\mathcal{T}$hey spend the morning curled on the couch, like they used to. She tells him about her family. Subsistence farmers. How they moved from Benue state, into the wilds of another state called Taraba. How they were killed in the ethnic conflict that followed. The girl had been the only survivor, was rescued by missionaries. But then a kind rich woman who had been rescuing young girls had assured her that some members of her family were still alive, and that she would see them again if she got into her car. The Reverend promised her that an angel would protect her. The woman took care of her and some other girls for a month, feeding them but making sure they didn't talk to each other. A few weeks later, she found herself here.

Once she's done, he braces himself to tell her his story. He tells her about the accident at the textile factory and how he ran away, with only a bag of clothes and not much else.

"So where were you going?" she asks.

"I don't know," he shrugs. "I was roaming the continent when that bastard found me. I think the most important question now is: what about you? When are you planning on leaving?"

He smiles as he says this. The sun is behind his head, and as she looks at him, the girl thinks of an angel smiling at her, mesmerised at the cards fate has played. In that instant, she realises she could never leave him. Even if she did, the feel of his fingers on her skin is something she would never forget. She doesn't know that the notice is a hoax to lure her back into the hands of her traffickers. In fact, she will never know. For now, she says to him, "This is home." She shuts the door. "We make them like tea."

The Fates

Edwin Okolo

I remember my father as a wall of sound.

I was always listening for him. My arms wrapped tightly around my little brother's shoulders as he rumbled through the house, the steel toe of the shoe on his limp foot dragging against the cement floor. Doors creaked open, slammed shut. It was futile to hide from him, but I tried. I tried because I was thirteen and didn't know better, and in our house, you either hid or you ran, or you gave in to his rage. His rumbling would grow louder as he followed us through the house, towards my mother's old room, the bloated belly of our house. I would squeeze my eyes shut, breath tightening in my chest. He never entered her room. Especially now that she was gone. There was too much of her in that room, it frightened him.

That night, the last time I would ever see my father, he hesitated outside the door before crossing the invisible boundary. Dragging his foot behind him, he began to tear his way through what was left of my mother's life. Her clothes were a mountain on the bed and mulching the floor. Broken electronics poked out from the mess, silently bearing witness. He turned the room upside down, even taking time to upend the heavy orthopaedic mattress they used to share. Then he came for the closet, panting heavily as its wooden doors broke in his hands. Layefa had slept through everything, but the smell of him, my father, woke him up screaming.

"Papa, please!" I begged, even though I knew it wouldn't change anything. He dragged us out of the cupboard, me by the scruff of my neck, brother by the arm, through what was left of my mother's detritus, out the corridor, to the car idling outside.

It was almost midnight, but neighbours drawn by the commotion came to watch. I could see them squinting through the holes in our fence. I fell on my knees and grabbed hold of my father's leg like I'd seen my mother do too many times.

"Mama will come back, she promised."

I tried to find his eyes, but they were vacant even as they glared down at me. There was no emotion, only resolve. He pushed my brother into the back seat of the car, held the door ajar for me.

"Enter," was all he said.

I should have fought, but the neighbours were watching. I'd rather die than give them one last show.

*T*he taxi turned into a street lined with neatly trimmed trees and a quiet untainted by the low hum of generators, and I realised we'd been ferried into a different life. This had happened before; we'd come here, had a taste of this, and had it taken away.

I shook Layefa gently, raised him upright.

"We're here," I whispered.

The car stalled in front of a wrought-iron gate, a three-storey building peeking out from over its spiked crown. A small woman stood in front of it, her arms crossed over her wrapper tied high around her chest. In spite of her size, the massive gate seemed less imposing than her face. She pulled the door open, and scooped Layefa into her arms. He panicked for a second, but I met his eyes and gave the smallest nod. She grimaced as he wrapped his hand his around her neck, settled his head into the crook of her shoulder. I stared back, astounded that a face slightly weathered but still identical to my mother's sat on this stranger's face.

It hadn't occurred to me until that moment that there was life outside my mother, and our house, and Layefa. This woman, my mother's sister, was evidence of another life.

*S*he made me miss my mother, Auntie Philo. She had all my mother's tics. She spoke like Mama, shared her mood swings, her pettiness. She held on to the smallest slight for weeks, letting the resentment simmer. She had my mother's beauty, her hair, her smile. But Auntie Philo had also built a life for herself outside of her home, something my mother was never able to manage after the accident.

The other difference between Auntie Philo and my mother, I thought, as she led us through the house showing us what we were forbidden to touch and never to do, is that my mother had spent her life holding onto everything she owned. Auntie Philo held on to nothing. The floors were bare, the walls too. Even the chairs in the house were little more than skeletal frames, covered with cushions like muscle on bone. All her bedroom had was a miniature vanity mirror and a handful of suitcases piled by the door. She followed my gaze, shrugged when she saw what I was looking at.

"You can take one," she said, "they're all empty."

I found out later the suitcases belonged to her husband, his absence a question she refused to address.

Her only concessions to extravagance were the kitchen that sparkled with tile and shiny chrome, and the television, a monstrous square that covered one wall. Aunt Philo loved her television. And Layefa, who had never seen one, was drawn like a moth. Our aunt led me to the guest bedroom, my newly chosen suitcase in tow, and offered it to us officially. Then her face soured as she turned to the room opposite ours.

"Stay out of your cousin Edith's way."

$\mathcal{W}$e took aptitude tests. Auntie Philo drove us to the school even though we could have walked there. I think she was trying to make an impression on the teachers. I understood what school was, as an abstract concept, yet watching girls my age wrap their arms around each other's necks, their joy tangible as they gathered their skirts and chased each other across the dirt playground, showed me just how much I didn't know. It frightened and fascinated me. The tests also frightened me. I read through them and realised I understood them, but only in the way I understood school. My mother had never bothered with subjects, or sums, or continuous assessment. I answered the questions as best I could, turned the test over and awaited judgement. The woman who read through our answers kept pausing to look up at me. I fidgeted under her gaze.

Auntie Philo drove us to a restaurant afterwards, bought us lunch to celebrate. Layefa had got in, they were putting him in primary one. A class lower than he should have been, but not too far to catch up.

Auntie Philo took my hand and tried to make her voice light. It didn't work.

"They say you're intelligent, but have the literacy level of a seven-year-old. They wanted to put you in primary two, but I refused."

I nodded, swallowed. "I will find you a teacher, someone who'll come to the house for evening lessons. A year should be enough to get you up to speed. Things will be different here, you will be safe."

She seemed to be waiting to for me to say something, so I gave a small smile and nodded.

We ate our food while Layefa made plane sounds and guided his fork through the air. The silence festered, following us like a bad smell as we left the restaurant and drove home. We pulled into the compound, and Layefa bolted out of the car and into the house to go find Edith. Auntie Philo didn't follow. Her hands were closed around the steering wheel, veins rising on her arms. When she spoke, her voice was a rasp.

"She never took you to school?"

I tried to imagine my mother in a car, weaving through traffic, waving as I stepped through school gates. The image was too alien to conjure.

"She never left the house."

Auntie Philo seemed to sag in her seat, and her hands went up and hid her face as sobs coursed through her body.

"I didn't know, my God, I didn't know."

I taught myself to sleep deeply. It took months, but I taught myself not to worry, not to listen for my father's limp, not to think of my mother drowning in the detritus of her life. I taught myself not to worry about food or clothes or electricity. I taught myself to abandon my chores, to watch TV instead, or whatever children my age did. When school came I wanted to be ready, I wanted to blend in, I wanted to have "normal" stories. Auntie Philo let me get away with it most of the time. Edith, though, was another story.

"Mama, you're spoiling her," she'd say within earshot and glare at me. And Auntie Philo would ask me to do what it was Edith was nagging about.

But I never gave any lip about walking Layefa to school. It was the only time we spent together, and I savoured it. I told him about our mother and father, all the good things I could remember. She had an eye for beauty before the accident. She sought it out. The two of them worked in a hotel, Radisson Blu. That's how they met. It was a dead-end job, shifts as night staff, but she didn't mind.

She used to say, "I get to walk past some of the beautiful people, I touch paintings someone has paid millions of naira for. Everything there is carefully thought out, even the vases are carefully picked out. The nights are silent and I am surrounded by beauty. "

They were living in the house Papa inherited from his elder brother, so they didn't need that much money.

I never talked about the accident. Papa drove one of the big delivery trucks for the hotel. She was in the passenger seat when another truck came slamming into it. They were in the hospital for weeks. He came away with a limp, she at first seemed fine. The hotel let them go with a joint disability cheque. They might as well have given her a noose. Even before the accident, my mother had trouble holding it all together, but now she seemed to come unhinged. She bought things with the money, stupid pointless bric-a-brac. By the time my father realised something was wrong with her, the money was gone and the habit formed. Not just her disability cheque, but all his savings from their joint account. That was when he started drinking.

Layefa had taken to this new life here so easily that I worried he would forget how we came here, and why. I feared that something would happen, and this would all disappear like wisps of smoke.

I watched Edith and her friends from behind the curtain that hid the rest of the house from the living room. Portraits of my mother and Auntie Philo looked down on them from the walls. They were all sprawled on the sofas, playing cards, pretending to know more about the world than they did. They were the physical embodiment of youth.

"They're all crazy. She and her sister. Freaks. Pussy that drives men crazy runs in our family. My father was smart, he ran. The other one, Keren's father, that one just stayed there like a gbef and let that woman destroy him.

"My mother's OCD will force her to organise shit into neat piles, but at least she's clean. Keren's mother was a little piglet, bringing in trash from outside to pile in their house. One small car accident, the bitch hit her head and turned into a schizo. I heard when they came to take her away, they had to dig her out from the rubbish. That's why Keren's father went crazy too. All that dirtiness…"

I felt her gaze turn on me, even before I saw her head move. Quick as a snake she crossed the room and caught me before I could flee to my bedroom. She dragged me into the living room, in the midst of her friends. Their eyes bored into me like tiny drills.

"Keren, my mom said you were there when they came to take your mom to that hospital. What was it like? I heard her bones were like twigs, she was too crazy to say no. Didn't she shit herself?"

I stood there, unable to find words. Edith's friends waited in quiet anticipation, angling their bodies to watch me more closely. I fought the urge to cry even as my eyes misted, and I clenched my fingers at my sides, pressing my nails into the soft of my palm so hard they left marks.

Then the tall, skinny boy stretched out his hand, dragged me to him, and patted his lap. I didn't think, I sat.

"Leave her alone," he said.

Edith raised a brow, but she backed down and returned to their game of cards. I sat on his lap, still as a doll, and pretended to watch them play and when I felt him, for the first time, hard against my thigh, I wished I hadn't. I wished for Mama or Auntie Philo, or my father, anyone with enough authority to wrest me free, chase them away.

Edith was sitting on the sidelines, like me.

She hadn't gotten into university, for the second year in a row, and there was a year-long wait ahead before she could try again. That was why she and her mother fought all the time. Auntie Philo had decided she would be my tutor. Edith hated it, because it meant she couldn't leave the house in the evenings, go out with her friends. So they came to her instead: Negene, Francis, Anny and Sam. They arrived at two o'clock, almost religiously, following the exodus of primary school children let out of school. They came for the television. Everything looks better on a big screen. They were the first people even remotely my age that I got to spend time around. So I skulked, snapping up the crumbs of affection they fed to me. My reticence meant I was a weight around Edith's neck, and she was eighteen and angry at the world. She instituted a siesta for me and Layefa, forced us to lie in our room and stare at the ceiling until they left.

Auntie Philo was never around. She left for work before dawn, came back after dark. I knew no one, had no friends, didn't want to make any. A small part of me hoped my father would come, his limp magically healed, his eyes clear. He'd be remorseful, sweep me and Layefa into his arms, take us back home.

Of all Edith's friends, I think Negene noticed me long before I did him. He was the first to learn my name, pronounce it properly. The rest grunted in my direction.

I had caught glimpses of him, his legs splayed on the floor because Auntie Philo's chairs were too tiny and utilitarian to contain all of him. He always smiled, held my gaze. He looked at me like he could see beneath, inside me.

After the day Edith derided my mother for their amusement, he came for me, waited in the doorway as I put Layefa to bed. He took me by the hand, led me to the living room, and squeezed himself into a chair.

"What is she doing here?" Edith asked, glowering at me.

"She's a big girl," Negene said. "She wants to hang out with us."

I sat in his lap and we watched as Edith, Francis, Anny and Sam played Monopoly, paper money switching hands. Then he draped his pianist hands over my knee, casually, though under me the rest of him was still as bone. Then his hand moved higher, to my thigh, then finally under my skirt. And Edith watched, from the corner of her eye. She watched as I whimpered on top of him, tried to knock my knees, deny access. She glowered, her lips a taut line. I could see her anger rise. But she held it in check, met his eyes and held them as his hands moved faster and faster. Then his hand withdrew, slithering like a sated snake.

"Are you done?" Edith said, still holding his gaze.

She didn't look at me.

He laughed, a full, happy sound. I hated everything about it, even its timbre.

Edith turned away. That seemed to hurt her more than everything else. He put his hand, the other one around my waist, absently ran frets over my belly. And I stayed on his lap.

*T*his was how we woke from siestas, to the sound of Auntie Philo fuming. It must have been happening for years, because by the time we came to stay, Edith didn't care. The sound of Auntie Philo's car driving into the compound was her cue; she'd slip out with Negene and the others, and return when Auntie Philo was in front of the television, or in bed. Auntie Philo would barrel through the house, fuming about the same things. The dishes unwashed, dinner unmade, how Edith seemed to care about nothing. Most nights she would simmer, muttering under her breath as she did the chores Edith had abandoned. Slowly her rage would come to the boil, expressed in her taut spine, her hunched shoulders silhouetted by the glare of the television. She would stay that way till she grew tired.

But that night, she came home already bubbling over, and marched straight for Edith's room. Usually Edith was out the door by then. But that night, her luck ran out.

Seeing a grown woman consumed by rage is a different kind of terror. Whatever her hands could reach, Auntie Philo put to use. Brooms, the wooden spine of a mop, high-heeled shoes, the belt drawn from her waist. Edith never screamed. She tightened herself into a ball, the meat of her arms crossed to shield her face. Aunt Philo devolved to teeth and nails, tussled with Edith on the ground, barely human sounds coming from her.

Her rage eventually burned itself out. And afterwards, they sat heaving in opposite corners of the room, Edith's eyes shining with tears.

"Do you know the things I did for her, the things I suffered so she would never have to?" Aunt Philo said, her voice so raw it hurt to hear the words. "I worked so she could go to school, I stayed in that house even though it was hell. Even though our father beat me every day. I could have left, I had a business. But she was just a baby. Do you know what she did? She left the first chance she could. She ran away. After I had spent all my savings to pay for university. The money I had wanted to use to escape him."

Aunt Philo was crying now, unashamed, like a child.

"Even now, I'm still picking up after her. I am always picking up after her, raising her children. This is how she started, like this. This life that you think you have mastered, that's exactly how she started."

"I am not your crazy sister!" Edith screamed at Aunt Philo, her eyes wild. "I am your child! Your only child. Do you know what my father leaving did to me? What it's doing to me? Do you even care?"

"You are worse than her!" Aunt Philo screamed back. "She was a horrible, selfish person, but at least she accepted that, she didn't play the victim.

"You think you're the only person that your father destroyed by leaving? You think I didn't just want to curl up somewhere and not exist when he disappeared? Do you think I want to work like a dog, get humiliated in the office so I can pay for your education – that's if you ever do pass and come home to wash plates? Are the things I ask of you too much? I gave you everything I didn't have growing up. Everything! And you're throwing your life away because you think it makes me suffer?"

Then she laughed, pulling herself to her feet.

"What you are is evil," she said quietly, with the kind of malice you reserve for sworn enemies. "I look at you sometimes and wonder how you came from me. You're wicked, you're a... a sadist."

Edith didn't cry till Auntie Philo was gone, but once she started, she didn't stop. It haunted me, her sobbing, and the things Auntie Philo had said about my mother. Nightmares of that terrible rage turned against me robbed me of sleep.

Edith began to do the dishes.

*H*e didn't do it all the time. Often we just sat and watched TV. It was enough for him that I was there. Francis and Anny fought in Auntie Philo's living room, broke one of the side tables. Anny abruptly stopped coming to our house. I learnt how to stay still when Negene touched me.

I thought I knew all there was to him, until that day.

"Small oga, you're late today, oh," he said to Layefa, meeting him at the front door. I froze where I sat, in his favorite chair, pretending to be part of their circle.

Edith looked up, rolled her eyes and pointed to the bedroom.

"Before I count three, Layefa, siesta, now."

Layefa's face fell. I'd stopped picking him up from school and I had no idea why he was late. Negene helped him out of his school bag, carried the thing like it was a purse. He matched Layefa's short steps as they turned the corridor even though he was twice as tall.

"Let's get you out of your uniform and into bed."

I looked at Edith, stared until she noticed that Negene had followed Layefa. She watched them, a hunger coming into her eyes.

"He can change his clothes by himself, Negene," she called. There was no bite in the words.

"Okay," Negene replied and kept walking.

I hesitated for a moment before I followed.

They were by the bed, Layefa standing with his hands over his head as Negene pulled off his vest. I swung the door hard so it slammed against the wall.

"Layefa!" I called.

He sighed in relief and came to me. I undressed him, helped him into his house clothes. I was used to Negene's stare and I had become inured to its intensity, but seeing it directed at someone else made my skin crawl. I shuffled Layefa around so my back shielded him from Negene's gaze. Small mercies. I guided him to our bed, tucked him in and lay beside him. Negene sat on the edge of the bed, listening as I shushed Layefa and whispered him to sleep.

Then he crawled into bed with us.

I'd seen to it that there was no awkwardness in my movements as I rolled Layefa to the side of the bed, put my body between his and Negene's. He watched me make the switch, an amused smile tugging at the ends of his lips. He leaned in, holding my gaze like you do when charming a snake. He put his lips to mine.

He'd swindled me, laid out the bait, set the trap. And I had rolled myself right into it. The classic bait and switch.

I hoped wildly for the groan of Auntie Philo's car, the click of her keys in the front door. I even wished, impossible as it was, for the sound of my father's clunky limp. I heard Edith, her feet slapping against the concrete floor. She stopped in front of the door.

"Keren?" she said quietly.

Negene put his hand over my mouth, gently but firmly. His hand was wide enough to cover the lower half of my face. I stayed as still as I possibly could. Her footfalls grew fainter as she retreated back to the living room, and my heart sank.

I knew then why Edith wouldn't help me; she couldn't. The game was rigged against her, against us. Negene was her friend, she'd brought him into our house. Auntie Philo would have never believed that she didn't know that he would do this. Not after all the rebellions, after their fights. What worse way to hurt your mother than let bad things happen to the people in her care?

She too was trapped by her mother's perceptions.

Layefa.

If I talked, no matter what happened, I'd get taken away from him. Or worse, he would get taken away from this life, with school and uniforms and sanity. My year was almost up, I could almost see the classrooms, touch my uniform, feel the cotton undershirt against my belly. The newness of all of that. I… I couldn't.

My mother had gotten out. So had Auntie Philo. Maybe Layefa could get out too.

Negene reached down, breached the hem of my jeans.

I did nothing.

Keeping

Karen Jennings

*I*t was the first time that a plastic drum had washed up on the scattered pebbles of the island shore. Other items had arrived over the years. Torn shirts, bits of rope, cracked lids from plastic lunchboxes, braids of synthetic material made to emulate hair. There had been bodies too, as there was today. The length of it stretched out beside the drum, one hand reaching for it, as though to indicate that they had made the journey as companions and did not now wish to be parted.

Samuel saw the drum first, through one of the small windows as he made his way down the inside of the lighthouse tower that morning. He had to walk with care. The steps, made of stone, were ancient by now, worn smooth as silk, their valleyed centres ready to trip him up. Into those places where the stone walls had been yielding, he had inserted handholds, but the rest of the descent was done with arms outstretched, fingers brushing the rough sides in support.

The drum was the colour of workers' overalls and remained in sight, bobbing in the flow, all the way during his reckless hastening to the shore. The body he saw only once he arrived. He side-stepped it, walking a tight circle around the drum. It was as fat as a president, two-thirds the height of a man, and without any visible cracks or punctures. He lifted it carefully. It was light, empty. The seal had held. Yet the thing, despite being light, was unwieldy. It would not be possible with his hands, gnarled as they were, to grip onto that smooth surface and carry it across the jagged pebbles, over the boulders and then up along the sandy track, through scrub and grasses, to the headland where the cottage sat, abutting the tower. Perhaps if he fetched a rope, tied the drum to his back, he could avoid the effort of the ancient wooden barrow with its wheel that splintered and caught across the craggy beach, often overturning as a result of its own weight.

Yes, carrying the drum on his back would be the best option. Afterwards, in the yard, he would hunt out the old hacksaw that lived amongst sacking and rotting planks. He would rub the rust from the blade, sharpen it as best he could, and saw the top off the drum, then place it in an outside corner of the cottage where the guttering overflowed, so that it could catch rainwater for use in his vegetable garden.

Samuel let the drum fall, watching as it lurched on the uneven surface, thudding against the arm of the corpse. He had forgotten about that. He sighed. All day it would take him to dispose of the body. All day. First moving it, then the burial, which was impossible in the rocky island with its thin layer of sand. The only option was to cover it with rocks, as he had done with others in the past. Yet it was such a large body. Not in breadth, but in its length. Twice as long as the drum, as though the swell and ebb of the sea had left it this unnatural, elongated form. The arms were strong, disproportionate to the naked torso's knuckled spine and sharp ribs. Small, fine black curls formed patches on each shoulder blade, and another spot coloured the base of the back where it met the waist of grey denim shorts. The same curls, small, too small for a man of his size, grew on his legs and toes, across his forearms and between the joints of his fingers. They unsettled Samuel. They were the hairs of a new-born animal or of a baby who had stayed too long in the womb. What had the sea birthed here on these stones?

Already, as the mid-morning sun was rising, the curls were silvering with salt crystals. His hair too, was grey where sand had settled in it. Grains adhered to the only portion of the man's face that was visible – part of his forehead, a closed eye. The rest of the face was pressed into his shoulder.

Samuel tutted. The corpse would have to wait. First he would tend to the drum, then, next morning, if the body hadn't washed away, he would have to break some of the island's boulders, creating enough stones to cover it. There had been thirty-two of them, these washed-up bodies, over the eighteen years he had been lighthouse keeper. All of them nameless, unclaimed.

In the beginning, when the government was new, crisp with promises, when all was still chaos and the dead and missing of the twenty years under dictatorial rule were being sought, Samuel had reported the bodies that washed up. There had been fewer then.

Perhaps only one every six months. The first time officials had come out, with clipboards and a dozen body bags, combing the island for shallow graves, for corpses lodged between boulders, for bones and teeth that had become part of the gravelly sand.

"You understand," the woman in charge had said, as she looked down at a scuff mark on her red patent-leather heels, "we have made promises. We must find all those who suffered under the Dictator so that we can move forward, nationally. In a field outside the capital, my colleagues found a grave of at least fifty bodies. Another colleague discovered the remains of seventeen people who had been hanged from trees in the forest. They were still hanging, you understand, all this time later. Who knows how many we will find here? I am certain it will be many. This is an ideal dumping ground. Just wait. You will see. And that is when the healing will begin, for the nation, for us all."

But when the crew returned one by one, empty-handed, with only the washed-up corpse to show for a day's work, she was annoyed. She rushed to the boat, her departure abrupt, without the courtesy of a goodbye. Samuel did not hear from her, nor from her department. He did not know what had happened to the corpse, or who he might have been.

Months later, possibly as much as a year, he found three small bodies washed up side by side. A young boy, a girl, a baby in a blanket. In those days, the lighthouse's radio still worked and he'd contacted the shore to report the case. The woman called him back, her voice clipped by the static. "What colour are they?" she demanded.

"What?"

"What colour are they? The bodies. What colour?"

He was silent.

"What I am asking is, are they darker than us – their skin – that is what I want to know. Are they darker than you or me?"

"I think so."

"And their faces? Are they longer? What are their cheekbones like?"

"I don't know. They're children. They look like children."

"Listen, we're busy people. We have real crimes to deal with. Actual atrocities, you understand. We cannot come out every time another country's refugees flee and drown. It is not our problem."

"What must I do with them then?"

"Do what you like. We don't want them."

By then he had already started his vegetable garden beside the cottage, had used his wages to import soil from the mainland, ordered seeds and clippings. And to protect all of that new growth, he had begun to fashion a dry-stone wall around it. He gathered rocks, fitting them together one on top of the other, until they were high enough, stretched far enough to form a barrier. When all the loose stones of the island had been collected, he ordered a sledgehammer and used it to break apart the many rocks and boulders that comprised the coastline. Slowly the island began to change shape. Had a helicopter been in the habit of flying over, its pilot would note the widening of the small bays, the curves where serrated edges had once been.

Samuel continued with the wall along the perimeter of the island until everything was encircled. It was into this outer wall that he began to introduce the bodies, selecting spots for them on the farthest part of the island where the stench of their decay would not reach him. This attracted gulls, of course. For weeks they hovered and cawed around the wall, trying to peck their way in. With time he had learnt to make these parts sturdier, so that they bulged a little around their contents. Yet even so, sometimes the gulls managed to break the wall and pick at the body inside. In those places where corpses were left to disintegrate unaided, the stones often collapsed.

Most times before burying them, Samuel went through their pockets for objects of identification. But there had never been anything of significance. Not beyond an old man's fist, lumpen with a wad of foreign money squeezed to pulp in his grip. Samuel had buried him with it.

Beside the drum, the body stretched out still. Samuel half-nudged, half-kicked it with annoyance. The impact caused the arm to shift, the head to roll from its position and reveal the face. Both eyes opened briefly. The throat growled and fingers on the outstretched hand twitched, gripping hold of a pebble beneath them.

Samuel shuffled backwards. "Hello," he said softly. Then, "Hello."

The man did not move again. But there was now the visible slow throbbing of a pulse in his neck. Up-down, up-down it beat as the sea washed onto the pebbles and away again, mirroring the pulse.

Samuel counted. Fifty beats. Two hundred. Three hundred and fifty. At 500 he turned to the plastic drum, wrapped his arms around its middle and lifted it awkwardly in front of him, unable to see as he stumbled up the shore beyond the high water mark. He laid the drum on its side, chocked it with pebbles and then returned to the body, counting 100 more pulses before making his way up towards the headland through the well-worn paths he never altered.

*T*he gulls arrived while he was gone. They stood a few metres from the man, calling uncertainly, darting forward with low heads. One of them flapped its wings, approached the right leg and took an awkward peck at the man's shorts. But by then Samuel was on the sandy path, pushing the heavy barrow in front of him.

"Get away there! Go on! Get away!"

The birds rose, hovering low, as Samuel struggled through the boulders and onto the pebbled shore. He left the barrow beside the man and removed some rope from the bowl of the wheelbarrow, walking to where he had left the drum. He tied a rope around it, twice across the middle, twice along its height, and fastened it to a tall boulder. There were no trees on this part of the island. Only dry, leafless scrub that snapped if touched.

He returned to where the man lay, put a hand under each armpit, and tried to pull him towards the barrow. The body would not move. It was too heavy. Samuel grunted as he tugged, hoping that the body could be yanked loose from whatever it was that held it in place. Minutes followed, his arms aching, the small of his back aflame. He cried out, falling backwards as a pebble came loose underfoot.

Now the body was on top of him. The weight of it, and the smell too, decidedly foreign. A foreigner's damp hair, a foreigner's sweat and breath. Samuel pushed the man off, lifted himself up. The hair under the man's arms was coarse and long in contrast to elsewhere on his body. As Samuel heaved, he had felt himself pulling them out, those rough long strands. They stuck to the sweat on his wrists and forearms, working their way under his fingernails. He rinsed his hands and arms in the sea, before grabbing hold of the man again.

At length, he was able to lift the shoulders onto the wheelbarrow. His buttocks leaned against the wood as he caught his breath. Then, with an exhalation, he moved around to the side of the barrow, dragging the torso upwards so that the skin of the back caught on the splintered wood. The head lolled against one of the handles, both arms hanging down the sides. He stuffed them into the barrow, forcing them to fit in the space. But the legs remained extended, comical.

By now his own legs were shaking. His hands. He crouched in the sand a moment, looked over the water to the fog of the horizon. He thought it before he said it: "I'm old." As though frightened by the words, he stood up in haste, taking the cracked heels of the man and pushing until the knees buckled the legs into triangles. Bending, shoving, he positioned the feet so that they balanced on either corner of the barrow. Then he took the remaining rope and plaited it around and over until feet, knees, arms were locked in place, the entire giant body was trussed and shrunken and wholly deformed.

And yet, despite his precautions, the body tipped, it twisted, the head especially nudged Samuel's hands as the barrow cobbled over the pebbles. The wheel stuck with every rotation, so that soon he began to anticipate jolts, pauses, and put the barrow down in advance, clearing the obstacle, observing the damage done to the wheel, before beginning again.

Once the man groaned and Samuel waited to see if his eyes would open again, but they did not. So he pushed on, through the wet sand of the water-carved alley between the boulders, so narrow that the sides of the barrow rasped, and one of the man's knees grated against a jagged edge and began to bleed lightly.

Then they were out of the tunnel, off the shore almost, with only the steep incline up loose grey sand to halt them. But the wheel stuck again, it would not be pushed, and Samuel backed away, ready to give up. He had tried, hadn't he? He had done enough. He would untie the man, bring food and water if he woke, a blanket maybe, and that would be enough.

He did none of those things. He came forward again, tried turning the barrow around, almost hopeless in the soft sand. He moved backwards, pulling the barrow up the path, even though he thought his arms might tear, thin as paper they felt. And then it was stuck again, and he was back down on his knees, fire in his legs. He was all sand now. His shoes held it, as did his pockets, the creases of his neck, the arcs of his fingernails.

But then, at last, came the breath of the headland, of a soft breeze through yellow grasses, and a solid dirt track lined with clusters of small pink flowers and green-thorned weeds.

Above them rose the lighthouse. It had been white once, last plastered in the middle of the previous century, before the colonial government left them to their independence. Now it was flaking, dull, with orange swathes where metal fixtures had rusted and leaked their age. Around the base of the tower, short scraggly trees grew, their trunks and branches cast westward by the prevailing wind so that they seemed ever in flight, and Samuel often wondered, before he stepped out of the door in the morning, whether he might find that they had fled after all.

The cottage door was old and heavy. It stuck in the jamb, fat with moisture from the sea air. Samuel had to put a shoulder against its grey hardness to force it open. He pulled the barrow over the single step, and dragged it through the small dark entranceway with its clothes-hooks, anoraks, hats and worn-heeled boots, into the living area.

He untied the ropes that had kept the man in position. Then he slowly tipped the barrow over until the man fell out onto the threadbare carpet. Samuel repositioned the limbs, the neck, checked on the knee that was no longer bleeding, and took an old cushion, its original design faded to dun, and placed it under the man's head.

There was a couch in the room, a table with a television that did not work, and a bookcase full of video cassettes and old magazines. Beyond those objects there was only a three-legged stool, speckled with paint stains and long-ago trails of woodworm. Samuel sat on it, feeling the creaking unsteadiness of it beneath him.

He watched the face of the man where he lay. A wide mouth in a narrow jaw. He appeared to have no hair on his face at all, not even eyebrows. He might have been in his early thirties, though Samuel would not have been surprised to learn that he was in fact older or younger. How long might the man live? he wondered. How long would he lie on Samuel's carpet in Samuel's home? He rattled his fingers on the table, smoothed a hand over his face. Was it to go on like this, then? This incessant movement in his home. His home that had been his alone for eighteen years of solitude. Was it to be this? This breath, this youth, this life?

He could not bear it. It was taking over the small cottage, seeping into the floor and walls and he began to feel breathless, to gasp his panic. He tried to reason with himself. The next day the supply boat would come, as it did every fortnight. It would come and he would hand the man over to them. They would have to take him. They had that obligation.

But he remained unsettled. And on the floor, as though in mockery of all he was thinking, a vein seemed to emerge from the depths of the man's calf, to surface, swollen and alive, pumping life through him.

Samuel stood abruptly, and stumbled out the back door. He would go and fetch the drum. When he returned, he hoped, the man would be dead.

The Impossibility of Home

Izda Luhumyo

*P*rivately, I rename your city. I start calling it "the city of restlessness".

Everywhere I look, I see people who find that they cannot make a home here; people who are always on their way to better elsewheres; people on whom the city hangs like an ill-fitting coat.

Here, people seem to have little use for the present. Instead, everything is held to ransom by the regrets of the past and the possibilities of the future.

*P*erhaps Nairobi is simply an outline I am colouring in with my own restlessness. We humans have an uncanny way of imposing bits and pieces of ourselves on places. Perhaps this is my mark.

*B*ack home, I'm famous for my itchy feet. I've told you about that time my grandmother lowered her voice to a husky whisper and said to my mother: "I wonder what our girl did in her past?"

"Why?" Mother asked.

"Because God played a dirty trick on her," Grandmother said. "Why take with one hand what you give with the other?"

Mother's response was swift: "I've never known God to make mistakes."

*M*y name is Santa and this is what it entails: a gap in my front teeth, a laugh that can make walls move, an absent father, a love for lemon pickles, a talent for turning words into swords, and a body with only one leg.

I am finally in Nairobi.
   Nairobi: what we mean when we say "Kenya".
   Nairobi: brighter lights, bigger city.

*S*omewhere in my notebook is a hastily scribbled note: "It is easy to look; it is not easy to see."

I came all this way because no matter how carefully I looked, I could not see my home town. It was too close; everything was right there in my face.

But Nairobi is new to me. There is enough distance between the city and I; I can begin to see it clearly.

This city is not yet tainted with my memories. There are no places I avoid because of this one thing or the other. It is unmarked territory for me.

I want to learn how Nairobi works. I want to lose myself in this place, to see whether I can begin to build a life here.

To do this, I must find a way to understand its rhythms, and see where I fit in the chaos.

I need a guide. So I do what I've been neglecting to do all this while: I call you.

*A*nd now we are two.
 You are Sofia; I am Santa.

Together we are a nuisance, walking aimlessly around the city, being a pain to those who have actual places to go.

You visit my house in Umoja, and I show you the pride that is my apartment.

You ask: "Why Umoja?"

I tell you that I am fond of Umoja, even though its looks are against it. I like this quarter because it has the suspicion of a charming past about it. It makes me think of an elderly musician who was all the rage in his youth but has now been slowed down by time.

"This place makes me feel like I live in a time, not a place," I say.

You frown-smile, as if you suddenly stumble upon mirth right there in the midst of your confusion. Then you say: "And what colour shall we paint these walls?"

In my kitchen, I manage to impress you with my recipe of chicken cooked in coconut milk.

Later, we sit on the kitchen floor and you show me your tattoos.

You tell me that they signify the three great losses of your life.

"Everyone must have a record of their private aches," you say. "I get tattoos; you scribble in your notebook. It's all the same thing."

"You talk like a poet," I say.

We go through my wardrobe and weed out all the bright-coloured clothes. You've decided that I look nicer in blacks and greys.

I fish out blue hair dye from among my things, and we paint my bathroom blue in the process of dyeing your hair.

As we sit outside in the sun waiting for your hair to dry, you explain my face to me as if it were some kind of theory.

You say: "Your face is interesting to look at. What I mean is: you're beautiful in an interesting way. The features of your face are individually striking. You have gorgeous eyes, a lush mouth, and nice cheekbones. But it's all chaos. There's no harmony; you've got too many pretty things on your face and every feature cries to stand out."

"I'm not sure whether to feel insulted or not," I say.

You frown. Then you say: "Santa, I have decided that you are a woman on the brink of stunning beauty. And that's a compliment."

When darkness falls, we sit on my bed sipping tea and feeling like brand-new people – you with your blue hair and me with my grey and black clothes.

You start telling me about this place on Kimathi Street where they play Bongo music all night and where the light is always right and where if you perch on the long stools with your skirt riding up your thighs and your butt hanging off the stool just right, a man on his way home will ask the bartender to keep the drinks coming for you.

I say: "Sofia, let's go and try out our new selves on the world."

*W*e are outside this club on Kimathi Street. And we've been standing here for about a half an hour.

We've been shifting our weight from crutch to crutch, and our spirits have been falling further with every bewildered look that people give us.

One man raises his voice: "Why don't they just buy from a local and drink from home?"

Another man shakes his head. "I thought I'd seen all wonders," he says.

So it happens that as we stand outside the club, waiting to be deemed worthy to get in, we discover that we are a wonder. That our presence here is itself a wonder.

But we don't feel like wonders. We're just two women who want cold beers.

We know we should walk away, but that requires more courage than we can muster between us.

So we keep waiting and waiting, avoiding each other's eyes.

Finally, a man in a suit – the club manager, perhaps – steps outside and whispers something into the ears of the bouncers at the door.

They allow us to enter.

We get stools at a spot where we can watch the Nairobi night. The beers are brought and we drink in silence.

Then unable to bear it any longer, I say to you: "Sofia, these beers are not that cold and the stools are not even that high and come on, this place is not even that good to be charging us 350 for a beer. Can we please go?"

We find that we cannot say a word to each other as we walk to the bus station.

Later, when I get home, you call me. You say: "Soul sister, from now on, let's just stick to the places where we're actually wanted okay?"

"Okay," I say.

Here is the first lesson of the city: don't go where you're not wanted.

A few weeks later, I say to you: "Show me the places you like."

So you take me to bookshops and art galleries and thrift shops and museums. You take me to the oldest buildings in the city and watch me as I graze my hands over the old, mildewed stone.

We get on buses going to places like Londiani and Ndia and Gichugu. We travel just to go and see what's happening.

There is no method to the places we visit; we are simply two women who take our whims seriously.

We just want to keep moving.

We want our eyes to glaze over new places; we want new material with which to fill our conversations; we want new things to remember.

I tell you about my theory of Nairobi's restlessness. About this constant movement its people have, as if being propelled forward – always forward – by some kind of force.

"It's the only way," you say. "Here, you must keep moving. Otherwise, the sand swallows you whole."

On the buses, we talk loudly about books and people and places and ideas that only we know of.

You confide your weakness for men from the lakeside; I confirm mine for a man who knows how to roll his tongue around Kiswahili words.

We try not to think about the future, aspiring only as far as the next bus stop, as far as our next outfits, as far as our next meal.

We live out our lives as if we are in an Otis Redding song: full of longing and wistfulness and sappy melancholy.

And later, when the buses deposit us in nondescript towns that only appear on the nine o'clock news for bad things, we walk around and ask for the most outrageous of things, things that could never exist in such places: tattoo parlours, fish pilau, crop tops. We are secretly pleased when we are rewarded with the shaking of heads and confused frowns.

We spend some of our days sitting in small-town cafés, waiting for the next thing.

Somehow we've gotten it into our heads that we are the leads in an indie art film and we are roadtripping through lazy and dusty towns, drinking cup after cup of bad coffee, coughing our way through packs and packs of cheap cigarettes, and punctuating our sentences with curses.

When you call home, your mother hears the effect of cigarettes on your voice and only asks that you don't return home with darkened lips.

*O*ne afternoon, you look me in the eye and say: "Hey, soul sister, tell me about him. Even a little."

I tell you there's nothing to say.

You say: "Okay, what do you remember most about him?"

"I have no memories of him," I say. "Thankfully, he left before he could take up space in my life. Mother used to call it a kind of kindness."

You chuckle. "It can only be called a cruel kindness. Then tell me about your mother's memories of him."

"She never said much about him," I say. "It was too painful for her. They met and then they had me. He left right after I was born."

"Was it because of you?"

"I think so. You know, I've never even met the man. Yet here I am, lugging his name around with me."

*A*nother afternoon, another café.

You look up from the book you're reading and say: "Soul sister, where is he now, your father?"

"Here," I say.

"Is it why you came to Nairobi?"

"No," I say.

Then later I say softly: "I don't know, S. Maybe."

I dress in black, as if I'm on my way to a funeral.

Perhaps I am.

In Westlands, I get lost for about an hour before I find the building.

I choose to heave myself up the stairs so that I can have enough time to change my mind and return to my life.

I am a spectacle: this is the kind of building where concerned people ask to help you.

"May I please help you?" they say.

It gives me enormous pleasure to reject their help.

Sometimes help is just a bother. "Help me with my life instead," I want to scream at them.

I sit in the reception lounge of a large office and watch people walk past me, their minds taken up by what seem to be important things.

Then about an hour later, I sit across from a man who has poured himself into a crisp, white shirt. I watch shock travel up and down his face as his eyes travel up and down my body.

He looks like he's making a quick dash into the past to retrieve the connections that will help make him make sense of the reality sitting awkwardly across from him.

"I've wanted to meet you for a long time," I say to him. "I think you're my father."

He coughs and then falls quiet.

Finally, he asks: "How is your mother?"

"Dead."

"Oh my... I didn't know."

"Grandmother is dead too, so you can stop sending the money now."

"The money was for you... um... I'm sorry... God, I don't know your..."

"Name? Santa."

"Santa... okay... I see."

He goes quiet again. Moments pass. And then he says: "She named you after her mother."

"She also named me after you," I say. "I think she might have loved you."

He gets up and opens the windows. He goes to the other side of the room and switches off the light.

Anything but to sit still in this nightmare, it seems.

I search the lines on his face for clues. I'm trying to see if there's any trace of myself in this man.

He sits down and starts to talk about Mombasa, going on and on about the Mombasa of his younger days.

I get my phone out of my bag and show him a little of Mombasa.

"The Mombasa of the 1990s is long gone," I tell him. "Places don't remember people, you know…"

Then I show him pictures of mother's house, and the flowers she grew outside it.

"It's a beautiful house," he says. "And she got to grow her own flowers. She always wanted to do that."

"She built that house because of your money," I say.

"Santa… the money was all to provide for you. I am a responsible man."

My name is unrecognisable in his mouth. I regret handing it to him so easily.

I tell him I have to go.

"I only came to tell you to stop sending the money. It was not even difficult to find you," I say.

"I was not hiding, Santa."

"Don't call me that," I say through gritted teeth. "You don't deserve to call me that."

I get up and amble towards the door.

*W*hen a man puts on a white shirt on a Tuesday morning and drives to work, stopping at the usual place to fill up on fuel, he does not expect that the past he deftly left behind him all those years ago will catch up with him. He does not expect to find that some things cannot be placed in boxes and put away. Yet, when the past finally comes to find him in the present, he finds himself wondering why it took so long.

*B*ack home, I find that everything hurts.
I text you: "S, I think I just lost my father."

You come for me and take me to a tattoo parlour in town and hold my hand as the tattoo guy writes this first loss of my life into my skin.

Later, you hold me as I cry out the pain on my kitchen floor.

I say: "He wasn't even hiding, Sofia. He wasn't even hiding."

Sometimes you have to go on living with the knowledge that someone counts you as a mistake that they have to pay for – for the rest of their lives.

My apartment has started to feel strange. The novelty has worn off, and I spend less and less time in it. I only come to it when the city retreats into night-time. I know what this means. It means it's time to go.

I've been to a couple of places, and I'm on my way to more.
Home can only stop feeling like home if it has felt like home before.
This city cannot home me.

Insomnia comes to me like a messenger. Its message is clear. And in that state of sleeplessness, I pack a few things in my suitcases and leave everything else intact: the bookcase and the cushions and the carpet and the mattress.

You stop coming to my house when you visit one day and see my things packed in suitcases.

Finally, I dare to broach the thick silence that is beginning to wedge itself between us.

I send you a message: "Sofia, I'm leaving tomorrow."

"Flying or bus?" comes the swift response.

"Bus."

"Which one?"

"Mash. Bus leaves at 9:30 p.m."

You say you've got one more place to show me.

You take me to an ice-cream joint that is covered in yellow

and white tiles. You tell me that it has been in place since your parents' days.

"Sofia, you've never told me about your family," I say.

"You didn't stay long enough to hear it," you respond.

We order vanilla ice-cream and listen to the waiter tell us about his home – a village deep in Taita – where it is so cold that they always keeps flasks of hot tea at the ready.

Later, you say: "That explains a lot. I once dated a Taita man, and I swear all we ever did was have sex and drink tea."

"What happened to him?" I ask.

"Oh, he left," you say. "I'm actually surprised he stayed that long."

*Y*ou are there at the bus station when I arrive, minutes before the departure time. The other passengers are already in their seats and the driver has the engine running.

When you see me, you run towards me as fast as a person with one leg can.

We hug. You don't let go when I start to pull away.

"Sofia, the bus…" I say.

"Soul Sister," you say. "Your friendship has been a lifeline to me. Please stay. You can build a life here."

Your words are a rush.

"Sofia…"

"Santa, I've never asked anyone to stay in my life…"

"My father… he's ruined Nairobi for me. I can't stay… I…"

"He's an ass! Don't mind him. Listen to me… you can build a life here… I swear it's not that bad."

It's 9:30 p.m. The driver honks twice. The passengers are now craning their necks, trying to see who's keeping them waiting.

"Sofia…" I start. I cannot go on.

There is the bus engine running and the driver honking and the passengers waiting and you saying don't go don't go don't go.

And then there's me, shifting my weight from one crutch to the other, unable to leave and unable to stay.

BIOGRAPHIES

ABA ASIBON is a Ghanaian writer whose short fiction has been published in *Guernica*, The University of Chester's *Flash Magazine,* and *African Roar*. Aba has also had poetry featured in the *Kalahari Review* and was longlisted for the Ghana Poetry Foundation's debut prize. She currently lives in Malawi, where she works on public health initiatives to improve healthcare for newborns.

FRANCIS AUBEE is a Gambian, born in 1996 and a budding writer. He lived in Nigeria for five years, where he won the Kenneth Imansuangbon National Essay Competition in the tenth grade. Francis is currently attending college in the United States, with a major in Economics. He is interested in football, politics, and travelling.

TJ BENSON is a Nigerian short story writer and creative photographer. His work has appeared in *Transition, Jalada, Sentinel Literary Quarterly*, and in various other print and online publications. His chapbook of photography *Rituals* was published online by *Sankofa Magazine* and his collection of short fiction, *We Won't Fade into Darkness*, was shortlisted for the Saraba Manuscript Prize in 2015. He is currently working on a collection of photographs and poetry titled *Self.*

GAMU CHAMISA is a Zimbabwean writer based in Melbourne, Australia. She blogs (occasionally), watches football (religiously), and likes to take photographs. She is obsessed with the idea of home and the question of who gets to tell our histories. She is currently working on her first novel.

MIRETTE BAHGAT ESKAROS is a short story writer based in Egypt. Her work has appeared in various publications, including *The Huffington Post* and *Arab Spring Dreams: The Next Generation Speaks out for Freedom and Justice*. In 2009, she was awarded The European Institute of the Mediterranean Writing Award. She was also awarded the American University's Madalyn Lamont Literary Award in 2016. Her writing explores issues of identity, spirituality, mythologies, and gender.

SIBONGILE FISHER is a published poet and writer from Johannesburg, South Africa, with a higher certificate in Performing Arts. She loves working with teenagers and enjoys home-made burgers.

STACY HARDY is a writer, teacher, and researcher. Her writing has appeared in numerous anthologies and journals, including *Evergreen Review, Bengal Lights, Glänta, Black Sun Lit, Drunken Boat, Chimurenga,* and more. *Because the Night*, an anthology of her short fiction, was published by Pocko Books, London (2015). She is currently working on a new collection that explores the intersection of the human body and the body of text via the tropes of disease and animality.

KAREN JENNINGS was born in Cape Town, South Africa, but now lives in Goiania, Brazil. She holds Master's degrees in both English Literature and Creative Writing from the University of Cape Town, as well as a PhD in English Literature from the University of KwaZulu-Natal. Her debut novel, *Finding Soutbek*, was published in 2012 by Holland Park Press and was shortlisted for the inaugural Etisalat Prize for African Fiction. In 2014 her short story collection, *Away from the Dead,* was longlisted for the Frank O'Connor International Short Story Competition. Her memoir, *Travels with my Father*, was published in November 2016 by Holland Park Press. Karen is currently a Miles Morland Scholar and is working on a fiction manuscript.

BLAIZE KAYE is a writer and programmer from KwaZulu-Natal, South Africa. His work has appeared in *Nature*, *Fantastic Stories of the Imagination*, and *New Contrast*.

FRED KHUMALO is an award-winning novelist, short story writer, and the author of *Dancing the Death Drill*, *#ZuptasMustFall and Other Rants*, *Bitches' Brew* and *Seven Steps to Heaven*, among other titles. A seasoned journalist and a 2012 Nieman Fellow at Harvard University, Khumalo also holds a Masters in Creative Writing from the University of the Witwatersrand.

LAURI KUBUITSILE is a writer living in Botswana. She has had many short stories and books published in Southern Africa as well as around the world, for children, teens, and adults. Her latest book is a historical novel titled *The Scattering* (Penguin South Africa, 2016).

IDZA LUHUMYO is a writer and blogger from Kenya.

ANNE MORAA is a writer, editor and creative. After completing an under-graduate degree from the University of Nottingham, she completed her Masters degree in Creative Writing at the University of Edinburgh. Her works focus on feminism, "otherness" and the importance of voice. Her published pieces can be read in *Jalada*, *KikeTele*, and *Brainstorm,* among other publications, and her performances have taken her from South Korea (as part of Exhibit B) to Edinburgh (with the Loud Poets at the Fringe Festival) and Nairobi (StoryMoja Hay Festival, Festival CulturElles), where she currently lives and works.

MIGNOTTE MEKURIA is an Ethiopian writer, feminist and lover of international cinema. She recently completed what must be one of the most self-centred creative writing PhDs ever, focusing on her mother and her country: her two greatest inspirations. The time she spent studying abroad both strengthened her resolve to return to Ethiopia and her determination to unravel its secrets through her creative works, and to map the links and commonalities between her country and the myriad others on the African continent. She remains committed to her goal of writing about her country and continent as she sees it – central and necessary, flamboyant and fantastic – whether the setting is in an ancient empire forgotten by time or a futuristic settlement in the outer reaches of space.

EDWIN OKOLO is a writer and editor based in Lagos, Nigeria. He has written for several blogs and literary magazines, including the *Kalahari Review, The Lonely Crowd, Omenana, Sable Lit Mag,* and a wildly popular web series for TheNakedConvos.com. He is an editor at Stories.ng and he is currently working on his first novel.

MARY ONONOKPONO is a Nigerian-British writer and artist. Winner of the 2014 Golden Baobab Prize for Early Chapter Books, Mary is also a two-time shortlistee of the Morland Writing Scholarship. She recently graduated with a degree in history from SOAS, University of London. Mary lives with her daughter, an avid writer and mini-chef, somewhere in North London.

NYARSIPI ODEPH is a content creator, feature writer and magazine editor based in Nairobi, Kenya. She is also a wine and cheese enthusiast, and a champion daydreamer. Although she spends most of her energies trying to figure out how to be a functional single mother and adult, she is currently working on re-focusing her love for writing into memorable fiction.

MEGAN ROSS is a writer and journalist from the Eastern Cape in South Africa. Born in 1989, she would spend all day in the Indian Ocean if she could. Instead, she divides her time between writing fiction, covert beach missions, and chasing after a toddler. Her work has featured in *Prufrock, Aerodrome,* and several anthologies. Most recently, she was shortlisted for the Miles Morland Writing Scholarship, and also awarded the Iceland Writers Retreat Alumni Award.

ARJA SALAFRANCA has published three collections of poetry, *A Life Stripped of Illusions,* which received the Sanlam Award for poetry, *The Fire in which we Burn,* and *Beyond Touch.* Her fiction has been published online, in anthologies and journals, and is collected in her debut collection, *The Thin Line,* longlisted for the Wole Soyinka Award.

She has participated in a number of writers' conferences, edited two anthologies and has received awards for her poetry and fiction, most recently co-winning a SALA award for *Beyond Touch.* She has a Masters in Creative Writing from Wits University. She lives in Johannesburg.

OKAFOR TOCHUKWU's *Warscapes* story, "Colour Lessons", featured in *Columbia Journal* and *Vol. 1 Brooklyn,* has been shortlisted for the Problem House Press Short Story Prize (2016). His *Open Road Review* story, "Spirit", featured in *Litro Magazine, Juked,* and forthcoming in *Kweli Journal,* has been shortlisted for the 2016 *Southern Pacific Review* Short Story Prize. In 2014 he was awarded the Comptroller Charles Edike Prize for Outstanding Essays. His work has also appeared in *No Tokens, Aerodrome, The Bombay Review, The Kalahari Review, Flash Fiction Online,* and elsewhere. He is an alumnus of the Association of Nigerian Authors/Yusuf Ali Creative Writing Workshop and the Short Story Day Africa Migrations Flow Workshop and a two-time recipient of Festus Iyayi Award for Excellence for Prose and Playwriting (2015/2016). He is currently at work on his debut novel.

UMAR TURAKI is a writer and filmmaker living in Jos, Nigeria. His short fiction has appeared in publications such as *Afreada, Short Sharp Shots,* and *Aké Review.*

☙

EFEMIA CHELA was born in Zambia in 1991, but grew up all over the world. When she grows up she would like to be a better writer and literary translator. Her first published story, "Chicken" was nominated for The 2014 Caine Prize. Efemia's subsequent stories and poems have been published by *Brittle Paper*, *Short.Sharp.Stories: Adults Only*, *Prufrock* and *PEN Passages: Africa*. She is an editor for *Parrésia* and continues to write fiction whenever she can find a moment on the train and a working pen.

BONGANI KONA is a writer and contributing editor of *Chimurenga*. His writing has appeared in *Mail & Guardian*, *Rolling Stone South Africa*, the *Sunday Times,* and in other publications and websites. He was shortlisted for the 2016 Caine Prize and he is currently studying for a Masters in Creative Writing at the University of Cape Town.

HELEN MOFFETT is a poet, editor, feminist activist and academic. Her publications include academic essays, university textbooks, an anthology of landscape writings, a cricket book (with the late Bob Woolmer and Tim Noakes), and the *Girl Walks In* erotica series (with Sarah Lotz and Paige Nick under the nom de plume Helena S. Paige). She is the author of two collections of poetry, the latest of which is *Prunings* (uHlanga, 2016). She lives in Noordhoek.

ACKNOWLEDGEMENTS

A good writer possesses not only his own spirit but also the spirit of his friends.
– Friedrich Nietzsche

*E*very publication is the result of a team effort, and none so more than this.

Special thanks to the *Migrations* editing team, Helen Moffett, Efemia Chela and Bongani Kona, whose tireless efforts, keen eyes and dedication helped these twenty-one writers improve their stories and their craft. Also, to Jason Mykl Snyman and Shameela Essack, who were kind enough to spend December proofreading these pages. This year, we created an editing mentorship thanks to the generous support of Worldreader. I'd especially like to thank our Worldreader liaison, Nancy Brown, for her enthusiastic support of this crazy dream.

Once again the beautiful cover is the work of the talented Nick Mulgrew, who is also responsible for the page design and layout.

Over the years, Colleen Higgs of Modjaji Books has offered much in the way of advice and friendship. She took the project under her wing and helped us grow, then pushed us out of the nest when she knew we could fly. I am forever grateful for her support.

Thanks to Dan Raymond-Barker and New Internationalist for believing in what we're doing and taking our stories to new readers.

To Sindiwe Magona, Hawa Jande Golakai and Tendai Huchu for giving freely of their time and experience to judge the Migrations longlist.

To the team of readers that helped us whittle down the entries, and thus played a vital role in shaping this anthology: Aaron Bady, Ada Chioma Ezeano, Brian Asingia, Brian Jones, Carine Englebrecht, Cat Hellisen, Catherine Shepherd, Cebelihle

Mbuyisa, Charlotte Bossa, Cindy Page, Arinzechukwu Patrick, Elizabeth Kitego, Emmanuel Anyole, Esther-Karin Mngodo, Fiona Snykers, Harriet Anena, Helené Prinsloo, Isla Haddow-Flood, Jamillah Bisbas, Jane Morris, Jeanne-Marie Jackson, Jennifer Malec, Jonathan Cane, Kari Cousins, Karina Szczurek, Kate Sidley, Kerry Hammerton, Lauren Smith, Lungisa Noganta, Mack Lundy, Margot Bertelsmann Doherty, Mary Watson, Mehul Gohil, Nella Freund, Nnamdi George Okeke, Nyana Kakoma, Pamela Yori Stitch, Rahla Xenopoulos, Rayka Kobiella, Romeo Oriogun, Shameela Essack, Sima Mittal, Susan Newham-Blake, Tiah Beautement, Tolu Daniel AKA Tolulope Daniel Ojuola, Tracy Saunders, William Burger, and Zaheera Asvat.

With generous funding assistance from the Miles Morland Foundation, we were able to grow the SSDA team and our reach. Their assistance gave us the space to breathe, expand our ideas and achieve so many dreams. Thank you Miles, Michela, and Mathilda for believing in us.

In partnership with Goethe-Institut, we ran seven Migrations Flow Workshops across the continent, in Addis Ababa, Dar es Salaam, Johannesburg, Lagos, Nairobi, Windhoek, and Yaoundé. Many thanks to the participating institutes, the facilitators, and especially to Brigitte Doellgast, the Head of Library and Information Services for Sub-Saharan Africa, for being so open to our ideas.

The online writing courses given to writers who show great promise were donated by All About Writing. Funds for the monetary prizes came from the Miles Morland Foundation, Generation Africa, and Books Live.

Without the sponsorship, financially and in kind, of the following organisations and individuals, our scope would have been much smaller:

ALEX LATIMER • ALL ABOUT WRITING • ANGELINA ULZEN-CHELA ANTON ROBERT KRUEGER • ARINZECHUKWU PATRICK RODNEY AYOBAMI ADEBAYO • BELINDA DODSON • BLAIZE KAYE BOOKSLIVE • CHERYL NTUMY • CHRISTINE COATES

• CLAIRE ROBERTSONDUSTIN CROWLEY • EMILY BUCHANAN • ERICA LOMBARD FULGENCIO SANMARTIN • GBEZERA OLIVIER • GENERATION AFRICA GENNA GARDINI • GOETHE-INSTITUT • HELEN MOFFETT JARED SHURIN • JEN THORPE • JOANNE HICHENS • JUDY CROOME JURASSIC LONDON • JUSTIN C GREENE • KAREN JENNINGS KARLIEN POTGIETER • KERRY ANDERSON • KERRY HAMMERTON KESHNI NAICKER • KHALED EL SHALAKANY • KRISTIEN POTGIETERLAUREN BEUKES • LISA-ANNE JULIEN • LOTHAR SMITH • LOUIS WIIDMACK LUNDY • MARK BOULD • MARY ONONOKPONO • MARY WATSONMICHAEL NIEMANN • MICHELLE JOLIN • MILES MORLAND FOUNDATIONMODJAJI BOOKS • MONIQUE KWACHOU • N CROWDER • NEELOFER QADIR NERINE DORMAN • NOZIZWE CYNTHIA JELE • RAFIQUE KESHAVJEE RAHLA XENOPOULOS • REINER BARCZINSKI • RICHARD DE NOOY SARAH LOTZ • SHAMEELA ESSACK • SIMA MITTAL • STEPHEN EMBLETONSUSIE DINNEEN • THE DESIGN GROUP • THE KITSCHIES THE NAMELESS FOUNDATION • TRISHA MULGREW • VERENA LEE REIHANA WOLE TALABI • WORLDREADER • ZUKISWA WANNER

I am grateful to the members of our board – Nick Mulgrew, Helen Moffett, Isla Haddow-Flood, Karina Szczurek, Mary Watson and Rahla Xenopoulos – for their support and dedication. Also to Efemia Chela, Catherine Shepherd, and Jason Mykl Snyman for their hard work, ideas and effort. And to Tiah Beautement for her contribution to the project over the years.

The number of people willing to lend a hand grows every year, and I am, as always, amazed at the generosity of spirit in the African writing community and those who support it. If I've left anyone out, I apologise. Hence, to all the writers and readers of African fiction: thank you.

Rachel Zadok
SHORT STORY DAY AFRICA

DONATE TO
SHORT STORY DAY AFRICA

Please support African writers, editors, and publishers.
Scan this qr code on SnapScan to donate. Every cent counts.

To donate through PayPal, please visit
shortstorydayafrica.org/donate